BOOK EIGHT

FORGOTTEN RUIN

HIGH VALUE TARGET

JASON ANSPACH
NICK COLE

WARGATE

An imprint of Galaxy's Edge Press
PO BOX 534
Puyallup, Washington 98371

Text Copyright © 2023 by Jason Anspach & Nick Cole

www.jasonanspach.com
www.nickcolebooks.com

Production Copyright © 2024 by WarGate Books
All rights reserved.

ISBN: 979-8-88922-053-4

WarGate Books website: www.WarGateBooks.com

TECHNICAL ADVISORS AND CREATIVE DESTRUCTION SPECIALISTS

Ranger Vic
Ranger David
Ranger Chris

Green Beret John "Doc" Spears

Rangers lead the way!

CHAPTER ONE

TWO things before we get going on what happened next.

I love coffee, and I love being a Ranger.

PFC Kennedy has once again taken to reading select pages of my account of our time in the Ruin. He says I go on and on about *coffee*, still. Way too much.

Naturally. Who wouldn't. Amirite, Ranger Fam?

And that I use the word *Ranger* a lot. Even for a Ranger.

I disagree.

Hence the opening statement of this account of the strike on the high-value target that Captain Knife Hand and the command team had tagged as HVT Mummy.

Sût the Undying himself.

Anyway…

I love coffee, which I was drinking a cup of, recently exchanged for a few coppers off a local street brewer, of which there were many more than I'd thought in the city of Sûstagul. Fantastic stuff spiced with cinnamon and a little cardamom and fantastic orange floral honey instead of the usual valuable sugars of various colors ranging from molasses to cream that came along the spice routes and arrived in Sûstagul during the fall.

And definitely not the syrups. No, not ever those. I had learned my lesson there. Those syrups were courtesy of the witches of Caspia and little more than narcotic spells. More often than not they had some minor mind-control sorcery fused into them. If just to get you tipping too much and feeling giddy and not on your game such that you get mugged just down the alley by a waiting gang of thieves who'd insisted the street brewer spike certain targets with their Caspian syrup they'd paid dearly for in order to mug their victims the more effortlessly.

Work smarter not harder, they must have been thinking.

So, Talker's policy, that's me, nice to meet you: no syrups to sweeten my dark addiction. I'd fallen in for it once out by the Gates of Mystery in the eastern wall and ended up in a gaudy brothel on the verge of getting fleeced of everything and becoming the personal plaything of the six-armed beauty that acted as the house madame, as it was rumored she wanted a Ranger for her very own now that they were the latest power bloc in town.

Sergeants Thor and Monroe QRF'd right in there, beat the hulking bare-chested guards in ornate sultans' hats senseless, and pulled a babbling me out of there just in time.

She had me clutched in all six of her cobalt arms and was intent on smothering me with her… charms.

And that was on Day Three of my R&R.

That was the last day.

Next day, after my head cleared up from the syrup… and her charms… I reported to the smaj and he put me right to work.

There was a lot to do, as most of the detachment was on leave. Prep for the war. Gather intel. And hall-monitor for the Rangers running amok across the desert port city.

How the Rangers got R&R and ran amok in the desert

port city of Sûstagul before getting into a serious tangle with the last of the forces of Sût the Undying came about like this. I was there in the TOC when it went down.

"Sar'nt Major," said Captain Knife Hand. "In my experience in combat, a Ranger company needs rest after stand down of battle, and this company needs at least two, if not three or more, months of such before they're ready for the follow-on missions we need to execute to throw grave dirt on the HVT. The North African campaign has been nothing but *bang-bang-bang* sea and land battles one after the other, culminating with the taking and subsequent defense of Sûstagul. I know the boys are burnt out and need rest. I know that…" He seemed to say this last part to himself and then faded off for a moment, which he'd been doing more and more of lately. Whether this was due to the weight of a seemingly endless command, or his past intruding on the present, I, the nosy linguist, and collector of all things Ranger… did not know. But I saw it nonetheless.

He continued after the briefest of pauses.

"The whole unit needs to stand down and refit. Broken equipment needs replacing, ammo needs to be stockpiled, giant holes in the MTOE from casualties need to be filled. And my Rangers need time to decompress, get drunk, chase women, and get their heads back on straight. They need that. But I can only give them two weeks, Sar'nt Major, before the Accadion legions are staged and ready to push onto the final objective in the south."

Our captain didn't say, "Sorry about that, Sergeant Major." But the look was there on his rugged and tight face. Right there next to that perpetual look of indigestion and fatigue paid for on credit and promises that would never be fulfilled.

Other partners, assets, and even intrigue and politics among the Accadion court, our allies, were forcing the schedule.

And the Saur were massing their own allies from all across the northern deserts of the Land of Black Sleep. Tribes of monsters and hordes of enemies were responding to the offer of open Saurian caskets filled with gleaming gold and priceless gems. In time, they'd have enough to move from defense… to offense.

But you could tell the captain was sorry all the same.

The rock, the granite tablet of all things NCO and Ranger, keeper of the flame, the smaj… merely nodded.

"They'll be ready, sir. We don't forget nothin'."

And he didn't need to add, *You have my word,* because the smaj's word was… his word. It would be so. Come hell or high water. It would be so. We would be ready to Ranger.

Like it was some law carved in the stone of some ancient mountain that could not be moved.

We would be ready to fight… after two weeks of trying to kill ourselves with pleasure.

In our defense… we did our best.

So there I was, in the Pit Fighter's Last Stand, a "bar" run by a one-eyed old gladiator named Marios who liked the Rangers very much. It was open air, a deep pit of seating, and covered by massive, salvaged canvas sails to ward off the beating sun even as the Ruin turned toward the harvest season.

Music and slender beauties were everywhere as the Rangers reveled.

"I like deez guys. I like dem very much," crooned the ragged old one-eyed gladiator who ran the place. "Remind me of me when I fought da t'ree-headed dog for dat emperor and everyone but me died dat day on de sand in each other's blood. Each one o' deez Rangers is purest gladiator. I know my kind!" Then… and this was courtesy of me using the word *Ranger* way too much, Marios the old and many-criss-cross-scarred owner and barkeep gustily proclaimed at the top of his lungs, *"Ranger gonna Ranger!"* And then fetched more drinks for those of the detachment currently destroying themselves in his vast sprawling tavern as best they could.

The Pit Fighter had become the place to be in the city of Sûstagul for the two weeks the Rangers were given leave by the captain and the smaj.

We had gold coin coming out of our assault packs after the many battles and subsequent plunder of many a dead monster out there in the Savage Lands' forests, and along the ancient temples, lost caves, and rocky granite of the Atlantean Coast. Not to mention the plunder of the Saurian navy and armies we'd stacked here in the city. And the big bruisers we'd blown to pieces—or *Carl G'd into the Shadow Realms*—during our long hump across the Ruin to reach this final staging point for the mission we had set for ourselves.

Strike a blow for the Cities of Men against the Big Bad that plagued whatever chance civilization and mankind, and elven kind, and dwarven kind and a whole bunch of other kinds we'd barely met, had against the Nether Sorcerer who ruled from a dark tower in the shadowy land of Umnoth to the north.

Sût the Undying.

The Big Bad of the Ruin himself.

Smoking him here on his home ground before he had time to march his elite Saurian forces forward into battle, augmented by the southern orcs of the Desert of Despair, would definitely disadvantage said big bad Nether Sorcerer against the struggling legions of Accadios and the hearty dwarven tribes of the Stone Kings.

Or so Vandahar had assured us.

So, we were doing our part, slaughtering our way across the coast of North Africa, or what the Ruin called the Lost Coast, taking the only active port city on the southern edges of the Great Inner Sea, and destroying a Saur attack force that was due to set sail to the north and join the orcs marching forth from the slopes of Umnoth.

After taking the city, we'd held the desert port against a massive Saurian counterattack from the south and were saved at the last second when the main general of the Saur, a powerful medusa, suddenly switched sides and used her aberrant *Medusa Power*—she can sing and turn people to stone—against her own forces to decide the battle.

Then… we slaughtered her army and sent them running south, as Vandahar might say, *muchly*.

Very few of them made their escape, for the Rangers are pure predator when it comes to hide and seek.

And there are no second prizes in that game.

I played my part, too. But it was a small part. I was with the Accadions and Captain Tyrus, and we smashed right into the vanguard of the Saurian praetorians and fought a huge battle for about two hours that left every jacked Conan lizard dead and hacked to pieces.

I went forbidden popsicle on the SAW I was carrying. Don't tell anyone. And… if you ever get the chance… ride the lightning and don't look back. Seriously. I could be a support gunner forever.

It's as close to *as fun as it gets…* as it gets.

So, I love coffee. Love being a Ranger. Those were my thoughts, standing there with Sar'nt Hardt watching the bacchanal and chaos underway inside the Pit, as it was being called.

I had arrived at my destination of what my life was.

The coffee because I'm Talker. You must know that by now.

The part about being a Ranger…

If you haven't figured that part out after reading this far, I don't know if I can explain it to you after this.

At first pass someone might think it's because I started a fanboy, then became one of them. They might dismiss me as merely some booster for some college team I once played on, or that some address happenstance had me living near, and this is how I get my validation. Somehow. Cheering for the guys wearing my colors. Regardless if it's warranted or not.

You would be wrong.

They were my brothers. Are. And we had… I'll borrow a line from a cool movie I once saw. Saw it one rainy Saturday evening when studying Arabic was hurting even *my* brain. And I'm good at this language stuff.

Big Trouble in Little China.

A perfect adventure movie in which ordinary folk do extraordinary things, in the course of a strange rainy weekend.

And as one character in the movie put it, looking back

and knowing, like some Henry the Fifth delivering his St. Crispin's Day speech cut for an action movie flick on a Saturday afternoon, that what they had done, there in that adventure in the foggy streets of Chinatown, they would always remember having done. Having been there at that moment in time when few were. Even when they were someday old and the ungrateful young sat at their broken knees and wondered how this old grape of a vaguely human being had ever once been young, and brave and afraid at the same time, and done incredible deeds and fought in strange battles.

Fallen from the sky.

Rangered.

Soldiered.

Soldiers understand this. I bet the other services do too. Like when the Air Force DinFac served chateaubriand and orange sherbet on Tuesday after the polo match, or the Navy reached some port where they could drink themselves blind and participate in some new debauchery that would make even a Ranger shudder… and that's saying something.

I jest.

I know they have their moments when, as Rudyard Kipling put it… and yes this is inherently Navy, but it captures what it's like to serve in the collective human endeavor that is any form of military service, dying to yourself and serving that greater cause… so indulge me.

> *We pulled for you when the wind was against us and the sails were low.*
> *Will you never let us go?*
> *We ate bread and onions when you took towns, or*

ran aboard quickly when you were beaten back by the foe.

The captains walked up and down the deck in fair weather singing songs, but we were below.

We fainted with our chins on the oars and you did not see that we were idle, for we still swung to and fro.

Will you never let us go?

The salt made the oar-handles like shark-skin; our knees were cut to the bone with salt-cracks; our hair was stuck to our foreheads; and our lips were cut to the gums, and you whipped us because we could not row.

Will you never let us go?

But, in a little time, we shall run out of the port-holes as the water runs along the oar-blade, and though you tell the others to row after us you will never catch us till you catch the oar-thresh and tie up the winds in the belly of the sail. Aho!

Will you never let us go?

"Song of the Galley-Slaves," by Rudyard Kipling.

That's what it's like to serve alongside your brothers no matter what service you're in. It's just like the poem I memorized, and then used as a test in every language I know to ensure my mastery, summed it up. But I never understood the words fully until I watched my brothers have the time of their lives, as I thought about everything we'd been through. Together. Knowing I would never ever… forget.

And remembering those who were not among us.

We shook the pillars of heaven.

That's how the character in *Big Trouble in Little China*

put it.

That was the line.

Shook the pillars of heaven.

And in that moment, watching Monroe charge into a suit of tattered patchwork armor of some beaten gladiator as merchants in fine livery and rich silks from all across the Ruin shouted in triumph and victory at the betting on the outcome of the Ranger smash, or sneered and cried fraud and bought the rounds of drinks anyway as payment for lost bets…

And Tanner, half his face less horror show now that it had gone bone-white and skeletal underneath on that side and the other half still the roguish perpetual Ranger PFC who'll fight anyone anywhere no matter the odds, smiled that rake's sneer, surrounded by three voluptuous and clutching whores who were fallen beauties, each marred in their own way. One missing an eye. One who had the scar of having once had her throat slit by a customer as payment for her gifts. And one who seemed sheltered in Tanner's embrace not for lust or mere charm, but for the fact that his arms about her, even knowing that this man was half-undead dying… were some sort of safe harbor in a world that terrified her with the horror of each new terrible day.

She was young and haunted and pretty like a stray and beautiful dog that's been abused and only needs shelter to come back to life, and love.

There was the Air Force TACP there among us who had come and joined us in our party, the young Rangers making him one of their own now, which is good. He would die at the Steps of Fate calling in an airstrike on himself to hold off the Eld guardians Sût would summon forth from his vast and haunted tomb that was the Grand Pyramid when all seemed lost for our task force.

But that was to come.

And this was now. This was leave.

Rangers drank, gambled, hit things hard, climbed stuff, then wandered out to find more trouble and women across the sprawling desert port city after so long at our crossings and warrings.

We were finally given some time off before we'd soon go south and join the Accadion legions already digging in against the swelling forces of Sût the Undying before the Grand Pyramid and the City of Death that lay at its feet. Or the sleeping horrors of the Valley of Kings and Priests. Or Priests and Kings. Or sometimes just Valley of Kings. Also Valley of Tombs, as long as I'm cataloguing.

In that moment there at the Pit…

Amid chaos and revelry…

Coffee in one hand.

Hardt's right-hand man playing cop while everyone had their fun as best they could before it was time to form up and march…

I thought to myself, this must be my destination.

These are my Rangers. My brothers.

That's all.

That's why I use the word so much. Ranger. It means that to me. It's how I mark that time we shook the pillars of heaven.

Literally.

And that's how the battle that would soon be fought, began for me.

CHAPTER TWO

HOW did I end up the R&R cop?

Well, getting close to losing my marbles due to a narcotic coffee and a six-armed demi-human whore who had plans for my body and her future, was part of the story.

Part of the reason I took a good look in the fountain I was splashing cold water onto my bloated face in, and looking at it with no little amount of contempt.

But... remember, something had happened. Something... unexpected.

Listen. After the night with Autumn, I was restored and ready to go. If the smaj would have told me to head out into the Southern Waystes with my threaded-barrel Glock and start cleaning a way right to Sût's necropolis all on my own...

I would have done it.

As Sar'nt Chris says, Rangers can do anything.

Hey... Ranger gonna Ranger. Amirite?

Coffee.

Ranger.

Coffee Ranger.

Take that, Kennedy.

Center yourself, Talker.

Drink of coffee. Pen in hand. The account continues...

That night with Autumn was...

After everything... after the loss of Kurtz and Brumm

especially…

It centered me. Being in her arms. With her now and our shadowy terms.

All the questions I had were answered after that night. In fact, the big question I had unknowingly been asking myself throughout every challenge, relationship, every new language under my belt, joining the Army, going Airborne and RASP, call me whatever you want to call me… but it was answered for me when she told me the terms of the evening.

The challenge.

The offer.

And a promise of some tomorrow for… us. One day. After all this. After… a lot of stuff.

A tomorrow to march for.

The question I'd always been asking myself was…

Where was this going?

I'd always asked myself some version of that in everything I was doing. And to be honest, a lot of the time I ignored the question. The asking and the challenge were enough.

But then after that night with her in the tent, after the battle and the slaughter and even going otherwhere down a dark alley with Tanner going undead and leading me to… Summer… to Kurtz and Brumm and knowing they were… okay… now…

After the siring of an heir for the Shadow Elven throne in a tiny hut between the desert and the sea, filled with my collection of books and my resolve to never feel again…

It was answered.

That question I'd been asking myself without ever knowing I had been.

Where was it all going?

In the morning silence, listening to the surf out beyond the walls of the city, before the city itself moved, and just feeling the ghost of her going in the dark scent of the sage of morning and salt water, the answer was…

It was going right here.

I thought about how we both remained silent after all the talk we raced through knowing time was short, and that time was also forever for us… just not right now.

Knowing that in the darkness before the dawn she would be gone.

It was going right here, was the answer.

Us.

Apart. Yes.

But together. Forever.

And some day, on the other side of all this. Together. And together. And together.

That was the deal she'd made with the wounded Shadow Elven king. A mere cored-out husk of the once-brave and dangerous knight he'd been. His years in the dungeon of the dragon had broken and shattered him. He slept much and watched the shadows.

He was afraid and could not do what needed to be done.

But, because he was a leader, he would make a way, even if he could not.

Could not do what needed to be done.

And if he didn't, the throne would vanish.

Autumn had made her deal as queen with the ghost of the man she once loved. She would provide an heir to her people. And she would reign as queen. But one day, she would be allowed to withdraw… to wherever I was on whatever edge of the world I ended up in. Not in plain sight.

But it wouldn't matter then, because it would just be us. And there would be a new Shadow Elven king in eighteen years.

She wouldn't age as I will. That didn't matter to her.

Lucky me.

I would grow old as humans do. Or die in some pile of expended brass among my brothers.

She asked me in the dark, her voice small but firm. "Those are… the terms?" Her English soft and broken. She told me she would speak it better and that was how she would communicate with me for the rest of our days. That "someday" I had seen when it was just that boat I had dreams of. Visions once. Visions of her in the bow and me rowing for the Cities of Men that lay beyond the forests and caves of the Shadow Elves and all that is required of thrones and kings and brave queens who found the Rangers when they were lost and surrounded.

"Do… you… accept?" she asked.

Silence in the darkness that lay all about us. You know… that morning silence when the world seems afraid to make its first sound. Knowing that soon, every bird and every life will begin some grand chorus that is unheard unless you know how to listen. All the life and death and horror and happiness that can be contained within one day.

That silence before all of it.

"I do," I answered.

And yeah, that was a vow. I knew it then. Know it now. And I was glad Sar'nt Thor was able to yank me out of the arms of the six-armed cougar who was trying to make me her very own personal Ranger concubine.

She was a looker though.

And after all, I am very charming, handsome, and a Ranger.

LOL Kennedy. I cannot be stopped.

Coffee!

So I said I do, and she was gone with the dawn tides on a galley back across the sea and to the fortress the Shadow Elves rule from. Perhaps there would be an heir. Perhaps not just yet. I would enjoy the trying to provide if there wasn't.

I do.

Interesting words you never really think about. But sometime… when you get a chance… stop and think about them. Those two words. Odd. Not *I will.* But *I do.*

Very Ranger. When you think about it.

Perhaps I think too much. Perhaps Kennedy and all my critics about addictions and word usage are… right. And I am wrong?

Perhaps.

I'd blame coffee but coffee is blameless. It's too wonderful to be anything terrible.

So, in order not to get caught up in the Ranger Shenanigans of Leave and all the chaos we were causing there in the desert port city of Sûstagul, I reported to the sergeant major and he turned me over to Sar'nt Hardt who was more than happy to be everywhere all at once and attempting, and I would give him credit for this, rather judiciously, to prevent irreparable death and injury, and minimize the damage the captain was having to pay out on an almost daily basis to the locals.

Which was, as Vandahar might again say… muchly.

To list a few of the follies, and this is not a comprehensive enumeration of what went on as Rangers by their very nature are sneaky and surely got away with a lot more that was never caught and documented…

We turn to…

Recently demoted Private Soprano. Who, after several days of drinking in various dens, challenged a troupe of arrogant acrobats to a series of climbing feats. The acrobats were from Caspia, haughty, and decided Soprano's Italian accent made him Accadion. They promptly ridiculed him. Big mistake. Later, he told me the challenge was actually issued to impress the dark and very doe-eyed assistant, and daughter, of the troupe's fire-breather. Three days' challenges and gambling ensued across the city and reached a fever pitch daily as every day Soprano challenged the tightrope walkers and acrobats to climbing challenges more and more dangerous with each instance.

First, the assault on what was known locally as the Wall of Surgit the Mad. Surgit, an ancient charmer who had built his small tower atop one of the crumbling walls in much disrepair near the cemetery surrounding the old Legion fort. The tower had long since fallen into a pile of treacherous stone, but there was an ancient snake stamped in some of the high remaining bricks and it was said that whoever could reach the snake up there on the dangerous wall, a precarious climb out over the old refuse pits where sections of the early driedmud brick were prone to give way without warning, that they could have a wish granted by the stamped snake.

Legends and rumors.

That day Soprano made the climb and touched the snake. The troupe's acrobat fell far below into the refuse pit and broke both legs for his troubles.

Everyone laughed, much coin was exchanged, and Soprano was held aloft and carried off to a tavern for riotous amounts of drinking.

The troupe master, on the other hand, felt he was owed compensation by the Rangers for the maiming of a performer, and to prevent further trouble, Captain Knife Hand flung a sack of gold and told the man not to bother him again.

The next day the fat ringmaster was promptly back after Soprano had challenged another troupe tightrope walker to an all-new contest of feat and daring. Cross the High Tower Street from above, on a rope, with a blindfold on.

Wispo the Deft fell. And of course shattered his hip and arms and cracked his skull.

He should have been dead.

Soprano on the other hand made the crossing, and the fire-eater's daughter didn't come home that night.

Outrage and a small riot of the city's performers attacked a group of Rangers near the Pit, and much mountebank blood was spilled and broken bones were handed out in abundance.

No one got killed.

The next morning the fat and mustachioed ringmaster was back in the captain's tent fuming about ruined performers and dishonored young girls.

The troupe was demanding either Soprano be killed or marry the fire-eater's daughter immediately for damages probably caused.

The shy little beauty made moon eyes and the mobbed-up Ranger gunner said nothing.

She said, in Arabic, "*Hu yahibuni*!" Soprano smiled, and it was a guilty smile if there ever was one.

No one needed me to translate, as enough knowledge of street Arabic and the patois of the port abounded by now among the Rangers.

The smaj ended all further discussion by lowering his Kindle and issuing an edict from on high.

"Yeah, whatever, sir. Boy's a damn good gunner and that's where he's gonna stay."

More gold was flung. The girl disappeared and Soprano was told to cease and desist his feats of daring and challenges to the acrobat troupe.

And to stay away from the curvy little dark beauty.

On the following day Soprano challenged Windhammer Spring Step, yeah, that was the guy's name, to swing from one of the galleys in the port to a galley across the waters near a lagoon at the edge of the fortified bays where sharks would come and feed in the early evening.

One of the Rangers who happens to be a Shark Week enthusiast the way some people severely devote themselves to insane cults and/or wild-eyed religions, said these sharks were known as Oceanic whitetips and that they were very, very deadly… if not the deadliest… sharks.

Full disclosure here: I knew about the challenge and so did every Ranger and almost everyone in the city.

So we were there.

It was night.

The trick went like this…

Leap off the mast of the galley with a line, swing all the way around the galley until you're almost aligned with the other galley across the water, the shark-infested waters I might add right below, then let go and fly toward the… I think it's called a yardarm, or whatever, and catch it without missing or falling into the shark-infested waters.

The very deadly if not the deadliest Oceanic whitetip shark-infested waters.

So, long story short…

Soprano lived and Windhammer, who seemed to have some elven blood in him, didn't.

This Windhammer dude had tried to fight Soprano a bunch of times before this, we found out later, and the only thing that kept him from killing Soprano was the fact that Jabba was always around Soprano and had any one of the many weird goblin weapons the little gob keeps coming up with out and ready to stick the elf with should he try to knife Soprano in the back.

I should say half-elf. Windhammer was some kind of mix of human and elf.

The dwarves had said there were such and that they were not loved by their own Fey kind. Then the dangerous little gang of many-weaponed Amish bikers muttered among themselves and turned back toward improving the defenses and walls of Sûstagul.

But as Jabba put it in his own gob way, "Big Bigga no like… elfs!" As he spat this he worked a broken tomahawk he'd "repaired" himself over his bony arms, shaving his springy goblin hairs there and looking like some stone-cold killer straight out of the nightmare of all jungle wars.

He's not a Ranger, but he's learned the cold murder look solid.

Then he smiled his Jabba broken-teeth smile.

But I have to say this again… that gob was beginning to Ranger for sure. He had pure rage murder no-bull eyes and he wanted you to see them.

He wanted to stick that elf. Half-elf.

On that note…

The Ranger School at FOB Hawthorn has been running since before the Ranger company left for Portugon. There should be replacements showing up now in a continuous stream. The Rangers will need time at the team, squad, and platoon level to integrate these "replacements" so the whole unit still runs like a Swiss watch. So far, we've heard some wild stories about the Lost Boys and a few other creatures that have ended up going through the school being run by the Rangers back at the FOB. But it's unclear if they'll arrive before action in the south.

So, to get back to Soprano. It was rumored this Windhammer would marry the despoiled girl and… make her life miserable just to get back at the Ranger.

Soprano—let's not forget his family was mob—solved the problem by using the challenge and making sure he lost the contest and ended up in some netting he had conveniently arranged to catch his "ill-timed" fall from the yardarm line.

Or whatever it's called.

Laughing at the Ranger gunner's failure, the arrogant Windhammer made the yardarm-or-whatever on the target ship, catching it deftly because he was the troupe's best acrobat.

Then it promptly snapped because someone had made sure it would, and cartwheeling Windjammer went into the dark evening waters between the ships.

The very very deadly… if not the deadliest… Oceanic whitetip shark-infested waters.

By torchlight, with everyone along the beach and in small boats watching, Windhammer ended badly.

And someone else had put chum in the water because Rangers never go alone. And they play to win. And by win I mean, pretty much the other guy is gonna die.

Call it Ranger Checkers.

So it was a feeding frenzy for the next few seconds. But a short one. And a violent one all the same.

No one would ever mess with the girl, and she would… I don't know… be not allowed to moon along after the jacked little Ranger gunner and his mafia of one goblin with murder eyes and a growing collection of broken weapons the little gob had "repaired."

Whatever… that's Soprano's deal.

But seriously.

Ranger gonna Ranger. And he basically did it textbook according to Sar'nt Joe without waiting the year for Wind-hammer to go get a burrito.

Soprano solved that problem and got busted right down to private for his troubles.

He smiled all through the busting, even when he was in the front leaning rest for the better part of an hour.

It was said, and I was not there for this. But as the smaj walked the newly busted Private Soprano off to his extra duty, leaving the command tent, it was said that the old NCO muttered laconically, "Good on you, son."

And that was that.

The captain paid the money for the lost performer, but he did it in full were-tiger, and the greedy ringmaster literally soiled himself and passed out as he took the money from the man-tiger whose voice growled pure and sudden murmuring death as the money was handed over.

But that was not the end, or the only, of the troubles the Rangers caused in the port city of Sûstagul during those two weeks.

Initially we had the run of the city. That was, innocently I protest, when I sought to spend my days scouring every loca-tion, from street vendor to hidden dark pour-over concoction alcove, for various brews of coffee. I scouted and delved the twisting alleys and many secluded and hidden neighborhoods the city had to offer where such delicate aromas could be had.

Sometimes it took hours or even an entire day to tease out a particular location the locals wanted to keep to themselves.

I might have even joined some weird coffee death cult at one point. But they seemed mostly harmless. Mostly.

One day I saw Tanner heading out of the cantonment area near the old haunted fortress with a six-pack of Rip It and a plastic gallon jug of vodka he'd convinced the Air Force techs to gin up for him in their Forge and I knew… that way lay trouble.

But that was how Tanner had rolled long before the Ruin. Plus, there was talk of making him a specialist or even taking my corporal for a leadership position on a fire team. So I think he was looking to get busted down to private again, and Soprano inspired him.

Hence the plastic gallon jug of vodka and Rip It.

As I said… that way lay trouble. And I was a new man now that Autumn and I had a future. Someday.

So I left Tanner to his jug. I would be merely a tourist inside the twisting maze of the ancient city. Sightseeing and capturing all the ways and talents by which my particular dark addiction was brewed here in this crossroads of the world.

I even bought a leather journal to make notes.

I know… *nerd.*

I don't care. Coffee loves me.

Ranger!

But I had no intention of being drugged and becoming a sexual plaything for a six-armed cougar madame with blue skin and giant yams.

Thankfully I was rescued before things went too far.

Wait… thankfully? LOL. Talker, what happened to you?

I'll tell you what happened.

I fell in love. And I liked it.

Note: Never in a million years would I have thought I would ever write that sentence. But hey, there it is. Talker done gone legit. Sorry, girls. Show's over. Find someone else.

I do.

So, during my first three days I hit several stands and met interesting people and consumed enough coffee to smell colors and see time move backward. But by the end of the week, and my turning over a new leaf, the Rangers were kicked out of the port district after the city leaders appealed to the captain that this should happen to prevent more business establishments from burning down.

On one hand, you have the most disciplined fighting

force in the world, trained from day one to be the epitome of modern warfare and battlefield control.

Then the unit gets leave and they try to burn the city down with their antics.

As Tanner put it, "A commander like Knife Hand would definitely do what he did: drop that bag of gold to smooth things over after the first incident. But after that, gonna grab a bucket of leg breakers to round everyone up for a 'stand down.' That's how I see it."

Tanner's logic was solid. After all, Rangers were in short supply and the antics being done put combat-effective numbers at risk for the coming operation.

But then Tanner flicked his lighter, inhaled a smoke halfway, blew it out the side of his skeletal face, and offered this…

"Other side of the coin, Talk, is that these guys are technically 10K years past their ETS and they can do what they want. But I doubt Knife Hand gonna see it that way much longer."

This was late in the long afternoon just after the city leaders appealed to the captain for some kind of restraint.

The Rangers had been having a flaming tomahawk contest after they discovered a particular brand of liquor called Kurat Alraed, roughly translated as *Thunder Ball*, was ignition proof in a little drinking den down by the port where we'd slaughtered many Saur during the counterattack.

There were Rangerettes there of course. There was flammable alcohol, and most were traveling with their tomahawks when they reached the inn that hot and thirsty afternoon with too much free time and gold coin weighing them down.

This was Second Platoon.

Third and Fourth Squad to be specific.

So, the place burned down a little while later and the Rangers got banned from the port.

The Rangerettes.

These are the girls back on any post who have made it their quest to bag a Ranger. The Ruin generated them and the game continued. These Rangerettes were an offering of the city's most ambitious courtesans and the daughters of some of the richest merchants and even of the occasional powerful wizard. All of them stunners. They followed the Rangers around batting their long eyelashes and undulating in their gossamer silks for the attention of the swole and hulking Rangers dripping with unreal amounts of tats and scars.

The encouraging presence of the Rangerettes, combined with the alcohol and the massive amounts of testosterone the average Ranger possessed, made for much mayhem and chaos. It had always been only a matter of time before the Rangers were kicked out of much of the city. Even without the Soprano tightrope-walking blindfolded challenge that went so horribly wrong for the acrobat.

Then there was that "murder."

The falling acrobat guy—not Windhammer, the one before that, Wispo the Deft—destroyed a coffee kiosk I'd been meaning to hit when he fell, and one of the legendary brewers a few streets over, a timid little man, packed up and left the city now that Rangers were causing men to drop from the sky and ruin their businesses. He considered this some kind of sign that the world was ending, and the Great Winter of Death had come according to his religion.

The guy was rumored to be so good that I had ideas about

getting a horse and following the caravan he'd left on out into the deserts of the Eastern Waystes just to try a cup of his brew as soon as I could catch up to the camels.

But the smaj had his Goon Squad busy, and we were much so, steering Rangers away from the trouble spots they seemed intent on heading into, or getting them back to their places in the cantonment to sleep off the legendary amounts of liquor and other activities they were destroying themselves with.

Over those two weeks, Sûstagul got a lot richer.

Especially the tattoo artists in the Alley of Ink and Smoke.

Then there was a fire *there*, too… and no more tattoos.

Sergeant Kang was part of the smaj's Goon Squad, and he and I were out getting a wayward Ranger, Sergeant Rico in fact, who'd taken command of the gun team, back to his tent after he'd taken over a small butcher, drunk to high heaven, and demanded he be allowed to make his own "special recipe" carne asada tacos.

The special part about the recipe was the Thunder Ball.

Butcher knife in hand, Rico could not be denied his time at the grill.

Thunder Ball jug at the ready, he'd fed much of the street, urchins, whores, beggars, and anyone who wanted his "special recipe" taco, while keeping the butcher and his fat yet overly large sons at bay with his tomahawk—and a Glock.

This was quite a feat. But he was a Ranger, so… Tuesday.

Once we rescued him, hauling Rico by his arms as he snored and drooled, his bare feet leaving a bloody trail in the sand as we dragged him back to the cantonment, Sar'nt Kang asked in his own enigmatic and very sober way, "Did he go out without boots, or did he lose those somewhere?"

A minor detail but an important one to the grunting and seemingly tireless Master Breacher. But that's Sar'nt thinking, and technically, though I'm a corporal, I'm still *E-4 Mafia 4 Life*!

So who cares. Forge will provide.

I said nothing and grunted, dragging slobbering Sergeant Rico to his rack.

That was when the smaj crossed our path with his long-legged stalk, snapped his fingers, and growled.

He was pure dark storm cloud, and I was pretty sure someone was gonna die shortly.

He just growled.

Like a wild animal. A wolf.

And I'd been around long enough to know that wasn't good.

The normally stoic Sergeant Kang swore and said as much as I was thinking.

Then the smaj muttered a bitter, "Commons is missing. Drop that Ranger off quick and be at the TOC in less than five. Air Force is spinning up a bird for us to go look for him. Make sure you leave him on his side, otherwise he'll choke on his own puke."

CHAPTER THREE

COMMONS was missing.

Not everyone was on leave and not everyone was policing those on leave. A few of us had some details to get ready for the training and then the pump.

The dwarves were also building an obstacle course for the smaj once leave was over, and it was… the most hellish course I'd ever seen.

And I've run the Darby Queen.

Well, not the one ten thousand years ago. The one Hardt and Kurtz came up with around FOB Hawthorn. I don't know if it was worse, but when the people who'd run the original finished throwing up they told me it was.

So… I got that goin' for me.

Commons and a few others got some intel collection assignments once they'd had their fill of leave—or hadn't, if the smaj had some burning hot desire to know what was where and who needed to die around some particular grid square as the prep for the final invasion.

Now collectively known as "Aqua Ranger" among the Rangers, for good or bad, mostly good in that he liked it better than "Gill," which was nevertheless still in the rotation, Commons had singlehandedly been scouting what the Ruin called the River of Night. Or what the world had once called… the Nile.

Rumor was there was a sunken temple that contained some secret access into the fractured crescent that surrounded the Grand Pyramid. This was the Valley of Priests and Kings, or Kings and Priests, and it was looking like that would be the asymmetrical route that would allow the Rangers to pull their standard *Surprise, Ranger Smash!* trademark into the flank of the Saurian defenses at a critical moment to be determined later in the coming battle.

Now, Specialist Commons, or Aqua Ranger, or sometimes simply, "I got bit!", was overdue and missing. And the smaj wanted us on the SAR—Search and Rescue.

Mainly because there was no one else sober, and the dwarves had a hard time with the choppers.

Kang and I dropped Sergeant Rico at his rack, flipped him onto his side, told Bannister to watch him while the AG sharpened his knives, and then *di di mao*'d off to the TOC to get the mission. The AH-6 Little Bird was already dialed up for the hop, and Air Force crew were swapping the gunship loadout so more straphangers and less ammo could be carried into the search site. Another Little Bird was on standby in case things got hot, and that one was strapped for bear.

Generally, the Little Birds were on horde suppression duty, making nightly gun runs to the south in order to light up the massing clusters of orcs coming from all points of the southern compass to support the defense at the Grand Pyramid. There were orc cav flanking and scouting the deserts to the east and west, and no one was more surprised when in the dead of night a Little Bird came screaming over the dunes and dumping minigun fire until there was nothing but drooling corpses in the bone-white moonlight and bloating camels and torn-apart orcs in the brutal sun of the next day's heat.

Sometimes the pretty little blond ponytailed co-pilot found them with one of her predator drones and…

Death from above. Air Force style.

She was becoming known as a proficient killer, and all referred to her as Valkyrie. But the Rangers still called her Pretty Blond Ponytail too.

Word was she'd shift forward from the FOB and… Rangers' hearts and hopes were high.

Valkyrie was the best of both worlds to the Rangers. Icy beauty. Cold-blooded killer.

Or, to me… endless coffee.

So, besides playing Ranger Cop while everyone bacchanaled harder and harder by the day in some unspoken contest to see who could degenerate into little more than a Spring Breaker champion with a penchant for flaming tomahawks and street gang brawls… and then get challenged to bacchanal even harder… preparations for the invasion of the Valley of the Priests and Kings and the hit on the HVT were underway.

Mummy was gonna die. It was just a matter of how.

There were now three Accadion legions south of the city of Sûstagul under the command of Captain Tyrus. Still captain. The peacock generals of Accadios would not promote the formidable yet enigmatic warrior to general even though it was clear Tyrus was in charge and their best field commander. Ever.

Apparently because Captain Tyrus was not of Accadion blood, he could never be made a general. Rites and traditions and such of the Bronze Age savages of the Ruin. But he had been hailed as Imperator twice before on the field of battle, a temporary title awarded by the legionnaires themselves and holding some kind of Medal of Honor-esque respect required even by the throne of Accadios itself. So that was enough to give Captain Tyrus command of the three legions digging forts and laying siege to the valley while hordes of orcs and the Last Legion of Sût prepared to defend the besieged pharaoh.

Also, none of those generals, or the emperor himself, were bothering to get involved in the sudden conflict that had spun up on the enemy's flank thanks to our deep penetration assault into the Land of Black Sleep and the Empire of the Saur.

Side note, and a strangely interesting thing about the Accadion legions and their legendary commander… the Rangers were trying to download as much Ranger into the Accadions as they could. Op orders. Patrolling. Other tasks.

Captain Tyrus seemed to possess such an affinity for everything Hardt and Kang and the other NCOs taught the legionnaires that it was like he already knew it. And generally the Accadions, little more than Italian males, if you know the type, struggled with the tasks if only due to the fact that Al Haraq, and more specifically his succubi beauties undulating in their gossamer silks and preening while they cast long-lashed eyes of feigned disinterest… seemed to distract the legionnaires, who debated constantly the price of ten thousand years of slavery for "just a cool drink of dat water, Talk-ir!"

Another Accadion legion was on the march south to Captain Tyrus's command, and still another was due to arrive by fleet in the port any day. They would immediately march south, and once all pieces were in place, we would conduct the final attack.

There would be no more troops from the north, as already the war in the north was underway. And generally, the news wasn't good.

If five-to-one odds sounds great, it ain't. Standard Army doctrine indicates anywhere from seven-to-one to thirteen-to-one odds for displacing an enemy from an entrenched position.

And the Grand Pyramid was definitely that.

But Captain Tyrus and the Legion had… us. Rangers. And the Rangers had Little Birds and drone support from the Air Force.

Games could be played. Tricks were being placed up Crye Precision sleeves.

During the two weeks' leave, small bands of Rangers, along with some of the SOAR elements, had been conducting reconnaissance of the Giza Plateau and the Valley of the Priests and Kings where the Saur had centered their legion, supported by orc hordes and many other types of monster-slash-auxiliary units.

The scouting reports would have ruined most soldiers. But the Rangers seemed excited about overwhelming odds and tomb fighting in the dark against horrors from the unknown.

That's Rangers for you. They embrace the suck and wish it would suck more.

The valley was littered with tombs and traps and cursed monuments. Besides the sleeping dead and the small armies of guardians. As Vandahar put it, "Each of those black holes is a dire warren and a mad maze of Saurian thaumaturgic domination in which summoned horrors, or malefic guardians, along with the decrepit mummies of those powerful priests and necromancers, minor liches of no small amount of power to some greater or lesser extent, is just waiting to issue forth and provide counter to the main assault our legions will have to make up the valley to reach the plateau. And this does not include the vast temple necropolis that lies at the foot of the Grand Pyramid of cursed Sût himself. You should expect to lose many in your purchase of the damnation ground there. This… will not be easy."

Captain Knife Hand had made that perpetual look of indigestion when the old wizard stated this little tidbit. And so had Captain Tyrus.

The smaj merely muttered, "Ain't no easy days in the regiment," and then took a drink of his coffee.

That's the kind of Ranger I want to be. Mainly the coffee part. But hey, the promise of meeting the challenge with a simple statement of fact is cool too.

Instead I just sat there staring slack-jawed at all that scouted death on the map in the TOC.

But our two commanders, they were men cut from different cloth. Hard. Sick to death of their commands. And the only ones capable of executing orders and missions that would kill many on both sides. And willing to do it.

If only because it had to be done.

There's hard. Yeah. And then there's the leadership of the hard that will go and do the hard things that have to be done.

And these two knew all too well what the consequences would be. They didn't like it one bit. I had the distinct feeling that when the Rangers said, "Send me," their leaders would be right there with them. Leading the way.

Even if it seemed impossible.

And there in the tent with us was the fantastic creature that was the Accadion imperator's concubine. The medusa. A mythical and fantastic beauty, the third of the three mythic medusa sisters, her eyes wide and dark, luminous even in the thin light of the TOC as we studied the great map that had been drawn of where we would fight the battle. She merely nodded that what old Vandahar had said was indeed true.

The snakes in her hair were wrapped in an ornate dressing, but you could hear them hissing like some monkish chant in a high eastern temple.

With her bronze shield, stout spear, and fabled blade, she would accompany the man who had conquered her with a mere kiss on a battlefield in a dire moment. She would trail him into the arms of certain death that this battle was promising to be, if the map told no lies.

Yeah, Mummy was going to die. But it was probably going to kill all of us getting it done.

The crescent fracture that was the Valley of Priests and Kings had always been the Saurian last great defense. And in times past, even when the Saur had conquered most of the known world before being beaten eventually back to their last stands, the ancient and sleeping death that waited in that long valley, and all along the crumbling ruins of the vast plateau that lay under the glare of the incredibly massive pyramid, had proven a final dark salvation to the sleeping Saur and their long and unquiet dreams beneath the sands of a world resting, finally, under their cold claws.

And then there were the massing orc hordes.

These were unlike the orcs of the west. Savage warring

tribes sometimes sprinkled with four-armed fabled giants of their kind. We had beaten those and stacked them by the score.

These were not under the black flag and ghostly white eye of the Nether Sorcerer and the Great Orc Khan of Umnoth. Breeding by the thousands per year and swarming out of that teeth-bared land into the Cities of Men and against the slopes of the Stone Kings. A seemingly never-ending and relentless river of them if the words of Vandahar and the tales of the legionnaires were to be believed of the battles they had fought in Caspia and Umnoth.

The orcs of the southern deserts were different.

We hadn't faced this kind yet.

But because we were Rangers it was something we were— in that quiet, taciturn, murder-stoic way, working dip and staring off into the horrors we had planned for these orcs— excited about.

That was your average Ranger. Of course.

Some of them were downright giddy about getting it on with these southern desert orcs.

I was still enough "me" that I had... concerns. Still, I was gonna go and see who was who and what was what. Hell, who am I kidding—I was gonna go and stack southern orc, and if not... then that pile of expended brass was good enough for me too.

Like I have said in the past...

Ranger gonna Ranger.

Just let me have one last suck of cold brew before it's Winchester on mags and tomahawks out for the last line of defense.

Okay?

That's my bargain with the universe. A cold brew as final protective fire starts up with a vengeance never before seen.

And then, right there in the TOC, I thought, for the first time—ever—that despite thrones and succession and smart sexy little Shadow Elven queens whom I love, that there might soon be… a boy… a little boy… who looks a little like me… even if it could not be formally… *acknowledged.*

It was like a bolt of sudden and unexpected lightning out of the blue right there in the TOC as I stared at the map where there was so much death waiting for us.

That thought, right there as Vandahar laid out how screwed we were going into the Valley of Death, which was probably the best name yet for the dead and deathly place, and the preferred nickname among the thieves and expeditions who attempted to plunder yearly, striking out from the City of Thieves across the gulf to the east… that thought right there ran through me like cold lightning river ice water and for a moment… I realized my mouth was just hanging wide open.

"'Cause," I whispered to myself slowly. "That's what we were doing. Weren't we?"

I was talking about Autumn. And the one night in my shack before she was gone with the tide in the dark of dawn.

Making… *a child.*

I may be smart. But sometimes I am stupid dumb.

"What was that, Corporal?" snapped Captain Knife Hand in the silence of the very important briefing regarding our impending deaths in order to save civilization.

I took a deep breath and realized where I was. A briefing

in the TOC.

Everyone was staring at me.

Including the smaj with that cold emotionless *I could just murder you and get away with it and no one would ever know, Talker* look.

You know the one.

I hope you realize this account is not about me, as much as I've tried to make it be. That's a failing on my part. It is about, of course, Rangers.

But because I'm writing it… it sometimes *seems* to be about me. Like I'm the main character. Again: I'm not. It just seems that way.

Why else would there be so many words devoted to coffee.

And sometimes, in stories, the character, the main character, has this moment, this same moment I'm having now in the TOC. I've read books where that happened and then they song-and-dance, rope-a-dope, whatever, and say something brilliant to get out of it and no one's the wiser.

Because they're the main character.

And because they're the main character, the chungo hack writer not only lets them get away with it but he even makes it so it turns out brilliant in the end, and later in the plot it somehow saves the day.

Stupid chungo writers.

Because that writer is a hack and that's not what happens in real life. This didn't happen for me.

If you are in a room with Rangers and you happen to be one of them, then you have no choice but to tell the truth.

Captain Robert Rogers spelled that out in his Rules of Ranging.

Don't ever tell a lie to another Ranger.

So…

I didn't.

"Sorry, sir. I just connected the dots on some personal matter that had nothing to do with this briefing. Focusing… sir."

The air in the TOC went arctic cold if only because the smaj seemed to "un-see" me.

Oof.

Captain Knife Hand, who could turn into a were-tiger and rip your guts out with his claws, merely nodded and asked Vandahar another question about the Valley of Death we and the Accadion Legion would fight our way through to reach the Grand Pyramid and take on Sût.

I focused, and forgot about… the future. A future I might never see because of this valley filled with mummies who couldn't be dead, had magic, and summoned demons and other horrors to defend their god-pharaoh.

But, for one last second, I thought about my dad, and how he'd never given up, even when my mom made it impossible, on being a part of my life.

He made all the deals, even the one that was the very definition of who he was as a man, for two weeks of summer with me.

He was there. Always.

So… I'd be too. Even if the elven king kid never knew what was what. Regarding me. I'd be there.

I connected the dots and swore an oath to myself. Even if the dead were going to come crawling out of every dark hellhole for me and my brothers…

I would be his dad. Even if it could never be said aloud.

Thank you, Autumn.

Bring it, Valley of Death.

CHAPTER FOUR

THE captain was all jocked up and ready to go on the SAR for Commons like he was going with us. And… surprise, he was.

We were receiving the op order in the TOC when all this became clear as the bird began to spin up her rotors outside and suddenly there was the feeling of loose electricity and imminent danger in the air.

I was… yeah… scared. And excited. Which I think is where you want to be.

The SAR team was Kang, myself, and Chief Rapp, the SF Green Beret medic and Doctrine Warfare specialist whose idea of leave was more skills training, more PT, and then squeezing off obscene amounts of rounds as fast as the Forge could print them out for him to lug them off to the range.

He smiled, always, and would train anyone who wanted to tear themselves away from leave in order to improve themselves.

Now here's a funny thing. In Chief Rapp's presence, most of the Rangers who spent a day of leave with him felt more refreshed than they did during the downward spiral of their trouble-seeking leave days in which feats of drink and battle were pursued relentlessly as some kind of "rest." But on Chief Rapp days, running the perimeter with the SF operator, him calling cadence and laughing in that deep voice then doing some weird version of SF CrossFit halfway around that involved a lot of body weight exercises, finishing the run, and then range time, almost to a Ranger all agreed that one walked away with a clearer mind, not to mention points to pursue better mastery of the gun among other things. Afterward there was usually some meat on the street with a clutch of urchins gathering about and wanting to play the "Ranger Rugby" that Corporal Monroe had taught them.

The Rangers always obliged, and a long game usually lasted well into the darkness of the night.

Then…

The Rangers often remarked that that day with the SF chief was the best day of leave.

Like it was real rest and that training and perfection and physical punishment and meat on the street were… sort of their natural state.

And the Ranger Rugby with the kids.

"I felt… human again," as Tanner put it. "Don't know why. Don't know how. Just did. And I'll tell ya, Talk. That ain't a bad thing always. Even for a Ranger… 'cause there's that line we all know that's inside us."

"What line?" I asked.

Tanner was silent for a long moment as he burned a dart and thought about what he was going to say next.

Then, in that dead voice he sometimes dropped into, he spoke.

"That line you cross where you can become like them, Talker. Those monsters and devils out there in the dark we goin' to fight. Beyond the wire out there in the madness that's this place. Monsters like us, Talk. Chief Rapp… he's different.

The Light, like it's a person, it comes through him… and keeps all that terrible endless dark back and away from… from you. Even I can feel it, Talk, and I'm almost all spent up on being human. I ain't got long now. Sorry 'bout that."

I felt a cold river of ice wash over me. And then, because I didn't want to deal with it… I pushed it away and…

I'm not even going to deal with that right here and right now.

There's no room.

Later.

Maybe never.

Maybe Tanner's just weird.

But it's odd. My undead Ranger buddy is… getting *odd*. More odd by the day. So, this is just a new level. Right? That's all. It doesn't matter. He's my best friend. I'll take whatever he's becoming and we will make it, and I'll be grateful because the Ruin without him… I don't want to think about that. Can't. Not right now.

Here, universe, Talker's sliding his credit app across the table. Let me have this one on credit, please. I can't pay now, and I'm not sure I ever can.

Okay?

Okay…

But…

"What's the Light, Tanner?"

Because that was interesting the way he referred to it. I felt the capital letter. The *Light*. Something else other than what he'd just said was coming.

I had to know this thing too. It all goes in the book. Even the things I don't want to. Just give me time. I will do what

I've said I would.

Just… not right now. Not yet.

Tanner turned to me, slowly. In that undead way. Then smiled and it was Tanner, it was him, the real Tanner that used to be, coming back through the other side of that half-dead face.

That sly smile the whores in the tavern knew he was good by. Cut-up women seeking safe harbor in the arms of an undead soldier. Somewhere. Just this once.

"Light of the Hidden King, buddy," he said slowly. "Chief's like… a doorway for it. That's what we feel when we spend that day doin' those SF tricks with him. We feel… the Light. Like he's some good… I dunno… preacher… who's preaching a good word without using any words at all. That's what it seems like to me, Talk."

Interesting.

Kennedy indicates that the Green Beret is some kind of *cleric*. A powerful holy man. Who has powers like Kennedy has spells. But how in the Ruin Revealing did that happen?

How did the divine… intervene?

And again, I don't believe in anything. And so this is a mystery. One I'm not sure how to deal with.

But I can tell you, regardless of the Light… Chief Rapp is good. And around him… you feel like… you can do the impossible.

I felt it when I was going out to stand second for Captain Tyrus. Felt it when the Green Beret came out from cover, movements concise, and just held my shoulder, putting one hand up and letting his rifle dangle on the sling.

"Lord," he said. "Help my man here."

That was all. I don't know if anyone had ever prayed for me in my life. But I gotta be honest. I felt something.

Some peace.

Some confidence that everything was… going to work out.

It all goes in the book. Even if I don't believe. It's been marked down. You deal with it.

So Chief Rapp, all six foot six, jacked and strapped and ready to go with all his high-speed SF gear, was there, smiling, and his white teeth and the whites of his eyes were brilliant in the desert light against his dark black skin.

Situation.

Specialist Commons was missing down along the River of Night. He'd scouted much of the area south of our position and was getting close to a sunken temple some of the Saurian captives indicated might be a way into the valley without having to fight our way through the main defenses or going in by air and suddenly getting lit up by magic meteor air defense from every bandaged-wrapped mummy high priest and undead necrotic Saurian sorcerer crawling out of their dusty black holes of burial tombs all across the Valley of Death that surrounded most of the Grand Pyramid.

"He was here above these rapids yesterday after we got our last check-in," said the smaj, pointing to the locations we needed to note on the projected map. "This temple entrance could be near these cliffs here, and we thought these two great statues we captured on drone recon might be an indicator of the entrance nearby, if they aren't flanking the entrance itself. He was going into the waters near there around dawn this morning. But he was ordered not to go into the temple if he found it."

The smaj flipped two high-res black-and-white photos captured from drone recon out on the briefing table. The two monolithic statues against the red stone of the massive cliff wall. They were immediately reminiscent of the ancient carvings of Ramses the Second. Typical Egyptian stuff, seated, knees together, gazing out imperiously at all the mortals that bowed and scraped in the carving and the serving. The Nile River and the reeds gathering in ornate steps that led down to the waters of the River of Night.

Or what we once called the Nile.

The steps were cracked and broken and half-sunk in the tranquil dark waters made somehow more inky by the black-and-white nature of the captured drone recon image.

But the faces on the statues weren't the human faces of ancient pharaohs from some lost dynasty staring impassively at the lesser mortals who dared approach their final resting place.

They were Saurian.

Almost crocodilian.

Reptiles.

The teeth of these giant carved lizard men seemed to smile in greedy death and hatred. And their eyes, even carved in stone, were alight with some sinister evil inhuman fire that bore no semblance to anything that could be thought of as an emotion or feeling a man or a woman might have.

Remember: *The Ruin… reveals.*

These monsters, just like the Saur, every one of them, had once either been animals or humans like us… before the nano-plague cut loose thanks to some long-lost coder known as "The Spider Queen." Changing everything and everyone. Granting powers and abilities, turning some into orcs and vampires and others into elves and dwarves and all kinds of monsters based on some insane logic known only to her, whoever she once was.

We'd learned all this in the fragments of the *Book of Skelos* we'd managed to collect.

And by *we*, I mean really just me and Vandahar. Kennedy didn't seem too interested, and I found that surprising.

"That's just lore, Talk. From ten thousand years ago. I'm not interested in that. I'm interested in *creating* the lore that will come to be those fragments ten thousand years *from* now. That stuff... it's just old news. We know that stuff. Let's make new stuff. That's what I wanna do, Talker. You know?"

I didn't. Kennedy is weird. But he's my friend too.

Ranger Wizard Specialist Kennedy. Sometimes he's just as alien to the rest of us as those carved Saurian titans that guard the resting place of some once-powerful servant of Sût.

Sût the Undying.

HVT Mummy.

The smaj landed his finger on the area we were going to search for the missing Ranger who got bit by a sea hoochie and became... one of them.

Breathe underwater.

Talk to fish.

Swim fast.

Aqua Ranger.

"Commons is good," grumbled the smaj. "But he's a young man. And young men do what they want no matter how hard you try to steer 'em away from the stupid they're intent on getting up to. And being that he got turned into what you guys are calling… *Aqua Ranger*… by one of them damned sea hoochies… that gives him a special skill set none of the rest of us have. That's why we had him scouting the river without support. He's better on his own. But like I said… he's a young man. Course he was gonna wanna go into that temple once he found it and try to get something to impress the rest of us. That's what young men do. So…"

Then the smaj swore.

"That's what young *Rangers* do. That's what makes 'em the Achilleses and the Ajaxes."

Mission.

"We're going south to find him, or find what happened to him," said the captain tersely as he made last-second adjustments to his gear.

I didn't like the last part of that. It was a possibility. *What happened to him.* But the captain was saying it… which made it a possibility.

And I didn't like that.

Sometimes you pray even when you don't believe.

Execution.

"We take the bird and fly over the target area," continued Captain Knife Hand. "We see sign of him, we try to extract him right then and there. If not, we land on this small sandbar out here in the river and cross the shallows and look around for the temple entrance. If we find the entrance, then we go in and look for him. That's how we're going to do this, and that's my intent. We find him and bring him back."

Then without break, the commander knife-handed each of our duties at us and the Air Force crew chief entered the

TOC and nodded to the captain that the Little Bird was ready to take us in.

They were ready to go, but range was a problem. The window for insertion and extraction would be tight due to the distance the Little Bird needed to fly.

But the captain had an answer to that.

"If we insert on the island, Sergeant Kang you're on security. Strap a SAW and be ready to hold the perimeter. You see a red flare from the direction we go in to find Ranger Commons, you order the pilot to spin up and get out of there. That means we've met a significant enemy force and will E-and-E to a safer location. Copy? I do not want the bird in *any* kind of jeopardy. It's irreplaceable for future operations in the coming operation."

Sergeant Kang nodded and spoke quietly. Rarely did emotion enter his solemn, almost seething demeanor even though he seemed to boil with some quiet anger and contempt for all.

Then again… that's pretty standard for most Rangers.

I have learned to accept it as basic programming for the operating system.

So far no one has accused *me* of it though. I'm still pretty happy and talkative and I'm waiting for the day when someone asks me, "Who pissed in your Wheaties?" That's when I'll know my journey to the Ranger-side is complete.

That murder scowl and cold impatient stare will become as permanent on me as the features on those carved alien Saur down along the River of Night.

"Copy, sir," said Sergeant Kang. "Hold the perimeter. Receive red flare signal, get airborne and RTB."

Captain Knife Hand turned and knife-handed me.

"Commons was talking with the locals, Corporal. If we encounter any…"

Clearly the were-tiger killing machine that was our commander was having trouble with this part of the order as he made that permanent indigestion face and rolled his eyes for the briefest of seconds.

"… *locals*… then you engage with them and see if they know his current or recent location." Another knife hand. "Chief Rapp, as a certified combat diver you will assess the river and see what we can develop there regarding Ranger Commons's whereabouts. I'll scout for a trail along the river and toward the possible location of the sunken temple for any sign of Specialist Commons. We target the steps and entrance to the temple and search from there. And stay on commo as we go, sitrepping every five minutes if our tasks take us in different directions. Thirty minutes on the ground and we make our way back to the bird and get out of there.

"Again, if I fire that red flare, wherever you're at, get back to the bird immediately and exit the AO. You'll have about five minutes for the pilot to get spun up once I give the signal. I suggest you use this time to do just that as the red flare indicates things have mostly gone pear-shaped sideways and, again… we cannot afford any losses with coming operations in the south."

He looked at each of us in the twilight of the TOC. Outside the day was heading to a sunburnt red afternoon. Soon it would be night, and the moon would cross the sky and the wind would cover the land once again with more blowing sand.

We had NODs for the night work and the search.

"Affirmative, sir," each of us replied, and then we exited and were moving to the Little Bird, clipping into the airframe and hanging our feet over the skids.

For me… this is as Ranger as it gets.

And yeah, I was worried about Commons and the air felt electric and my rifle was comfortable in my hands.

Chief Rapp patted my leg and smiled.

"Here we go, my man. We in it now," said the Green Beret.

Then the Little Bird hauled herself skyward and we were headed south to rescue Commons.

It was the only outcome I would accept.

CHAPTER FIVE

STRAP hanging off a fast little helicopter capable of dumping blistering hot death from above or dropping death itself in the form of Rangers… is about as operator as operator gets.

It's not often a linguist gets in on the juice.

Or, as Tanner puts it…

"Action's always the real juice, Talk. Everything else, booze, women, fast cars, and whatever you wanna test the edge of life and death with, when you ask the real pipe hitters, the chief and the captain and a few others in the detachment that's born to go dark… everything else is just a nicotine patch to pipe hitters. They just burnin' smokes and waitin' for the next chance to get it on. That's all."

Pipe hitters.

A term I should discuss for whoever ends up reading this account of our time in the Ruin. But for now, let's say they're the guys who pull the trigger in the dark of mornings when everyone's asleep and debts have come to be collected right there where those debtors thought they were *absolutely* safe. Pipe hitters are the real deal, and not everyone in Special Operations is one. But a ride on an AH-6 Little Bird into a dangerous and very tense situation, outnumbered and beyond the wire, tasked with pulling off the seemingly impossible, once again, is very pipe hitter, if not the epitome.

This was something they did and in so doing did not nec-essarily include the detachment linguist. There wasn't much talking on these kinds of operations.

Probably some real up-close and personal heartbreaking and life-taking though.

Unfortunately, currently all the detachment pipe hitters were busy throwing flaming tomahawks or trying to get it on with the local girls regardless of what flavor of demi-human they were, and yeah there were some strange and otherworld-ly beautiful girls, orcish ones even, "thicc" with some shapely quads, who danced in some of the seedier taverns, and defi-nitely the product of interspecies *relations* of an orc raid some twenty years back.

Some of them were downright smokin'. And spoiler: they likey-like Ranger-boys. "Not break easy like some," they'd murmur in their seductively hoarse raspy bedroom voices as they unabashedly shook their goods.

But I digress.

"Are you…" I asked Tanner when he told me what a pipe hitter was, "one?"

Tanner was always, when I look back on it now, teaching me the delineation between the various shades of operators, when at first I would have told you they were all the same and better than me and that was all I could comprehend just out of RASP and dazzling the upper brass with my gift for speaking in foreign tongues.

Pipe hitters were different than all the other operators, and they could be found throughout SOCOM. They were the ones that got called on when it absolutely had to be done, No Fail protocols in effect.

Chief Rapp was *definitely* one, despite the generally positive demeanor.

So was the captain. Or he had once been in another life not the one he wore in front of us. And I could see that.

Hardt was on his way to becoming one, and had things gone the way they had been going before…

Well, if things had kept going that way, both Kurtz and Hardt would have been lured into the Super Friends, some call them the Green Berets, to track and become such.

Many of the Rangers would definitely qualify and ran their game of death with a ruthlessness, savagery, and Ranger-smash cleverness that made them the stone-cold shock troops of the Pipe Hitter class of special operations warrior.

And now I'm gonna insert something that might clear things up for people who wanna understand where Rangers are in the pipe hitter hierarchy and why everything I'm writing down might just be wrong.

It's a quote Tanner butchered badly by just saying, "When they all in troubs, Talker. They call us."

I asked him where he got that, and he said some old Ranger command sergeant major named Birch. The exact quote I didn't have to scout around too much to find, because every Ranger NCO in the detachment knew it and said it with a rare smile. Brief. Not their usual hardboiled killer. But something they were proud of and said briefly and quickly.

Later, I would note one other thing about the way each Ranger NCO recounted the quote to me. It wasn't just a compliment. In the eyes of those state-of-the-art, tip-of-the-hardcore-spear killers I'd become part of by paying the rent on the scroll, the quote, in the eyes of those small-unit combat leaders, was something they knew they had to live up to every day. Because when the whole card that was the Rangers needed to be thrown down on the table, they needed to be worthy of it. So that smile of pride at what CSM Birch had once stated passed like a summer storm in their eyes, and then the realization of what it meant, what was required, replaced the smile and rested there next to all that cold, no-joke murder they were ready to lay down at a moment's notice.

The quote…

I know. Get on with it, Talker. I hear ya, Tanner, Kennedy, occasionally Corporal Monroe. I get it. I go on…

The quote…

"When SEALs are in trouble, they call Rangers. When Delta is in trouble, they call Rangers. When Rangers are in trouble… they call more Rangers."

So sayeth Command Sergeant Major Birch.

Who is legendary, even among Rangers.

And yes, there were pipe hitters in the elite line units as well as legs, which is what we call non-airborne troops, infantry line units. Or as Heraclitus would have put it…

"Out of every one hundred men, ten shouldn't even be there, eighty are just targets, nine are the real fighters, and we are lucky to have them, for they make the battle. Ah, but the one, one is a warrior, and he will bring the others back."

The pipe hitter is the one you can count on to go out and kill when it has to be done for the mission to continue and others to survive. And fortunately, they have a tendency to collect in the Rangers and then eventually get sucked up the shadowy ladder into the darker and darker realms of Special

Operations units, including some never heard of.

So, on a streaking AH-6, over hostile territory and headed deep, deep behind enemy lines, everyone on a strap is usually a pipe hitter because the Little Bird can't carry much. Thus, everyone on that ride into the whirlwind needs to be highly capable.

Lucky me, much of the usual *everyone* was drunk.

So I got to roll on this one.

All those killers were on leave and Commons was missing and that was drop-everything important as far as Rangers were concerned.

Our brother was downrange and beyond the wire and he needed help or retrieval.

I looked across the deck of the vibrating jumping little helicopter that seemed to want to shake itself apart through sheer energy displacement and watched as, with barely a movement of his powerful frame, and total, utter control, the captain, hanging from the opposite strap, transformed into his were-tiger form.

Discipline beyond imagining.

White-and-orange-striped fur burst forth along his exposed arms and neck where his Crye Precisions, chest rig, and expanded plate carrier didn't cover. His muscles grew, and the gear that had been developed for him specially, tailored in the Forge's menu, chest rig and plate carrier and even the war belt, accommodated the half-man half-tiger carrying a dialed-up M4 as the fast-moving helicopter clung to the desert deck and entered sharp canyons and desolate wadis to the south, twisting and turning while the SOAR pilot laughed and told us to, "Hang on, this is where it gets fun, Ranger boys...

Gunfighter Two to Playpen, picking up course track getting dirty. Here we go…"

Then he whooped like a real live cowboy riding herd and picking up the strays.

A sound I knew from my father's world.

And Gunfighter Two wasn't joking.

The pilot straight-up and flat-out flew the AH-6 like he stole it, and that was good because we needed to get close without attracting a lot of attention.

To our west, circling near some tight canyons on thermals, we saw a swarm of large crows and Vandahar had said, "These serve the dark pharaoh and are his eyes and ears in some of the more remote wastes of his necrotic empire."

The pilot got closer to the deck, and we followed a dead tributary, streaking over burnt-out husks of reeds and fractured canal ruins and the remains of once-fertile fields. It was lifeless, and despite the day's heat it made you feel cold to see all that emptiness where life had once been.

It was like looking at the results of what the world would become if we failed somehow to do what we'd come to do.

Kill Sût the Undying.

An inhuman thing as old as the Ruin itself, if the rumors were to be believed, who had already, somehow, defeated death itself.

On the other side of the ancient farms, we entered a line of bright broken mountains and followed a pass, climbing higher for a bit. The chopper twisted and turned and at points rolled hard on its side to follow the narrow pass as the sun flared through my Forge-printed Oakley Shocktubes. I turned once again and saw the captain making last adjustments to his gear, pulling the Vickers sling tight on his M4 with precise movements he was no stranger to.

I remembered the smaj dropping hints about how the man we knew as "Captain Knife Hand" had been up some very dark alleys in his unrated time.

The implied hint was that whoever the captain was, he'd once been with what many simply knew as… The Unit.

Delta.

First Special Forces Operational Detachment—Delta, or First SFOD-D. Sometimes called Delta Force or Combat Applications Group, CAG for short. And also, occasionally, Army Compartmented Elements aka ACE, or, within Joint Special Operations Command… Task Force Green. Yes, that super-secret special operations force of the Army that most simply know only the name of—Delta—and little more than that. They do, or so it is rumored and never confirmed, the most important counterterrorism, hostage rescue, direct action, and special reconnaissance missions. Their targets are often the highest-value targets.

So… pipe hitters. The very definition of the term.

Next to the captain, seemingly unconcerned that the man next to him had just, with little to no effort, transformed into a man-sized humanoid version of nature's most dangerous predator, a Bengal tiger, was Sar'nt Kang, strapping the tight MK48 super-SAW firing seven-six-two. The Tasmanian devil of a Ranger master breacher was draped with at least three belts around his impressive shoulders. And then there was that ruck loaded with a ton of fun and games the explosives expert was seldom without.

Sergeant Kang seemed almost meditative as he hung his

boots over the fast-moving landscape, loaded for bear and sitting next to an apex killer made more so by the Ruin doing its revealing…

Then Kang hung a stream of dip into the wind as the bird rolled ground toward us, a pro move as the dip went high and away from the bird, executed so beautifully it was like the sergeant was some movie actor who'd nailed his take like it was a thing of beauty and disgust all in the one moment, saying everything about the lifetaker the actor was playing the part of.

I know. Talker, seriously now, you're waxing eloquent about spitting dip off a bird…

Yeah. I am.

It was… beautiful. Don't @ me.

Sar'nt Kang… pipe hitter. For sure.

And then there's me. I considered being sick for a second at the sudden wash of vertigo as engine wash and exhaust, and a screaming turbine practically howling and beating everything to death at the same time, added a shifting-world perspective presenting a new puzzle every other second that had me suddenly staring at the racing desert wadi we streaked over, or at burning blue and red sky…

And that thought that you might get sick… surfaced.

Then I realized I'd never live it down and this was my once chance to "Pipe Hit" at the introductory level.

So I imagined coffee.

Coffee.

Coffee don't judge. Coffee don't @.

Chief Rapp's big hand was on my leg as though he knew where my mind and body were telling me I should be despite my best efforts to Ranger, verb, and not hurl off the bird into prop wash.

No one will ever confuse me with a pipe hitter, was the thought I had, and it was brief and startlingly clear.

I looked up, and Chief Rapp smiled that big, friendly, confident, "We got this" smile the SF must learn in order to convince the indigs they fight with that the impossible… might just be possible.

The jocked-up-for-war-mode Green Beret nodded toward the human were-tiger on the other side of the deck of the airframe.

Part of, and leading, our element into the darkness on the LZ.

"Ain't the strangest insert I ever had, Talker. But… it's up there."

Then he laughed loud and the whipping, beating Little Bird began to climb, hauling for the lip of the end of the small canyon we'd been flying.

Seconds later we were over flat desert, and a camel train of orc raiders was scattering in every direction. The armored orcs waved spears up at us and shouted orc stuff, probably blasting their Uroo Uroo horns.

I swallowed hard. I would not hurl.

Ran my hands across my M4 and made sure it was ready to go, pushing on the mag and feeling my thumb against the safety.

A flick and we'd go live.

I'd go live.

Select fire on the ground for security and conservation of ammo.

What we had was on us.

No resupply until we fly.

Anyone got hit, I'd go to full auto and lay as much suppressive hate as I could because immediate first aid in an ambush is to return fire. Hard.

On the ground we'd get away from the bird and establish a perimeter. Then move on the search area.

Thoughts of vertigo vanished as I focused on my part and contribution to what needed to be done on the ground.

I could do that.

Didn't make me a pipe hitter. Not by far.

But it did make me an asset to the mission. And for me that was enough.

I could do this.

CHAPTER SIX

THE ride south into what had once been Egypt was illuminating.

Before I tell you what happened on the SAR... I know, I know... rabbit trails. This ain't one about coffee... or Rangers. But those terms might show up, so thoughts and prayers for your tender feelings.

This is probably a good time to let you know what we would be getting into soon. The situation on the ground as it was.

What we were streaking over in the AI1-6 Little Bird, boots over the skids and clipped into the airframe, was the area we'd invade soon. Much of the resemblance to the lost and ancient lands of the pharaohs of Egypt was gone, even though the Saur seemed to have taken the development of their post-cataclysm nano-plague culture from that ancient society that was old even when the world was the way it was ten thousand years ago before we'd gone through the QST and leapt forward in time from Area 51 to save the world.

We missed our insertion and...

One hundred centuries later, and a major comet strike on the planet that changed significant parts of what we once called Earth... or the Ruin now... will do that to you.

Much of the Saurian civilization, and I'll talk about it later in depth...

I know what you're thinking.

Yeah, lucky me. I bet he mentions coffee and Rangers. A lot.

That's where you're right, kiddo.

Anyway, most of what I've gleaned from the many hours I've spent in the company of a very wise and very old sage in the Learned Districts, as they are known, of the City of Sûstagul, a frail wisp of a man with a singsong papery voice who is supposedly the foremost in knowledge regarding the Saur and how they came to be—a sage named Hazzim, who may or may not be completely crazy—revolves around the Giza Plateau.

The stuff he tells me sure sounds crazy, and I've seen some crazy stuff. But he's a good storyteller, he seems to enjoy my visits, and his wife grinds and brews a mean bean.

She also makes fried honey to go with it. So of course I'll listen to crazy, because coffee.

Never change, me. Never change.

And yeah... there's some oddities there in the story of the Saur that were mysteries even in our time ten thousand long years ago, and I wonder... I wonder deeply... what exactly we're getting ourselves into and what's been going on long before we ever showed up here in the Ruin to save what remains of civilization from strange otherworldly sorcerers and their mummy allies.

Near Giza is the Nile River. In the bird, that's off to our left as we head south and should be making an appearance here soon before dusk. The Nile, or what the Ruin now calls the River of Night. The ancient city of Cairo once lay there along the River of Night, or the Nile, where the pyramids of Giza once were.

They ain't there now.

That's all gone. Cairo. The pyramids, once one of the Seven Wonders of the Ancient World.

But the plateau where those wonders once were is still there. As is the river, with a few minor alterations. But that's rivers for ya.

River gonna river. Ain't like rocks.

Atop the Giza Plateau there is now… one pyramid. And it flat-out dwarfs the old crumbling ones that were once great enigmatic mysteries lying there among the sands and the wind for thousands of years.

This is the Grand Pyramid of Sût the Undying. And it's just not some tomb… even though when you consider the Lich Pharaohs' undead nature… it kinda is.

It's more. Apparently.

And an understanding of the Saur, as much as can be understood… will explain that. Later.

As much as they can be explained.

And seriously… it's nuts. I've listened to it hour after hour, coffee after coffee, fried honey keeping me awake and wired to write down all the crazy.

It's madness.

That's all I can say.

The Saur, the Lich Pharaohs, who they once were, the best and brightest of us or so they told everyone, all it is, was, and is, is an end-of-the-world death cult that never ended itself and found a way to stay right on the edge of terror and apocalypse forever… in undeath.

The lizard people they really were, *but now with undeath*! Like they're some new and improved feature on some old and tired food product.

Frosted Flakes, but now with *green energy*! Save the planet, tastes great! Or no, it was, *They're grrrrreat!*

Whatever.

No one needs Frosted Flakes and no one I knew ever ate them.

But it's a real hat trick the Saur have managed to pull over ten thousand years, and if it weren't for the Nether Sorcerer and his strange, and seriously his crazy makes the Saur crazy sound sane and rational, outer dark and other dimensions and all… if not for him, the Saur and Sût the Undying were the undisputed bad guys of the Ruin until that being calling himself the Nether Sorcerer showed up.

According to the ancient texts.

Oh no. Now I sound like Vandahar. I should just grow a beard and carve a walking staff. Then it's hippies' walks and the smaj's undying contempt.

So the Saur are from, using the undeath concept, actually our time. And the Nether Sorcerer… this'll be funny later, and if it's true, well, apparently, he's not from around here.

BWAHAHAHAHAHA!!!!

And if that's not weird enough you, well, you don't even want to know what the few fragments of the *Book of Skelos* we've discovered have to say about the Saur.

Bad stuff, and unfortunately an indictment of what we once were as a civilization and who it was exactly that ruled over us.

Hell, half the time I'm hearing this stuff, and this is part of my work for the smaj, developing intel on our enemy, I don't even believe it.

And I've bought art from guys selling it out of the trunks of their cars. Long story, not important. First paycheck as a kid working at a Togo's.

In my defense, "Charlie rhymes with Gnarly" told me it was "an investment."

But this is the Ruin. You embrace the fantasy. Even the sucky parts of it you don't like.

So, the guy the Rangers have come to kill, HVT Mummy, Sût the Undying, is southeast of the desert port city of Sûstagul we are operating out of.

Put that on your mental map.

That's the port we took away from the Saur and smashed their war fleet in. Effectively denying the Saurian contribution to the End War in the north, with the Nether Sorcerer and the Black Prince, he's a vampire out of the Crow's March and may have been running McCluskey the scumbag SEAL against us, versus the Cities of Men.

Seriously, that sounds cool. I would have watched that Netflix series.

Man… if I were back in the world… said every deployed soldier ever.

Ten thousand years ago I could've turned all this into some cheap fantasy series and got myself a big old publishing contract with some New York City publisher, martini lunches at some cool places, book signings at The Strand, maybe even a movie deal while sitting around drinking coffee and making this stuff up like some loser chungo screenwriter who lived near the beach and had a serious actor-model-dancer-weathercaster-newsgirl problem between royalty checks.

I coulda been a contender.

But instead, I Rangered, and here I am Rangering.

Take that, Kennedy. The blows will never stop. I will make it rain in the club of your mind with the usage of that word.

Because I am small, mean, and a Ranger, and this is my gift of non-fatal burritos for your little review about me using the word "Ranger" too much.

If I am known for nothing else, then let it be that. I have a calling. I can live with it.

But with coffee, because me. Hey, Talker here. Nice to meet you. Have I told you about coffee? Come, join my cult. Stay a while. Don't care if you do, or do not. No coffee, then more for me.

Lucky me, yay!

In other words… Easy Street. If I'd gone back in time and sold everything that happened to us to Hollywood, people would watch the hell out of that show.

And there'd be dope action figures.

So… just saying… it's a dream. But it is mine.

And…

I would have become weak and soft and not Ranging or even pipe hitting at the introductory level as we raced toward the Nile, or the River of Night if you prefer, at one hundred and eighty some-odd kilometers south of our foothold in the Land of Black Sleep.

Ancient Egypt, or what it once was. But now filled with undead lizard men who dream terrible dreams of conquering the world. Again.

Yeah, they conquered a lot of it a long time ago before we ever showed up.

Lizards. Undead ones. That's the important part to who

they are, not once were, but that too. But who they still are. Or so Crazy Hazzim says.

But then again, he's crazy. And he's my source. I'll get into that later.

The Ruin reveals. That and lizard men and undeath and you've almost got eighty percent of the whole crazy picture of what the Saur really are.

Now I sound like Crazy Hazzim.

Is that an improvement over sounding like old Vandahar?

I don't know. Jury's out.

Coffee. Not hurling.

And not everything in Ruin Revealing is a pretty-but-dangerous were-tiger Ranger captain or a jacked minotaur Ranger.

Sometimes what the Ruin has revealed… was right there underneath it all.

The Saur.

Undeath.

Keep those things in mind as we go. Remember when I told you it gets crazy, friend?

Yeah.

Well, here's where it starts…

Heading south and beat to death by the wind and adrenaline of the mission, the day fades and the sun falls like a dying red star in the forbidden west. We are flying the Nile now. Or the River of Night, if you prefer. East of the Grand Pyramid of Sût the Undying himself and the Temples of the Dead up there higher in the bloody murder of the Giza Plateau.

The Temples of the Dead is a vast "living" necropolis that's really a series of powerful fortresses guarding the approach to the sacred plateau of the Lich Pharaohs. It's here that the last legion of Saurian warriors, the best according to our medusa ally, intend to make their final stand against the assault from the north we are putting together more and more by the day.

That's the punch. We want them to see that.

It's the knife between the ribs we're still trying to figure out if my attendance in command team briefings has told me anything.

But that's beyond my scope. I just accept it will be a fight either way, and I will be in it. And I will win it.

Energetically will I meet the enemies of my country. I shall defeat them on the field of battle for I am better trained and will fight with all my might. Surrender is not a Ranger word. I will never leave a fallen comrade to fall into the hands of the enemy and under no circumstances will I ever embarrass my country.

Before the pyramid and the River of Night and the Temples of the Dead begins… *begins* is the important word here in the geographical description of what we've gotten ourselves into… is a vast crescent that's known as the Valley of Kings and Priests.

This crescent wasn't here ten thousand years ago and is the result of some ancient fracture in the Ruin, or the Earth if you prefer, formed by that long-ago comet strike that brought, or as old-man wizard Vandahar would put it, "*heralded* the coming of the Nether Sorcerer and the dragons."

Heralded.

That's such a Vandahar word.

The crescent makes its way around the entire Giza Plateau south and then heads east toward the River of Night.

The Nile, as it was once known. I know, I keep making that point but I'm reinforcing it so I can give you a mental picture of the layout of the coming battle.

The crazy of the Saur will distract you, it does tend to do that now that you know, or will know, what they are, so getting the geography and the operations and what we have to go through to accomplish the hit on the HVT will make things easier.

I'm hoping to make a mental sand table for you like a good little small-unit leader. If I get a "go" it's because you had a good picture of operations and were able to follow, and understand the stakes, of the coming operation.

This valley, the Valley of Kings and Priests, or Valley of Death, is filled with the "sleeping" Saur of all castes and powers.

It's mainly for the players. The movers and shakers. The powerful in the Saurian cabal.

Many are necromantic priests of their death cult, but there are also "practitioners of great wizardry," as Vandahar would put it. Did put it. Besides these there are the lower priest classes and the warriors of great renown and even fabled heroes of the past who lay dreaming the undeath sleep for the next epoch when once again the Saur would crawl forth from their dusty old carved tombs and conquer the Ruin once again.

Just like they almost did before.

Tooth and claw and slavery and death, unlimited death forever…

It makes no sense.

And that's because it's crazy, and *they* are crazy.

One more thing to keep in mind as we discover who they really are.

Power tends to corrupt, some old guy who wasn't a Ranger said.

Insertion: Tanner said Lord Acton said that. But he's drunk and so… this information is suspect. We both agreed Lord Acton was not a Ranger, though.

The Saur ruled much of the known Ruin for a long time a long time ago, and in that very long dark age long ago, they accumulated might and magic of great and now unknown power.

Seriously, it was an age of epics that makes the epics of the past look like TikTok videos about how to braid your hair or cook an egg.

The Saurian priests still lying in those temple deeps carved within the crumbling stone of the valley know great… prayers of power. *Prayers to whom?* Talker asketh. But prayers and powers to cause mass death or raise whole armies of bone and dark spirit against us. Diseases that once ravaged continents and lost kingdoms of fable at the farthest ends of the Ruin are rumored to be buried with these diabolical Saurian clerics deep in the vast silent tombs far below the sands and broken rock walls carved with their images in stone titan relief.

Their wizards, on the other hand, according to Vandahar and the council, once knew spells "to stop time itself. To make reality their plaything. And to even cause great destructions to fall from the heavens as though the heavens themselves must yield to their terrible wizardings."

Terrible wizardings… where does he get this stuff? You

guys complain about me using the word coffee once or twice and never minded this overheated wizard word salad Vandahar comes up with like some bad English tragedian trying to make the most of a terrible script being shot in Romania on a budget.

C'mon!

And apparently there is terrible magical stuff even wizards of Vandahar's rank are said not to know anymore.

"Lost to time and the ravages of tyrants," murmurs Vandahar as he stokes his long-stemmed pipe looking at things unseen and once long ago.

When I reported the sage's crazy tales to our resident Gandalf wizard after a late-night interview with the sage…

Hazzim keeps strange hours and only begins his consultations after the moon has crossed the night…

But when I reported this to Vandahar, the power of the Saurian sorcerers, he only chewed the end of his long-stemmed pipe and seemed worried as he saw things in his memory that I could not.

And what he saw seemed to confirm what was said and worry him further.

Then, as if coming to himself and not realizing I was there, old Vandahar only murmured, "These things would be true, Ranger. I have forgotten them if only because their memory was so evil."

After that he seemed not himself for some time. Worried. Alone. Vexed by some question only Vandahar knew the answer to and did not like at all.

So, the Temples of Death. A series of powerful and well-guarded fortresses connected into one vast necropolis.

It guards the stairs and bridges that lead up from the River of Night to the Giza Plateau and the Grand Pyramid of Sût the Undying where our HVT waits for us to do our best to kill him.

And over these bridges and these stairs, guarded with towers brimming with horrors and enemy forces, are the crescent canyons of the Valley of Kings and Priests. A moat, really, for the whole plateau.

The Valley of Death.

Here there are the powerful priests and their small undead holy armies waiting and ready to attack should we try this route. There are powerful wizards with spells that were so terrible and evil, the workers of magic collectively sought to forget these things.

And then there are the warriors and fabled heroes of the Saur who lie in state, waiting to be called into battle once more by their master, the Lich Pharaoh himself.

These warriors were their Achilleses, their Ajaxes, their Robert Rogerses, and all the Medal of Honor awardees that ever were.

If the crazy is to be even half believed.

Seriously, some of the stories I've heard Crazy Hazzim tell of these guys are… no joke.

"Then Phaz-Amuun took his great spear, seven feet long and weighing the weight of three men in full armor, and laid waste unto the enemies of the Pharaoh, destroying ten thousand himself that night with pestilence and lightning emitting from his mighty weapon."

Pestilence and lightning.

Sign me up!

Not.

In the long conquering of the Ruin, and the time under the claw of the Saur, these fabled warriors had accumulated weapons of great power.

So, long story short, each of these guys is pure stud.

The Accadion legions are building their small fortress to the north at the edge of the Temples of the Dead.

To attack, they have to break that dead necropolis, defeat the Saur legion, and then fight their way up onto the Giza Plateau to give battle at the foot of the Grand Pyramid.

The Valley of the Kings and Priests is a moat, and it cannot be used as an avenue of assault or bypass.

And… it's possibly a near endless troop resupply for the enemy. Consider ten thousand years of undead priests, wizards, and guys that kill thousands with a magic spear.

Oh, and there's lots of monsters.

Or temple and tomb guardians.

Then there're the slaves, humans, who can be compelled to fight against us.

And the Katari.

Remember? Cat ninjas that guard the tombs for the Saur.

And finally, there's the Tomb of Sût himself.

And if Crazy Hazzim is even half sane in what he thinks that is…

I don't know how we can fight our way through that.

I relayed all I was told to the captain and the rest of the command team.

In the silence that followed, the captain cleared his throat and said, "If that's where he is, that's where he dies. We will go there, and we will kill him for good. That's what we do."

And then I was all, "Rah! Rangers! Coffee!"
But I kept that part inside.
This time.

CHAPTER SEVEN

THE Little Bird came shooting into the search area, flying nap-of-the-earth protocols up the River of Night, just after full nautical twilight.

It was the perfect time for Rangers to get... Rangering, and that meant stalking and tracking with good moonlight and time.

I anticipated, optimistically because of course I'm me and I totally would do that, that we'd pick up some clue on the OBJ, find some trail, or even Commons just there and ready to go. That we'd be on the ground way shorter than the thirty set aside once we got some kinda clue about what was going on down there along the river we used to call the Nile and the old half-sunken temple Commons was doing an area recon on.

Normally, no Ranger would go alone. At least a four-man team. At the least. But Commons was special. And we didn't have a second Aqua Ranger and supporting equipment, scuba gear and rebreathers cranked out by the Forge, down that far south... impossible under current conditions.

But we needed that way into the Valley of Kings and Priests. Or Priests and Kings. We needed that angle for the hit on Mummy.

On the way south in the Little Bird...

We had one weird incident flying fifty feet over the river

and coming into the AO, area of operation, farther to the north. We spotted something frankly unbelievable—embrace the fantasy—and the pilot wisely decided to fly the low hills on the far side of the river away from the Land of Black Sleep. We deviated off the course track and there was some back and forth over the comm between Captain Knife Hand, call sign Warlord, and the pilot of the AH-6, call sign Gunfighter Two, as we dealt with the new… weird… enemy asset in play and very near the area we needed to search to find our missing Ranger.

Later, when I talked to Ranger Wizard Kennedy about it, the thing that caused us to deviate, we found from our wizard that this monster was called… a dracosphinx.

Half sphinx. Half dragon.

Fun.

Apparently there are other kinds of sphinx—sphinxes?—according to Ranger Wizard Kennedy.

Generally, sphinx are large flying lions with a weird interest in pursuing the truth, or general knowledge, and generally the accumulation of wealth through tough questions. Riddles might be a better word here. Or, in the case of the dracosphinx… they were sort of the gas-station dangerous loners of sphinx-kind. They enjoyed loitering on sunbaked rocks near rivers and pretty much robbing—read killing and then just outright stealing from the dead—what they wanted.

Hence gas-station loner analogy.

They were lazy and mean. And they were dangerous. Especially if you were in a helicopter with no weapon systems to defend itself because it was carrying too many troops loaded with all the ammo they could do.

"According to D&D," Kennedy would tell me later, talking about his game of strange dice and pens and paper, "it's pure predator. Avoid at all costs. Avoid, avoid, avoid."

We had already guessed as much, pretty much at a glance. Sometimes Kennedy's "intel" is just stating the obvious. *If you see a giant dragon-looking sphinx monster, stay away from it.*

Yeah, thanks Kennedy. What would we do without you.

I watched as the captain reversed his wrist and checked the Timex there, weighing mission clock against the aerial danger as the AH-6 hovered low over the sand hidden by dunes from where we'd spotted the winged creature circling on the last of the early evening thermals coming off the river, spreading its large wings and sweeping over vast sections, fast, like streaking death itself, intent on something in the area we needed to get into.

Clearly… it was searching for something too.

And I didn't need an op order to tell me that probably wasn't good.

But… good vibes. Commons was wily. And the water was a kind of "safe" for him in the adult game of tag we call reconnaissance. He hit that water, he could bolt. We'd clocked him underwater doing thirty miles an hour.

We didn't know what that was in knots because we're not Navy. But… it was fast according to Chief Rapp, who was a combat diver.

But with that monster out there searching the very area we needed to be in… I had to wonder who in the City of Sûstagul might have tipped them off, via communication spells, crystal balls, or whatever magic allowed our enemies' sorcerers to talk over vast distances. Someone had flipped the

Red Queen on us and squealed about one of the Little Birds going south, overloaded with Rangers out to hunt bear.

Avoid, avoid, avoid.

Yeah, Kennedy was "a dungeon master" in the strange little game few of us had ever played before the Ruin, a game of myths and monsters and make-believe for adults… but we'd learned in our time in the Ruin to heed what he said even though he never failed to remind us that "It's just a game, guys. Reality might not match the rulebook. Don't bet the farm, or your lives."

He was pedantic to a fault about that warning.

But the clock on finding our Aqua Ranger was burning, and I could tell that the captain was once again dealing with a situation that refused to be easy.

Rangers…

And this is me being serious and not just using the word to piss you off, whoever you are reading this. But this is the part you really understand because it means A LOT, all caps, to them.

Once again, we go back to the creed.

I will never leave a fallen comrade to fall into the hands of the enemy and under no circumstances will I ever embarrass my country.

Of all the things in the creed, that's the one that's as close to religion for them… I mean us.

I have carried a dead Ranger wrapped in his own poncho rather than leave him to our enemies.

It's one of the few things I've ever done… that was right. That's all I can say.

So… we weren't leaving him behind. In whatever state

he was.

And the captain was one of us. We didn't know a lot about him, and I doubted we ever would know his full story. All his stories. Even the dark ones beyond what the smaj hinted at.

Officers aren't supposed to tell you their stories.

They are men.

But much, much more is required of them. And so, the guy who orders everyone to march to their death, and then leads the way… he's got to be… aloof. Mysterious. Different.

The power of life and death require such things.

And he's the one who decides who lives… and who dies.

But he is a Ranger. We know that about him.

I wanted Commons to be on the ground when we came in. Alive. And smiling like he does.

He smiles when anyone says "I got bit!" at him.

He knows that's how you handle some of your not-so-finest moments. We all have them.

Trust me, "Talker" isn't that flattering of a nickname in a hardcore Army unit of stone-cold grim-faced killers.

But I wanted him to be there on the ground.

As in, "Hey there," says Commons. "My comm went bad. I figured you'd come looking for me. No worries. Gimme a new radio and I'll continue on mission."

The hardened features of the captain explained to me, without words, "easy days" were something he'd never known in all his strange life.

And he didn't need your pity. He would just do his best until there wasn't anything left of him. And then… rest. Finally.

But that meant death for a man like him.

For a hot moment the captain stared out into the dark and contemplated his moves as the bird hovered, blowing sand and burning fuel it didn't have too much of to spare.

He spoke to the pilot.

"Pop up and take a peek on night vision to see if we can pick this thing up, or if it's moved on, Gunfighter."

"Copy," noted the pilot. "Popping for a look-see…"

Power was added to the helicopter's collective and the AH-6 crested the dune that blocked us from the wide river out there to the west, gleaming like blue and silver beaten armor in the early night as the moon began to ride high in the darkening skies.

Nothing.

The strange beast was gone now.

"Clear as far as I can tell…" noted the pilot over the comm. The dull hum in the transmission seemed like an entire universe as we waited for the order that would either send us in… or… RTB.

Return to base.

The captain simply said, "Take us in, Gunfighter," and the pilot pushed the bird up and over the dune and we were headed back down to the river, fast.

Time was burning. And so was available fuel.

A few minutes later we were down on the sandbar we'd selected for an LZ. It was mostly bare except for a small lagoon of reeds and papyrus stalks grown and clustered on the side of the river we needed to cross to reach the remains of the sunken temple.

The AH-6 shut down on the sandbar, its turbine spooling slower and slower, the blades windmilling to stillness as the instruments finally ticked into bare murmurs of silence.

We were out of the AH-6 and on all four points in a short patrol halt conducting our SLLS, stopping, looking, listening, and… smelling, as the bird and the island got quieter and quieter, and we became one with the night in the Land of Black Sleep.

A river in the desert that had once been the land of Ancient Egypt. One of the cradles of a civilization that was now so gone, and so alien to the present, the Ruin, that the ancient past might as well have been some made-up fairy tale about a place called Atlantis.

So this is what I saw as we waited on one knee, scanning the darkness out there, watching the night, and taking it all in as we slowly became acclimated to the ambient light courtesy of the moon and the night.

We'd save our night optical devices, or NODs, until it was time to either go into the temple or go hot.

Knife Hand had covered that in the op order, and so far I was operating within minimal straphanger standards… standards I had decided must be met so as to not out myself for what I really was… not a straphanger. Among straphangers.

But I was doing my job and not ruining it for everyone and so… Talker is bigga straphanger, as Jabba the goblin might say.

Note, for some odd reason, in goblin-Jabba speak… one bigga means small.

Gobs are weird. And ours gets weirder every day as he becomes some amalgam of murderous little goblin slash community dog meets Rangers meets G.I. Joe World War 2 Dogface guy. Also, he just eats dip and he thinks coffee is disgusting.

Obviously, he's an uncouth savage.

But I digress…

What I saw on the *look* portion of the SLLS, there in the classic Ranger short-halt take-a-knee position…

Like hunting animals on the African savanna, watching for prey in the moonlight. Rangers have always struck me as such when this short halt occurs. They are totally dialed into their environments in ways people, normal people, will never be.

Never try.

Never attain.

Never experience.

And it's so weird… it's so easy to get here to where we were as we became the night. All you have to do is stop. Look. Listen. And smell. The night.

The land.

The world.

All the life and death in it. Plants and enemies. So many things…

Suddenly, the world you're in… becomes much bigger than you've ever imagined with all your distractions, concerns, and things you think are important.

The night was simply beautiful as we conducted the SLLS.

In the silence of the aftermath of the Little Bird's constant destruction of air molecules in order to achieve flight and haul us to our objective, the night that lay out there before us was like something Van Gogh might have painted in his most lucid moments when the insanity fled as he communed with the divine that gave his tortured mind… comfort. It was a beautiful and strange painting of things I never thought I'd ever see. And I'd spent much of my life dreaming of all the places I'd go and speak languages in. I like going places. Like seeing things…

There was the temple across the reeds and murmuring River of Night. Looming in the dark like some unquiet thing that made no sound at all but was there nonetheless.

There was the land on both sides of the River of Night. The land on the side of the Kingdom of Sût the Undying was the current extent of the Saurian empire, the river serving as the demarcation of that empire's boundary according to all the fading yellow maps and ancient traditions. It was rocky and full of cliffs there, with strange features like dark monoliths over there across the water.

And… teeth. The rock walls were like teeth in the night. Teeth of a wild and dangerous animal. Teeth waiting to consume you…

The very nature of those features over there was foreboding. And… a challenge. But maybe that's just the Ranger in me.

But I wanted to go in there… like it was some edge. Some edge that would show me who was better… it, or me? And I had to know that answer.

Oh mama. I'm turning into ultra-Chad adventure junkie Sar'nt Thor.

I calmed myself from delusions of edges and facing grinning death in the temples and tombs of that land by reminding myself coffee was probably in short supply over there and so…

Not a Top Ten Talker Edge to test Talker by.

I need something more like a fifteen-city tour of the greatest coffee plantations in the Ruin complete with daily tastings, jazz ensembles, and perhaps a good book and some local dialects to get into for bonus me points.

That sounds like a better edge for me than certain death in a land of curses and sandstorms and rotting mummies and undead pharaohs that may be eight to ten thousand years old depending on how crazy is the wife's bean brew old Hazzim is on that particular night of sagely recountings.

As the moon rose and my eyes adjusted to the night, across the sparkling waters in the lunar light, beyond the reeds and the shadowy murk of the far shore, I could see those massive carved statues I'd seen in the drone capture images.

Night vision would reveal more.

But for now, the gargantuan carvings were... sinister in what little could be seen of them. As though they were mere dark giants out there in the night close by, patiently waiting for us to come and fall into their greedy cold grasp, and be made meals of later when vast hellish bonfires were made and they roasted us... singing songs no mortal should ever hear.

So... reading back over this... that last passage... that's oddly descriptive for me. But that's what I was thinking right there as I conducted the *look* portion of the SLLS and watched those unquieting things in the quiet dark of the night.

The story of that place was that image to me, and it made no sense because the pharaonic statues, ancient Egypt meets Saurian lizard men, were just statues, carved into the red rock wall of the shattered cliffs that guarded the Kingdom of Sût from us.

Now... as I look back on it... I realize that was kind of

the first hint that my… powers… which I must state I don't like at all as they give me really awful headaches no matter how much Vandahar tells me they'll go away with practice… and they don't… but that was the first hint that my mental powers were coming online just when I wanted them least.

If I was gonna straphang, I didn't need that superpower baggage. I needed my skills, focus, and everything the Rangers had patiently taught me all along the way from where I'd come from to here.

Now, in a little while, they'd come on full, hard. But that first feeling in the dark of the night of what those statues would do, really the dark… entities… they were made in the image of… *represented*… that's what they did in lands of night far darker than the realm of Sût the Undying. That's who they were when they were home… and no one was watching.

…There are other realms of nether darknesses…

That's a phrase that still sticks from the impression of that moment thanks to my Ruin Revealed psionics.

Other realms of nether darknesses…

But over there in the rocky and dark land of where we would go and fight soon, frightening as it was in its dark and mysteriously guarded beauties, it all paled in comparison to the ancient Nile that surrounded us on that protective sandbar.

The River of Night.

Commons didn't suddenly surface out of it and say, "Hi, guys."

Or give his report to the commander.

The river just murmured its way to where it was going just as it had always done.

Suddenly, and now I realize this was the psionics talking… my *Ruin revealing*… the river was awash in history for me, and I could feel just how ancient it was and how so many lives and deaths had been…

Marked…

Here. On a map none of us had ever seen.

It was… beautiful. Simply. It's just a wide river. But… there's more to it than that. And I think the psychic impressions were making it so, making it more, more than it was… inside my fracturing head.

Here, on this night out on the sandbar, it was almost placid and gently telling some lost and forgotten tale. Tranquil even though statuesque dark titans of crocodilian death loomed across the river, guarding the ancient temple with their toothy carved smiling death grimaces.

Daring us to come in. Daring us to come for them.

The River of Night was more than all this pettiness of empire and armies on the march. It had seen such things and seen them buried in the sand, murmuring and chuckling its tale of such prides.

I know… I'm getting poetic. And yet it's not… not enough. Words aren't capturing the Ruin Revealed of my… insights… in the moment.

The river was like some vast and twisting silver road in the night that babbled its way from the south to the north. And… it seemed to want you to stay on it and listen to all the lost stories and buried languages it knew. And to follow it to where it knew great treasures and mysteries were hidden. Follow it all the way up into the vast darkness that was the central African plateau.

Or whatever the Ruin called it. Which... it didn't. The maps didn't mark it. Didn't know of Lake Victoria or any of the mysteries there.

Those lands were beyond civilization and the maps they thought were certain.

Africa was dark and mysterious even ten thousand years ago.

Who could ever really know it.

But ten thousand years of Ruin later, the maps and the talk and whispers and rumors inside the Cities of Men didn't even touch it.

It was just a blank space on the map.

But here, on this sandbar, the Little Bird a shadowy hulk seeming stranded here, the four of us watching our assigned sectors, it was like the murmur of the river over its stones closer to the shores, eddies in the current and around the temple steps and sunken columns, was whispering of so much more to be found to the south.

Lands and peoples never dreamed of.

Languages Talker never spoke in the Cities of Men.

And...

Probably coffee. Africa *was* coffee if you were a true believer like me.

I bet, I thought, there's some version of a Kenyan Huehuetenango brewed down there by Ruin-revealed lion-people that would knock your socks off.

And then I knew I wanted to go. Felt that call. And it was strong for one hot second... so strong, it might have been stronger than anything I'd ever felt.

Or maybe I'm just a junkie with a particular addiction.

You decide. I had to shrug it off and it wasn't easy.

I'd found my edge. Thank you, Sar'nt Thor, for getting me boiled in some lion-people cannibal pot and my head shrunk to boot because that's what they probably do to make their magic weapons.

The river that night was like some murmuring monkish wizard casting a spell of seduction, whispering those dark addiction temptations to me of other lands and strange coffees…

And I was cool with it all.

I shook myself and returned to my *looking* portion of the SLLS.

Straphangin' and operatin'. No addicts here, Sar'nt.

The eastern side of the river, the farther side for us, was endless dunes and peaceful oblivion in the blue moonlight. And even so… it was seductive in its own way too.

I'm telling you, in that short halt, and my knee usually gets tired the longer the halt goes on even with the kneepad inserts for the Crye Precisions, that halt was one of the top ten most magical lightning bolts of the world… the Ruin… I ever got hit with, and I will remember it forever.

Listening…

Silence.

The murmur of the river. Yes. Almost like a soundtrack for such a place. The wind in the reeds making a hushing sound here and there. The murmur of the water over ancient stones. Constant and reminding. Mesmerizing and… something else I can't describe. But it was there.

And still that wasn't the thing I found myself listening to the most that night. What I was listening to… disturbed me on some level even now I'm not wholly comfortable with.

There was a vast, almost like it was a sound even though it wasn't *really* a sound, but a deathly silence pulsing from the Lands of Night on that side of the river we'd soon make our way into. Where the temple and demon-carved Saurian pharaohs watched the river and dared the foolish to come and violate the tomb there.

That silence was huge. Like it covered the whole Land of Black Sleep. Like it wasn't just a silence in the here and now, but a vast monastic hum that resonated into other worlds not this one. Shadowy worlds closer and more connected than we might like to think.

That silence had a kind of quiet and dark power in it, and I could hear it, and I think everyone on the search and rescue could hear it too. But we didn't say anything because it was bad juju even for Rangers. They weren't afraid of it. But they knew it was… wrong. And evil.

And that they were going to go there, into it, and kill what they'd come to kill anyway.

I heard the pilot, still seated in the little chopper, murmur a quiet, "Creepy."

Sergeant Kang shot his head around with laser-like contempt and raised one assault-gloved finger to his lips reminding the warrant officer, who outranked him, not to violate noise discipline as we acclimatized to the surroundings we'd soon have to stalk and survive in.

Being 160th SOAR, the pilot should have known this and was most likely trained in it if not already a graduate of the Ranger School back in the world ten thousand years ago. But in his defense, that vast monastic silence radiating out over the river and the blue sand dunes into the bone-white cemetery moonlight, had a rumbling evil menace in it that was, in fact… creepy.

Very.

So I'll give him that.

That was the *listen* portion of the SLLS.

And yes, there was a smell too.

The air that night smelled of desert and dust and distant eucalyptus. The papyrus stalks were heady and almost sweet in the stink of decay where they clustered and refused the river's boundaries along the shore near the vast sunken monuments, proud hieroglyph-covered columns and cracked broken steps that had once received burial flotilla and dark rite processions of birth, rebirth, and death.

The endless cycle of this dark and ancient land, abundant in every broken and unbroken stone where you could smell the ancient dust of the place, the burial spices and the decaying rot of the undead… passed us by on the bare breaths of night breeze. You just quietly breathed it all in and it blended with what you'd seen, and what you'd felt, and what you'd heard… and then told you you were getting into something dark and dangerous, old and wicked. Something that had prevailed where so many others had failed and now lay buried out there in the sands of time that never stopped sweeping it all up and burying everything.

There were no enemies one could see out there in the night.

But you could *feel*… you could feel that someone, some*thing,* was out there, with bad intentions. Waiting. Just waiting for you to try and come in where no man should ever dare. And that beyond those unseen predators and waiting tomb guardians… something else darker, deeper, and much, much older… had been waiting for you all along. For a very long time.

You could feel that in the night among all those senses.

But regardless of all my artful alliterations and poetic perceptions… that's what we were really conducting the SLLS for.

Enemies.

Enemies out there and waiting to oppose us.

Signs of Commons, who surely would have heard the chopper and come swimming out to us, weren't readily apparent. He didn't show, and that was something we had to consider in all of our constant updating of mission with each new fact and facet as it came our way, the mission clock continuing its unbargainable advance.

I chanced a sip of my cold brew as we came out of the halt, and then it was time to make our way across the shallows toward the looming entrance of titanic leering Saurian guardians watching over the secrets and mysteries within the remains of the old temple they'd carved along their sacred river.

No one freaked out about my hit of coffee, and it was worth it anyway if they had.

We started across the shallows.

Chief Rapp on the right of the captain who took point. I was rear security.

Sergeant Kang would guard the chopper and we had our orders and signal for eventualities.

We set out, wading through the river, making our way

through the reeds, staying low inside the papyrus as we made the shore, following our weapons and looking for the danger we knew was there and waiting for us, to rear its ugly head.

Then we'd kill it. Then we'd search for our Ranger.

CHAPTER EIGHT

USING hand signals, the captain directed Chief Rapp to conduct a search of the river over near the ceremonial steps leading inexorably up to the entrance to the temple carved into the impressive and looming cliffs rising above us in the night dark.

The captain put two fingers, claws really, on me, pointed to himself, then pointed forward toward the temple.

We'd search there.

He pointed toward his eyes, then me, then the sector I should cover.

I picked up my sector as we moved forward and did my best not to disrupt stones or the dried-out reeds that littered the hard ground and sand drifts that lay before the black oblong dark square of the entrance into the cliffs and the foreboding and silent temple carved into the dusty stone of the land. I could hear the captain's tiger's nostrils scenting the night. And occasionally a low growl, and this was somehow darker and creepier than the Lands of Night and the dark necromancy of the Saurian empire.

It reminded me that the man… thing… predator… I had the six of… was an animal. A killer.

His cat's eyes scanned the night and the ground all around.

There was no sign of Commons here. No tracks. No shell casings indicating a firefight of some sort. No dead. No broken weapons. Just lifelessness and shadows mixing among the ancient stone columns, cracked steps, strange snake-like glyphs, and even the carved Saurian titans.

Beyond all this lay the dark depths of the temple. Hazzim had said there was such a temple as this and that through its chambers one could reach the Valley of Priests and Kings, or Kings and Priests, or Death, undetected by forces on the high desert above.

Rumors and ancient writings on yellowed papyrus scrolls said as much.

But there were many such temples of great lich-priests sleeping in death and waiting to be summoned, tombs of fallen Saurian heroes carved into the rock walls that guarded this section of the River of Night. Expeditions from the City of Thieves, vast parties of robbers and trains of slaves and specialists skilled in the plundering of tombs, often had ways through these tombs that let them into the wonders and fantastic treasures within the valley beyond. Many tombs had been plundered and for a time were merely used as passages, roadways, by the clever thieves of that fabled city on the other side of the gulf. But in time the Saur would come and lay traps in these, or cast powerful warding spells that would send entire expeditions off to the damned realms never to return.

Or bury them alive underneath all that living stone deep down in those plundered tombs of their heroes and priests.

The Saur guarded their empire of death jealously, but the thieves could not resist the temptation of wealth beyond dreaming.

There were many tombs.

Ten thousand years of tombs.

"For the Saur were rich indeed," crooned Hazzim. "So rich, for they have stolen all the wealth back to the beginning of the great dark that announced the Ruin. And some say… even before then. They are greedy. And they do not share. No, they do not."

But *this* temple, according to Hazzim, had never, ever been plundered. This temple was a tomb, as so many were, and its guardian was rumored to have been once very powerful.

"One of the greatest slaves the Death Pharaoh ever possessed for his unstoppable armies in the years of the Golden Age. Some say… one of the nine, even. One of the nine indeed."

But I didn't find out who "the nine" were because Hazzim got crazy talking about some detail of this particular tomb and the light was coming into the sky that morning after a long night of listening and even I was too tired to get it all down.

In hindsight… I should have found out who the "the nine" were.

CHAPTER NINE

CONTACT came from the ruined river temple pretty fast after that.

"Watch it!" growled the captain fast and suddenly, as he sprang for cover faster than I would have thought possible carrying that much gear. The first arrow hissed in from the Katari assassins guarding the temple.

Aaaaaannnnnddd… I caught it right in the chest plate. Even with a warning from Captain Knife Hand and all.

I'm pro like dat.

In my defense, running with the gun teams and the scouts we usually just shouted, "Suck dirt!"

Arrow fire ain't no joke. Knocked the wind right out of me and I took two steps backward, sat down hard on my butt, and tried to catch my breath as everything went kinetic all at once.

So… that was the extent of my cool guy straphanger contribution. Thus endeth my audition to be an operator.

The arrow shattered, hitting me with the Bronze Age equivalent of frag and spall.

In my defense… and yes, there seems to be a lot of that going around in this account… the captain told me later he was impressed with my shooting skills because even though I got sat down hard by arrow fire, and the incoming cat-humanoid Saurian temple guardian's arrow shattered, and I could feel fresh blood on my face and that probably meant something bad…

Spoiler… it didn't.

But at the time… you don't know that. You just have a decision, one decision, to make when the incoming starts up and you catch one: you're gonna forget the injury until you can get some cover and have it checked, return fire, and contribute meaningfully to the response against the attack… or you're gonna let the blood and pain become more important than your survival.

I decided to return fire like a boss. And bonus, I threw in some anger and spite 'cause why not.

Fear. Don't let it get comfortable.

Shoot. Kill someone. Punch back. But whatever you do… don't let it stay for tea. And we don't serve tea here. So get the hell out and get yourself a prize outta the prize drawer, Talker, for returning fire even though you were hit and couldn't breathe. Or at least you thought so at the time.

I sat down, unable to breathe effectively, and ignored impending death and the black gaping void that identified itself as such by shooting the first Katari assassin to come running through the soft sand gathering in piles along the features of this lost and forgotten temple. The cat-humanoid assassin, in grave wrappings of either bandages or grave shrouds that made it look like some movie ninja, leapt at me over a long-ago-fallen thick column carved with fading runes and the damned glyph tales of the greatest hits of Saurian atrocities from the old-timey times when they'd tried to snuff out all other forms of life.

Lizards gonna lizard.

The *cat-ssassin*, hey cool new word, Talker approves, landed on his cat feet like it was the most natural thing in the Ruin. I spat what I was sure was blood and drilled him center mass, pulling the trigger on the M4…

Twice.

Slow and smooth.

Which means fast in operator cult.

The cat didn't like getting punched by fast-moving lead hornets and tried to scramble away from me, drooling blood and yowling like any house cat that didn't get its way and was indignant about it all.

Later we'd find it made it another few feet off in the sand and weeds trying to put distance between me and it before its pump and pipes asserted domination on the reality of life-beating processes and gave up the ghost.

Never mind, more coming in.

The captain had already gone hot and was firing short controlled effective bursts into blurry shadows flinging knives at us, shooting arrows from tight little recurve bows, and making dancing little jumps and gallops to get close enough to stick us with those weird and shiny crescent blades they all carried.

If you've been reading this account, you know that I'd murked a ton of these into the shadow realms that one time on guard duty just before the dragon hit the FOB.

Murked. New Talker word. Meaning… *yeeted* unto the murky shadow realms of death and the nether.

Remember… me with both thumbs on the triggers for the Mark 47, linked with belts of spin-detonated grenades… that gets you that high score for sure.

We had a long day of flinging dead cats off the precipice crumbling old FOB Hawthorn rests on. Of course the Rangers made a contest out of this. Who gets the dead cat the farthest down the crag.

Then we had crows for days.

Meanwhile back in the cat fight, literally.

"On your feet, Ranger!" growled the captain in full were-tiger form. Then he took his firing claw off the trigger, lowering his dialed-up M4 to low ready in a machine-like moment of pure lethal efficiency, and swiped at a sudden Katari cat ninja who'd appeared of the nether of the night in a flying attack, crescent blades out and shining in the bare moonlight.

They say the reflexes of a cat are faster than almost every other creature. I've seen videos of them letting deadly vipers get impossibly close…

And I've seen a ton of cobras strike and snap in the marketplaces of the Ruin… and I'm always fascinated. Hey, don't @ me. I'm a *turista* at heart even if this is a Bronze Age murder hole where everything is deadly and twice on Tuesdays…

But I've seen those cats let that cobra have its way all the way into a strike… then suddenly end the serpent's existence in a blur of cute kitty kat now lethal murder machine.

They say only humans, dolphins, and cats kill for sport.

I can believe that about cats. But they're faster than we'll ever be in pure reflexes. And now, the captain is one of them. So, an already dangerous operator is now… even more deadly.

Dolphins though… c'mon. There's a Murder Flipper? I'll have to ask Commons if he knows.

Anyway, the captain straight up disembowels that leaping

flinging-itself-into-battle temple cat guardian the Ruin calls the Katari… half cat half humanoid ninja. Knife Hand tore the creature in half and… *murked* it right into the shadow realms.

It was fascinatingly horrible, especially when it happens not four feet from your face and you realize that that deadly assassin was coming in to finish you off.

Then like some terminator from the movies, the captain, with zero emotion, is back on the gun, dumping short controlled bursts into more unseen cat assassins closing on our circle of trust.

"Get your NODs on and cover our six!" shouted the captain as he gunned down another screaming hissing cat that tried to fire a power shot straight from its flexed recurve not ten feet from us.

The rounds, center mass, shattered the bow and tore the thing's chest cavity to shreds.

I could breathe now, some, but it didn't feel like I really could. It was better through my nose as I jerked my NODs down, went live, and caught two cats coming up from the rear who'd circled around us to get in and stick us from behind.

One caught several shots, hits or misses I don't know, it all happened too fast, but after putting enough fire onto it to make it change shape…

Catching fire is not an option with a non-magical M4.

It was confirmed dead as far as I was concerned.

I picked up the other *cat-ssassin* and without a thought… it was waaaay too close… flipped the selector to full auto and sprayed it as it cartwheeled knives out to get at the captain. Its pretty cartwheel turned into a barrel roll and then just a bundle of rags fluttering and lying there on the desert floor near the river in the night of our battle.

The attack was brief, but brutal.

The captain had two arrows sticking out of his assault pack, meaning they'd got angles on him from behind and only the ruck had protected him from getting killed. And he'd taken a severe slash across the tiger-striped fur of his forearm.

His tiger blood mixed and matted with the white and orange there.

It didn't seem to bother him.

We fell back toward the river and covered behind two fallen columns, each taking a sector to cover our improvised defense. Chief Rapp called sign and got the countersign from the captain as the Green Beret came up along our rear from the river where he'd been looking for signs of Commons having been here.

I knew it was him in the thermal vision of the NODs. The captain probably could tell by tiger vision and scent. Again, he was pure predator and watching him become one made more stark and startlingly clear the stories I'd copied down from the Rangers who'd been right there beside him in CQB. He was a fearsome thing to behold. He was death itself in were-tiger form and you really could feel that raw animal ferocity and the primal terror he spread oozing out into the air all around you like live electricity, as others had said.

Now I knew.

Out there I counted thirteen dead or dying *cat-ssassins*. Most were down and out. Two were torn apart…

I wonder by who?

Blood dripped from the captain's claws but it wasn't on

his mouth.

Which I'll be honest… is disturbing when it happens, or so others have said.

A few of the cats were either rolling in the sand or badly wounded. Or crawling away leaking blood and guts and clearly not gonna get much further than a bloody trail a few feet farther along.

"Found this down by the river hidden in the reeds. Marked and stashed jes like I showed him," rumbled the Green Beret softly in the night.

Chief Rapp held Commons's dive bag in his off hand. The other ready on his rifle, strapped tight by the Vickers sling.

Our Ranger had made it this far.

Now… where was he?

CHAPTER TEN

AFTER Commons got bit…

"I got bit!"

Or to be more specific, after the vampiric sea hoochies attacked us as we made the beach assault against the citadel way back in this account, well, we didn't know Commons was gonna become Aqua Ranger then.

We just thought the bite was bad and he'd picked up some kind of infection from the sea hoochies.

Mermaids.

Sea vampires really.

Hoochies of the sea apparently in the Ruin.

But, in their defense… they were super-*hawt*. So, they had that going for them.

I think they'd been up to that particular trick for a long time before we came along and trashed their little trap. The waters and harbor around the citadel were actually the remains of an ancient sunken city that had been buried under a tidal wave by the cataclysmic destruction caused by that comet, or meteor, actually I think the right term may be meteorite, but who really cares, certainly not the people who get hit by one, that hit the Ruin several thousand years ago before we showed up.

This made the approach by sea to the area of the Lost Coast treacherous, and we saw the wreck of many a ship as our galley was suddenly sucked into the harbor by a magical vortex.

Yes, there are sentences I put down here I never thought I'd write in a million years. But wherever you are… be there.

Embrace the Fantasy.

My guess is the Sea Hoochie Vamps had been preying on foundering ships and lost sailors for some time using their beauty and hypnotizing songs to lure shipwrecked sailors into complacency, then feeding on them as they waded in toward shore having just escaped their doomed wrecks.

Unfortunately for the sea hoochies… Rangers have a kill-everything switch installed and when it's not *on*…

Which is most of the time…

Be polite, be kind, have a plan to kill everyone in the room.

… then it flips to *on* pretty darn quick.

Hell, let's be honest. It's probably on all the time.

So, Rangers being Rangers… meaning hypermasculine males who likey-like pretty girl… didn't have a problem killing the sea hoochies once they started biting and dragging their brothers under the surf in order to have their way with them via some weird frenzy of kisses and drowning.

So, Commons. He survived, got sick, and then started to grow gills. Which was a new one for us.

Hence *Gill.* That's what we called him before *Aqua Ranger* caught on.

But… he seemed to be expiring. Chief Rapp assessed the situation, took him down to the ocean on what was the north coast of Africa which the Ruin calls the Lost Coast, waded the gasping Ranger out into the water, and held Commons there until he began to come back to life.

Miraculously.

Then… the giant Green Beret dunked Commons under and held him down… this is the funny part and I watched it even though it seemed kinda horrible at the time… but I laughed because I couldn't believe what I was watching which seemed to be Chief Rapp drowning Commons under the surf.

There was a brief struggle in which Commons tried, that was the funny part, to fight the six-foot-six super-jacked special operator. Chief Rapp smiled good-naturedly, ignored Commons's best Ranger combatives, and held the struggling specialist under water until…

Commons began to breathe.

He was still gasping raggedly like he had asthma up until that point.

Then, when Commons figured out he could actually breathe… *under water and all*… he calmed.

And within a few minutes Commons was swimming all along the beach without surfacing and having the time of his life like near death had never happened.

Chief Rapp had his Dräger LAR 8000 closed-circuit rebreather brought out to him via Sergeant Thor who seemed both amazed and… kinda jelly… which he manifests as pissed-off contempt, that the young Ranger could do what he was doing.

Breathe underwater without gear.

You could tell the hulking Ranger sniper was envisioning how far and what could be seen down there in all those hidden canyons under the ocean human eyes have never seen.

Thus… Aqua Ranger was born that early evening along the coasts of North Africa.

A pack of tiger sharks came in toward shore later in the evening and Commons again ran from the water screaming, "Shark, shark, shark! I don't wanna get bit again!"

Apparently, besides being able to breathe underwater, he can also sense other fish nearby. Like he, as a *merman*, as Ranger Wizard PFC Kennedy termed it according to the lore of his game with funny dice and pens and paper, Commons, or Gill as he was already by then being called, had the abilities of those fantastic creatures already. Later we'd figure out he would have deep water vision, water sensitivity, and possibly ampullae of Lorenzini like a shark. This would allow him to sense, and see, things underwater. And even communicate with them on some sort of fish-telepathy level.

Crazy stuff.

A few days later Commons started getting freakishly strong. And… he hated talking to fish.

"They're really stupid, Talker, and they have like the memory of a gnat," he said with disgust and contempt as he worked some dip after an early dive, or swim for him, with Chief Rapp who was amazed at what Commons could do underwater. And thinking hard about the potential this had for the unit regarding future operations.

Meanwhile Commons waxed on in his rant on how stupid fish really were.

"They're like, 'Oh hi, my name is,' they have weird names, Talker, like *Ixxcthyias* was one I remember. But they're all like… 'Hi, my name is… weird name… what's yours?' But there's like a school of them and after I *think* my name at them… 'cause that's how we communicate… they ask you the same question again. Six seconds later. Like they have *no clue* we just did this. And *it doesn't stop*. It just keeps going and going on and on and repeating over and over. It's… super annoying, Talker. Super. Annoying."

Anyway…

The sharks Commons heard that first night were screaming for blood and food like howling wolves out there in the deep waters of the ocean, but in fish language, and that freaked the Ranger out as he stared off into all that misty green nothingness beyond the shoreline and realized they meant him and were coming for him.

So… Aqua Ranger ran from the surf and Chief Rapp followed, laughing all the way as he did so.

Later, the Green Beret explained what this meant for the unit. Having our very own Aqua Ranger that could do all this crazy underwater stuff like talk to fish with severe short-term memory problems.

"This increases significantly," began the chief in the TOC one night, "our unit effectiveness potential regarding underwater operations, mainly travel, target, and termination of enemy assets or even designated HVTs. We can train him to sabotage waterways and craft, even salvage operations, and especially landing point reconnaissance."

Which is what Commons did in the weeks leading up to the assault on Sûstagul. And he did it so well, he found a little gang of urchins, all of them the products of sea hoochie and sailor relations, making them just like him, and turned them into a significant scouting and messenger force during the battle. They became crucial to our plans, and a large part of our subsequent success was due to Commons's efforts to recruit them into our force. He was absolutely the right guy to connect with them. He was still young and had a sense of fun.

If Hardt or Kurtz had been turned into Aqua Ranger they probably would have turned the urchins off with the contempt for everyone they seemed to broadcast from their own personal radio stations of hatred and Ranger Standards.

Many of the Saurian war galleys were crippled. The Saurian fleet was unable to maneuver during the battle, thanks to Commons and the urchins working with Monroe masquerading as a stevedore.

In a city of mostly men, no one really minded that the minotaur was literally a day laborer. Undercover.

Embrace the fantasy.

And we did for the win.

Later, as Chief Rapp continued to improve Commons's skills and understand his Ruin Revealed talents, I asked the chief about combat divers, which I really didn't think the Army had…

SEALs, I mean c'mon… isn't that what they do?

The Green Beret laughed and didn't expound on the topic of SEALs.

Then…

"Listen, my man," said the operator.

Green Berets are so groovy. They're the opposite of the tightened-down ready-to-kill hardboiled Rangers.

"Listen, my man. First and foremost, this is one of the most difficult courses taught in the services. Army Combat Diver. Hard stop, Talker. Anyone who tells you differently, they lyin' to you. Typical classes of potential divers start back in the world with sixty to ninety operators from across all special forces, Rangers too. School has an eight-five percent attrition rate. Start with ninety dudes who are usually the unit studs… and you'll get ten to twelve who'll finish. That's jes' facts."

"What do they learn besides swimming and the equipment?" I asked, with visions of surfacing with a knife, stabbing a dude, and dragging him under swamp water.

That's pretty Ranger, you have to admit.

I have those thoughts now. I have joined the cult. I have gotten all the way out of the boat.

But I dismiss the possibility of getting another badge because… everybody prepare yourselves, gird your loins… there's no coffee underwater, so… Talker will not be interested in this particular badge no matter how cool it is.

Chief Rapp chuckled again because his cleric Ruin-revealed self probably detected my evil thoughts of surface and terminate bad guys all cool-style.

Or my psionics broadcasted it so loud and clear because it was a pretty startling image and I'd had a sudden… let's call it… *electric thrill.*

So… maybe. Dunno yet. Write the future in pencil. It's safer that way.

But the Green Beret seemed to sense what I thought Combat Diver would be all about.

Then he proceeded to set me straight about the training he was going to put our Aqua Ranger through to make him become Combat Certified Aqua Ranger.

Emphasis on *Ranger.*

Take that, Kennedy!

There'd be drown proofing. That didn't sound fun.

Deep water diving, free and under gear.

"I can pass on teaching him operations in closed- and open-circuit breathing devices like SCUBA and RBS that I have to use. But I gotta put him through an individual confidence course…"

Full stop.

If you haven't been in the military, then you probably think that's some kind of cool motivational presentation in a cheap hotel out by the airport about how to live your best life and be the best *you* possible.

It ain't.

Take for instance… the gas chamber in Basic Training. In which they take you into a gas chamber filled with live gas, really potent tear gas, then tell you to take off your mask and breathe deep. In the gas.

Spoiler… your lungs feel like they just filled with acid concrete, and you're absolutely convinced you will never again breathe. Ever.

This gives you confidence in the mask you were just wearing that protected you from the poison gas. The one you were wearing before they told you to take it off and breathe deep.

Now you know the mask works.

Okay then.

This is Army training, and it's got a certain brutal, yet eloquent… *eloquence*, Talker can't find another word, to it.

What kind of training?

Army training.

It's an old joke from an old movie but it's pretty standard as a reply among us when a bit of grim humor is required as the suck abounds.

So, *confidence course* means abuse of some sort once you've been trained in your skills to have confidence in those skills and use them under pressure to survive and stay on mission.

As Chief Rapp explained what they do in Combat Dive School individual confidence, I came to understand what a kind of quiet hell this could be. Basically, you get two of your own instructors to just harass you, underwater, in the dark, continually pulling off your mask and breather, then messing with the settings on your tanks and tossing you around and making life rough as you struggle to breathe. Underwater. In the dark.

Hardt was more than happy to help, as he is Combat Dive rated, as are a few of the other Rangers, so they put Commons in a bag, tied it up, and threw him in the water at night.

Then they hit him.

First task was to get out of the bag.

He found his knife and cut his way free.

After untying his hands.

Yeah, they tied those too.

And they blindfolded him.

In the bag, blindfolded, he wisely chose not to get the blindfold off as he might have cut himself with the knife.

So, out of the bag—where he was instantly squirted with squid ink the chief had harvested.

The chief and Hardt were in rebreathers with masks. They continued to beat Commons and get a leash on him as he struggled to get free.

Then the chief dumped a mild neurotoxin from a local fish that made it extremely hard for Commons to breathe water…

He followed everything the chief had taught him, cut himself free, and kicked for freedom.

He can swim incredibly fast.

He swam off and they tossed some flashbangs at him and had some Rangers beating metal underwater to mess with the Ruin-revealed sonar he probably has.

Or whatever it is that lets him sense things underwater.

He grabbed the flag the chief had planted on the bottom and escaped the cordon they'd surrounded without ever needing to surface.

It was like water polo, but with Rangers. So there was violence and aggression.

Naturally.

First time go, and according to the chief… "most impressive."

Hardt said they should do it again. Just to be sure.

Commons looked Hardt straight in the eye and said, "Bring it."

Mad props among all involved.

Chief Rapp laughed and said it wasn't necessary for Commons, "but if you want a second crack you can try me, Sergeant."

Hardt worked dip and spat, then stalked off to go make someone else's life miserable.

He's hard to figure.

Different than Kurtz. But kinda the same.

After Commons passed his basic confidence test in his survival underwater skill, given his incredible Aqua Ranger Ruin-revealed powers, Chief Rapp started the next phase of training.

Underwater operations. Travel, target, and terminations.

Yes. Surfacing knife kills. It was cool. Then sidearms and carbines. Next came explosives, and Commons got real proficient in sabotaging waterways and boats and ships and even some salvage operations. Chief even spent three days teaching him how to do underwater repairs and medicine.

Crazy stuff.

Green Berets are about as training as training gets. They're excellent teachers, they seem to know everything, and when it comes to their particular skill set, they have a mastery level from which to download knowledge.

Just don't ask Chief Rapp about the goats he had to keep alive as a medic.

"Don't like that part at all, Talker. But it's what I had to do to keep you guys alive. So I did it. But… didn't like it at all, no sir. Never wanna do that again."

Commons finished Chief Rapp's School of Combat Diving for Aqua Rangers with studies in tides, subsurface geography and topography, weather, local chatter collection, and dangerous marine conditions. He would be talking to fish, his fave, not, and maybe friendly mariners. Portugonians were identified and noted as always helpful, as they were cool, but serious, and master, mariners.

Then Chief Rapp finished with some potential fault lines and geothermal activity in the areas of operation, and finally spent two weeks on security of any landing point, intel gathering on patrol and troop strength regarding beach operations, and potential recovery points for subsurface gear, or if the gear has to be ADP'd, asset denial protocol.

It was this last phase that I've been building up to as relevant to the search-and-rescue operation under the dark sky there in the River of Night. The agreed-upon protocols had been followed by Commons, and this allowed his combat diver sensei, Chief Rapp, to find his stashed gear and identify that Aqua Ranger had been in the area in the recent past.

The night was lit by moonlight as the captain and I watched our sectors in the impromptu defensive position and Chief Rapp came up silently from the river and showed us Commons's dive bag, still dripping wet with river water.

"He musta come ashore here," said the big operator, and pointed toward the temple.

I turned, saw the dripping wet dive bag, and went…

To Psionics Impression Land.

Terrible place.

Would not recommend.

One star.

CHAPTER ELEVEN

THERE on the small slice of beach that lay before the ruins of the forbidding temple in the night, Knife Hand was busy asking the chief exactly what Commons would do next according to SOP and the train-up they'd conducted for this portion of the mission… when I interrupted the Ranger commander and the warrant officer.

I repeat… the low on the enlisted and extremely low on the Ranger-slash-operator totem pole *interrupted the Ranger commander and the warrant officer.*

Currently I am a mere corporal.

In the world of junior enlisted, I am a rare bird and king of the great unwashed masses supported by the silent service of the E-4 Mafia…

Of which I am a member for life.

But I expect that status to change imminently. And not for the better. Farwell, E-4 Mafia. I shall return someday.

"Uh… sir. He got captured," I interrupted cautiously but quickly. I may have closed my eyes expecting to receive some sort of smiting from on high that would instantly reduce me to E-1.

My psionics headache was already killing me as the vision I'd just seen faded from my mind. I was trembling with a cold sweat that had suddenly broken out in its midst, and I rubbed my throbbing forehead to make the pain go away.

I had this weird idea about my psionic powers that it wasn't so much a headache that followed their unwanted appearance as much as sudden extreme muscle tension all through my neck and scalp as the… visions… impressions… call them what you want… took hold, and that kinda put me through some sort of muscular tension shock all of a sudden while I held on and went into a vivid reality of either the past, or the future, or somewhere other…

I'd asked Tanner if he noted anything different about me when I had these experiences, and all he said was, "I know you're havin' 'em, Talk, 'cause suddenly you get all quiet. Which, I don't know if you know this… ain't like you. You do have a tendency to go on and on. So…"

I don't know. But yeah, I do have a tendency to go on and on.

Talker. Kinda gives the game away.

Lately, I've tried to relax and… get groovy without fighting the psionics so much. Which was involuntary on my part. Vandahar had said as much regarding how to handle their appearance at usually the worst of times. But he said it in his own Vandahar way.

"Accept your destiny, one called Talker. I have found that fighting it only makes the journey you must embark upon… all the more unpleasant than it could be."

Meanwhile back at me interrupting the commander and the Green Beret right there in the middle of the dark-of-the-night search and rescue for Commons.

"And how do you know that, Corporal?" asked Knife Hand as humanely as a were-tiger dripping with fresh blood and strapping a deadly and very dialed-up carbine can.

I cleared my throat.

How to explain this? The chain of command knew I'd been "Ruin-revealed" into what Kennedy's little game probably called… a *psionist*. Mental powers *woo-woo* and all.

"You're Professor X, that's all, Talk. Don't let it go to your head. You get none of the cool scenes in the movie. If you was the Wolverine, then hey now…" That's how Tanner put it. "But you ain't."

The were-tiger Ranger captain staring at me and waiting for an answer with blood dripping from his claws on the other hand…

"You go somewhere else for a second, Talker?" asked Chief Rapp in that deep but gentle voice.

I nodded.

Headache was fighting to stay. I needed it to go. Not for me. Not for the pain.

But for what I'd just seen in the vision and the sudden imperative I felt having seen it.

Unceremoniously I put the commander and the chief on hold, reached for my canteen, and nailed as much coffee as I could in one massive Sergeant Thor beer-flagon gulp. So I pretty much drained it.

Coffee came and said nice things to me about all the fun we'd ever have if I survived this night much less the interruption of the mission.

Coffee. It don't judge you.

And it'll never let you down.

It's just there saying, *Hey… let's get real wired and do some crazy stuff. Whaddaya say, buddy?*

Holding the canteen because there might still be a few drops, I cleared my head once more.

And yeah… I always say yes to coffee's crazy talk. But that's me. Talker. Nice to meet you. Ranger much? Coffee anyone?

"Uh-huh…" I mumbled to the captain and the Green Beret staring at me like the stone-cold pipe hitters they were. "Yes, Chief. Yeah… had a vision when I saw Commons's dive bag. He… uh… made the shore. He made it this far. Then he got into his chest rig and plates. Got his weapons out of the dry bag, stashed the gear, and went in on foot."

"Where'd he go, Corporal?" asked the captain tersely.

I nodded toward the temple along the reaching cliff wall. The sinister crocodile titans leered like grinning demons in the dark, their looks knowing all that I knew. And approving of the evil being done even now. The black entrance to the temple, up crumbling steps and beyond a small column-lined pavilion, lay like a gaping mouth waiting to swallow all who dared. And it was darker than the night itself.

"Specialist Commons entered the temple, Corporal?" asked Captain Knife Hand, all business despite being a were-tiger. That fatigue and perpetual indigestion there despite the big cat growl his voice was augmented by and the subtle menacing purr he could not help.

That *purr*.

It ain't cute like some kitty kat.

No one had the guts to mention it to him. But he was aware of it. And so were all of us. I think if he could have done something about it, he would have. But…

The captain checked his Timex. Wiped away some of the

blood that had gotten on it. The dead lying all around us didn't seem to miss it.

"Twenty-two minutes. We go in and look for Ranger Commons until then. No actionable leads and we pull back to the chopper and depart. We'll go to drones and see if we can pick him up on the ground somewhere on the cliffs or the local area."

But I had this feeling…

A bad feeling.

That if we didn't find Commons in there then the captain was going to actually do the most un-Knife Hand thing ever and stay, going full jungle stalker to find his Ranger at any cost.

I could tell he'd do it. Maybe it was the psionics giving me that peek that it did into the hearts and minds of other men, even if they were lycanthropes… but I could sense that was already an option Knife Hand was trying to push back even now.

"One other thing, sir," I said, forcing my voice to be true instead of halting and unsure like it felt, as things got to the *woo-woo* and *embrace the fantasy* part of this whole conflict.

The captain said nothing and merely looked at me with those *Tyger Tyger burning bright, In the forests of the night; What immortal hand or eye, Could frame thy fearful symmetry?* pure predator blue eyes like burning sapphires as I felt a cold chill run through my whole frame.

"It was an ambush, sir. Katari were all around Commons in the shadows when he went in to do his job. He didn't see them when he went in to investigate."

Do his job.

That was an important tidbit I picked up in the vision… call it an impression… courtesy of the psionics. The older NCOs were going to rip Commons to shreds when they got hold of him for going into the ruined river temple alone. But I could tell he wasn't doing it to do what young men do. I could see in the vision that he'd spent a long time in the dark waters of the River of Night, watching the temple. Scouting. Observing. Recon. And that his scout of the river had made him aware of just how dangerous this land really was. Maybe more dangerous than any land we'd been through so far. There was a strong possibility Rangers were gonna die taking out the HVT. He wanted his brothers to have the best, and safest, way into the hit. He wanted losses minimized.

He had to be sure this was it.

And he needed to know if this collapsing temple along the river was safe enough before he called it in and the smaj sent the scouts down to find a way through.

That's what Commons was thinking when he went in to… *do his job.*

That's what Rangers do, and yeah they're violent and grim and brave as it gets, but they ain't stupid or foolish. They're in it to win it and Commons was straight Ranger that way.

That's the part the NCOs were gonna know when they were PT'ing him to death with white-line drills.

That's what Commons was thinking clear as a forty-thousand-watt radio station on a clear summer night broadcasting on full bandwidth. Playing all the songs you remember and thought would be forever when you first heard them.

Commons was doing his job.

And that's actually the most Ranger thing you can say about another Ranger.

Straight up.

CHAPTER TWELVE

WITH the captain on point and leading the way, following his M4 into the deep dark entrance of the old sandstone river temple, we went looking for our Ranger, following the clues in the vision.

My last glimpse had been Commons moving silently, stealthily, up from the river and heading straight for the temple. Surrounded by unseen Katari tomb guardians.

All the bad vibes I pushed away. But they were there. And for some reason they felt like they were growing in ways I hadn't felt since the first time I'd been in combat back at Ranger Alamo Bag-of-Death Island.

Damn… there were days I could still smell that orc-body-littered island.

Meanwhile, on the recon I'd been promoted to number two and took the captain's four o'clock in the three-man wedge we were running as we made our way forward. Chief Rapp pivoted this way and that to maintain our course track and cover the rear, following without a sound.

The place smelled of ancient dust, and just before we went into the darkness the captain ordered us to go to NODs and we did so with a quick head flip. The world went hi-res green, and we could see the narrow yet tall hall open up beyond the gaping mouth entrance into the river temple.

The captain would remain on were-tiger predator vision.

The interior was definitely Egyptian, but with that certain and unmistakable hellish Saurian taste for human suffering, chaos, slavery, and death.

Always death.

Always endless amounts of death.

That's the Saurs' thing. Death. Lots of it. And it, if the hard-won wisdom and lore Crazy Old Hazzim has acquired was true, is even worse than I ever imagined it could be.

There are some things you don't want to know. And I was already full up on the death cult of the Saur based on solely secondhand info.

Now we were getting into it for real.

I will get into the Saur. Download as much as I can in this account in the event I do not survive much longer, which, right there entering the ruined river temple and feeling the pervasive dread in the air… I had a growing suspicion might be the case. But if that happens, if I get KIA'd, then whoever picks this account up… hopefully the next Ranger to continue the fight… listen, you gotta end these bastards.

Straight up.

They're very bad. And if they get their way, even if they were once quote-unquote *human*, they ain't any longer and I have serious doubts they really ever were like us, but if they get their way… then they'll burn the whole world, the whole Ruin, if just so no one else will have it.

At the minimum they were all narcissistic sociopaths.

At. The. Minimum.

I say again to whoever comes next…

At all costs… end the Saur.

Use whatever phrase you want to read as this is super

important. *Terminate with extreme prejudice.* Whatever. Make it happen and smoke every last one of them, then burn the whole thing. Then pour salt all over it.

Go Roman. And then some.

But yes, *when* and not *if*, think positive Talker, I get a chance, I will download everything I've learned and you won't like it one bit either. Trust me.

But now ain't the time.

We tomb crawlin' now.

So just before the wraiths attacked us, coming out of dusty stone ceremonial sarcophagi stacked against the wall of the first inner chamber of the temple of some size, three on each side, I was being mesmerized by the unholy hieroglyph Saurian script etched and inked all along the walls in true Ancient Egypt style.

It was the story of ten thousand years.

The rise of the Lich Pharaohs.

The Great Overthrow in which Sût the Undying rose to power and became the permanent tyrant of the whole cabal.

Then the conquering of the known Ruin.

The slavery.

The death fields.

The grand monuments to themselves built not just by armies of captured slaves… but entire nations.

The great black "sun" they worshipped at the center of it all as peasants and slaves and priests and kings were "harvested" into its oblivion.

Thousands of inky stick figures in great insane scrawls suddenly sucked into that oblivion despite orderly hieroglyphs all around that talked of summers, harvest, rainfall, taxes, life, and death.

The NODs made it hard to read along the dark walls of the crypt as we threaded our way into the first chambers of the burial chamber, passing unmeshed urns and great orderly stacks of papyri inscribed with spells to protect the tomb, or so Hazzim had told me we would find if such a place was unviolated.

"But if you find such order, such organization, you must beware, for such places are the most dangerous of places," crooned the bent old sage in his singsong voice. "It means the guardians and wards are still active. And that where some many other tombs have been plundered… this one has plundered the plunderers."

So keep that in mind, kids.

Again, I never thought I'd be the one at the tip of the spear doing the "dungeon crawling," as Ranger Wizard Specialist Kennedy might have called it.

But there ya go… life comes at you fast, and here I was, right there just behind the tip of the spear about ready to get into it with Saurian wraiths guarding the first chambers of the tomb that guarded one of "the nine."

Whatever that was.

A great prize and a renowned warrior even to Sût the Undying himself. But we weren't yet aware of the fact that we were disturbing the tomb of the Saurian general who would lead the Lich Pharaoh's last armies in a final defense of the Grand Pyramid, and Sût himself.

We didn't know that yet.

All we knew as I studied the hieroglyphs along the walls and burial containers, couldn't help doing so as I followed behind and to the right of the captain down the entrance hall to the inner ceremonial death chambers, was that some of the glyphs bore a strange resemblance to things I'd once known.

It was a language after all. Hi, me, Talker. I do languages like no one else. And coffee. But you knew that already.

Cities with skyscrapers.

Computers.

Fighter jets.

You'd catch vague scrawls, but imagine these as the rude drawing of some child's art class, with the long delicate and near perfectly painted language in gold and black ink and lapis lazuli along the wall and think…

Well… that looks like a city. Like they used to look.

And…

That looks like an iPhone.

Or…

Odd. That looks like a nuclear mushroom cloud.

Buried within these lines of pictoglyphs lay Saurian over-seers cracking whips over the heads of slaves.

Tallying the harvest.

Harvesting the captured armies into the hungry black "sun" that seemed not like some mindless black hole, but instead like some dark entity you didn't want to think too hard about.

Or that's what it felt like to me. Something sinister about that black sun.

That was where my head was when the dusty old lids of all six sarcophagi slid open with a sudden grinding croak and fell to the floor, shattering into huge thick pieces each one.

That was when the wraiths pushed away the stone lids of

the sarcophagi and swarmed out at us.

But… we didn't see them at first because they were nether beings. Only that some unseen force had caused the lids to move as one and shatter along the floor.

We didn't see the near-invisible wraiths already swarming about us.

The captain raised one paw, ordering us to hold position. The air got cold and started to move like an autumn wind in the first cold mornings of that harvest season. It smelled of burial spices, heady and sweet with honey and lavender and even dry eucalyptus suddenly drifting about.

Spells of guarding and warding were being loosed.

"Feels like a trap," growled the captain as we studied the shattered stone lids that had all flung themselves away from what we saw as empty massive stone sarcophagi along the hieroglyphed walls of the inner chamber.

"It's the dead…" whispered Chief Rapp. "They guardians… and they comin' for us now, Rangers. Close your eyes and switch off your NODs."

The captain apparently embraced the fantasy more than I'd expected.

"Pulling back, Chief. Eyes closed."

Aaaaand mine weren't 'cause I'm pro like that.

But I did get 'em closed at the last second as the chief suddenly *Holy Flashbanged* the undead all at once.

"You are my Light, Lord!" the six-foot-six operator whispered like it was a prayer. All low. But the words as he said them… grew louder and louder like thunder because he was saying them rapidly… then… all at once I felt the room go suddenly hot, like a heat wave sweeping and surging from some unseen chamber to blast away the autumn death-cold all at once.

I swear I even heard the sound of dry leaves rustling… then beginning to crackle as they caught like in a bonfire.

The tiny world inside the chamber of entombed dead and the carefully inscribed story of the Saur exploded in released light and energy.

I'd just flipped my NODs up when it happened and suddenly, at the last second like I knew the explosion was about to happen, I closed my eyes just in time.

The light, now that I look back at it, had been growing already, and that was when I saw them revealed from their shadow-wraith state.

Six of them.

Six Saurian warriors, but wearing ancient armor of that long-lived race. More ancient than anything we'd ever seen them wearing in the battles we'd fought. Almost ceremonial. These were kitted like Old-Timers' Day for Saur. Wide shields. Big spears. Curved swords. Kilts of woven reeds. Leather helmets. In the instant before the Holy Flashbang ignited, I could also see they were rockin' full treasure drip. Arm bands of silver and gold, set with great turquoise stones. Torcs of gold, leering with demonic rubies. Magic snakes of red and black stripes slithering about the spears in their claws.

Their scaly green skin was jacked and swollen with muscle. Each was easily seven feet tall.

One was missing an eye and wore a fantastic diamond in the socket.

One was covered in tattoos like tally marks.

One had a cobra-headed crown. And the cobra was real,

but also a thing of magic as the serpent's eyes glittered like two massive slitted emeralds, darting this way and that as the deadly poisonous tongue flicked back and forth.

It hissed and struck out at us from across the chamber in that instant of growing light as the wraiths stood revealed and ready to attack and drain us of all life.

The holy light of the developing flashbang revealed them for just that half second before the detonation, and that was all I saw as I squeezed my eyes tight shut and braced for what felt like was going to be a tremendous impact. Kinda like when the rollercoaster tops the climb, and you get a good look at the fall and think…

Oh… this is steeper than it looks from the ground.

In the diminishing darkness they were wispy wraiths, pale, almost unseen shadows of what they had once been.

Then I closed my eyes and the world inside my head went a soft *kaBOOOM*.

A dull sonic strike like the witnessing of a JDAM from miles off.

I felt light. And intense heat broadcasting itself from some other place.

And peace washing over me at the same time. For a moment driving away that worm of fear that had been gnawing at me since the river.

I knew the ancient wraiths that had once been mighty warriors of the Saur weren't just dead. They were *damned*. Forever.

Disappeared by the holy strike from our special operator Green Beret turned Ruin-revealed cleric.

When I opened my eyes in the vast silence, I saw that

it was as though those wraiths of renown never were, in the grand scheme of things.

And I saw the light of the Holy Flashbang fading, faded, gone but lingering as a pleasant memory.

And here was the crazy thing…

It lingered here and there like it was a living thing, fading bit by bit as it went, wandering off somewhere else to do some good where it could be done in such a dark world. And the old, what must have been centuries-old torches left by the priests and ceremonial architects of this place, were now lit and guttering to smoky life, illuminating more the runes along the wall and the destruction the chief had caused when he damned the wraiths into utter oblivion.

The chief laughed in the silence.

"They gone now."

CHAPTER THIRTEEN

WHAT remained on the floor was the ancient and tarnished trappings of those once-fabled warriors of renown who'd once gone forth and slaughtered in the name of Sût the Undying. But their corpses weren't there. Just scattered piles of rotting bone dust courtesy of Chief Rapp's Holy Flashbang. The once bright and shiny spears were rotten and bent. The sharp and shining metal of the blades tarnished and ruined. The exquisite torcs and ancient bracers turned green and rusted into little more than battered junk.

And if that wasn't enough to prove to us that having these tomb guardians rise from the open sarcophagi hadn't been weird enough… then there were the shadowy outlines of the creatures that had permanently been burned into the walls as they were damned into nothing but exploding ash and disintegrating reality.

Their captured images, gray like rough charcoal sketches, were all that remained.

The captain turned his wrist over and checked his watch.

"Sixteen minutes. Let's keep moving forward and see if we can catch up with his captors before he gets too far out of pocket. Corporal…"

The were-tiger captain hesitated here and growled a little. An involuntary version of the perpetual indigestion look he wore on his face in human form.

"… any… more…?"

He was asking if I was getting any more psychic impression courtesy of the Ruin-revealed psionics.

"Negative, sir."

I could have added that I felt Commons was still alive. Probably not too far away. But that would have been conjecture.

Or maybe… just wishful thinking.

Truth was, I didn't really have any clue about my psionics and how they worked and whether the information was timely, as in actionable, or just some vision of what had happened at any time in the past. Commons's abduction could have happened at any time since his last radio check.

Which was eighteen hours ago.

So…

Vandahar told me there were monks who practiced my… *gift*… deep in the Eastern Waystes. And that given study and time, I could rise to some kind of acceptable mastery in Psionics as opposed to the hopeful lottery scratcher my ability currently bore more resemblance to than an actual talent that could be measured, applied, and relied on.

"A talent unmastered is not a reliable walking staff," was how Vandahar had put it in classic Vandaharese. "Serviceable until it breaks when you least need it to."

We proceeded out of the torchlit chamber and into a strangely shaped passage beyond and leading deeper into the mysterious Saurian temple that lay along the River of Night. The passage was strange in that its shape was oddly triangular, but off-kilter as though by design. To me, editorializing here, this hinted at the almost alien, no longer human, nature of the Saurian builders.

There were lamps, worked in bronze and filigreed in emerald glass, that lay in evenly spaced recessed alcoves along the walls, and whether these were lit by the chief's holy strike, or someone else…

Unclear at the time.

We proceeded cautiously down this passage and noted the Saurian hieroglyphs' absence as we delved deeper and deeper into the fantastic interior. Two massive bronze doors, stamped in writings and glyphs, lay ahead of us. I was amazed at how silently both Chief Rapp and Captain Knife Hand moved along the passage in the deathly silence of the place. Veteran patrollers, each slid his boots rather than trying the slow heel two step.

I had gotten better. But compared to them I was like a bear trundling through the forest.

The captain halted and I could hear his tiger's nostrils scenting the air, as though he was looking for a danger he sensed already and could not see.

"Sir," I whispered, indicating the two bronze doors ahead. "According to Kennedy those doors might be trapped."

Kennedy had given lectures on how doors and chests were trapped in his games. He'd even offered a few tests to determine if this was so. And then, as always, ended with his standard disclaimer.

"Guys, this is how it works in the game. Reality might be far, far worse, but… yeah, traps is just the start. If there are *mimics*… well… you'll find out if you run these tests."

There were mimics.

We'd dealt with them before, and they were… horrible

monsters that were simply unbelievable and startling.

Ever seen that movie where the guys are trapped at some research station and an alien from another world gets loose and starts taking control of them… like that doppelganger we met back at Ranger Alamo Island? There's a scene where they're gonna do CPR on a guy and as they expose his chest it suddenly turns into a mimic, a giant gaping fanged mouth of a ravenous and horrible monster and bites off… to the forearms… the guy trying to save his "friend's" life.

The friend had been turned into one of the aliens already. The alien had set a trap to consume more of them.

That's a mimic. But here in the Ruin they can be ordinary objects like doors or chests most commonly. Common objects that suddenly try to bite and then consume you.

Fun, huh?

"Roger that, Corporal. Remind me what the tests are?"

"Easier if I do it, sir," I told the captain. "Cover me."

I let my rifle dangle on the sling and moved to my assault pack. The captain didn't stop me. So… I took that as a vote of confidence and wondered if I was still straphanger material.

Shut it, Talker, and get on with the work, I told myself. Stop trying to impress everyone.

In my defense…

I know, I'm saying that a lot. But *in my defense*… I only want to impress the other Rangers because I respect them so damn much. The best way I can think of to show that… is to be worthy to run with them.

It's simply that.

Or, as Sergeant Chris would say… *Pay the rent on the scroll.*

So… I'm always looking to exceed standards.

Call me a junkie.

Then I had a brilliant thought as I got ready to test the doors for the traps as per Ranger Wizard Kennedy's instructions.

If this thing was a mimic and I got close enough with the tests I was gonna run on the two impressive bronze doors, and then suddenly the monstrous gaping, snarling, mouth of a thing appeared… think a pit bull but made into a door by either magic or Ruin-revealing… then I might need to get pulled out of danger real quick. Even if I did lose my forearms, or hands. Or just a slow finger. It'd be nice to be able to get away from it.

I took the Frog Personal Retention Leash we used to clip into the airframes of helicopters we ride in and handed it to the captain, mouthing a soft, "Just in case, sir."

Then I moved forward and studied the doors, feeling a bit like Indiana Jones.

Stamped in the bronze were hieroglyphs that, given time, and a system, I'd eventually learn to read. Because of my affinity for communication, I already had a very loose, and probably flawed, understanding of what the story of the Saurian hieroglyphs was trying to convey here along the stamp of the heavy and shining-by-torchlight doors. But the fact that I could not pick up the *nuances* of the language was glaring, and, as a perfectionist in my specialty of languages, this annoyed me greatly.

Let it go, Talker.

Here, along the artistry-worked surface in Saurian glyphs was a story stamped on the two massive, highly polished, and heavy bronze doors I stood before.

Bronze is the ancient symbol of judgment. That was the first thing I thought. The door had been made from that ancient metal… for a reason.

Keep that in mind, Talker. It's important.

That's what I told myself then.

Judgment was in play here.

The story of the door, starting in the top lines of hieroglyphs, was one of a great battle. Clearly the character used for Dragon Elves was in play. And the ancient Saurians with their brutal thuggish warriors and slit-eyed sinister priests were there too, telling their ancient story along the surface I studied.

And then there were nine figures that stood out also. Merely humanoid, in the most basic form, but stamped, or painted, in the blackest of ink and somehow stronger and different from the rest.

That stuck out to me.

Nine.

The next lines showed past harvests long ago forgotten. The building of a pyramid. The rise of a Saur of great power who I was sure was Sût the Undying as represented in the Saurian glyph language.

Then another battle.

This time Dragon Elves, men, the nine black humans, against the Saur along a great black serpent of a river.

The River of Night was my guess.

Then sacrifice to the black "sun."

Dragon Elves and men are tossed into it like summer wheat for the threshing. The sinister priests tally and conduct dark rites.

There are lines I can't understand that seem to involve perhaps magic and eventually betrayal.

These are nuances I'm unclear on.

The nine show up again a few lines later, but now they bow before Sût the Undying atop his golden and turquoise throne, and the malefic black sun.

The priests surround the nine and make them… minor pharaohs. Except… there are only eight.

One of the nine is missing.

Noted.

The last lines show that this… what lies behind the door… is the resting place of one of the nine.

And below this, Sût on his throne, smiling evilly.

Chief Rapp was watching our six for more Katari as I worked the riddle and made ready to test the door. I could feel the captain's eyes on me. Focused. Intent.

"Okay…" I muttered to myself, getting ready to probably do the wrong thing and explode into a thousand fast-moving pieces all at once.

I conducted the tests. Spit water on the door. Nothing. No discharged electricity. Tested various areas with a small wooden stick. Except I didn't have a stick, but I did have an MRE spoon because you should always have one.

Nothing.

The door didn't turn into a massive fanged mouth and bite my hands off.

It was as… *safe*… as I could determine.

I looked back at the captain.

"Clean, sir. Ready to breach."

The captain stacked to the right of the door, the chief moved to the left. Brief instructions were issued tersely with that tension that comes before violence.

The bronze doors clearly opened inward, as there were no scrape marks on the floor that indicated it opened outward.

"Corporal, put your shoulder into this area…" the captain muttered in a low growl. "Push it open and stay low. As soon as it gets far enough for me to slip through, pull back and go to your primary. Chief will take left, I'll take right, you come in and clean up the center."

"Affirmative, sir."

We got ready with as little sound and movement as possible. In my mind I rehearsed my actions and then waited for the captain's orders.

For five seconds we waited in position and slowed our breathing.

Then…

"Go, go, go. Go now."

CHAPTER FOURTEEN

I heaved my weight into the bronze door that wasn't a mimic and it swung open easier than I thought it would. I kept my feet under me and pulled back to my primary as the captain disappeared through the crack, then the chief.

Weapon low and ready I went in after, and was instantly greeted by one of the most surreal scenes I ever didn't think I'd see.

It was a long, low-ceilinged room, sunken in the center and lined with hieroglyph-scrawled columns. Torches angrily roiled from their sconces, and across the room with a clear view of the door…

… was a mummy in a chest rig and plate carrier holding an M4 with an ACOG scope just like the one Specialist Commons carried for recon.

It was immediately identifiable as our Rangers' gear.

Priests in white robes, their faces hidden, scurried from the room as the mummy faced us. Leaving via some hidden unseen exit at the rear of the chamber past the armed mummy.

The mummy even had the Vickers sling around its shoulder and waist, with one bandage-wrapped hand on the pull tab as though it had just released the tension to let Commons's M4 hang looser around the bandage- and grave-shroud-wrapped mummy. It wore a bronze circlet in the form of a snake, its head rearing. Two rubies for glittering venomous eyes.

Other than that, there was nothing else of note other than that the mummy figure looked quite ancient.

Two eyes like glaring red suns stared out from the dark slit in the bandages that covered where its eyes should be.

The captain had already moved to cover behind the nearest column on the right, and the chief had moved to one on the left. I faded, never crossing my feet, to the left and fell behind the chief, using the same column as cover and checking our flanks to make sure Katari or stray priests weren't coming up on us.

There was incense in the air.

Burial spices.

In the distance some great bell tolled.

Then the mummy spoke, its voice there… and not there in the same moment. It was real. I could hear its ancient deep growl, almost that dusty deep don't-mess-with-me rasp some of the hardest Rangers used.

It spoke English.

And I could hear it in my head, too. Close, and personal in the way something dangerous should never be. Still deep. But soft, a mere hissing whisper that seemed to echo what was being said in real-time and picked up by our ear pro.

"Stand by to engage," growled the captain.

And then…

"That would be… unwise… Ranger… boys," hissed the mummy with the M4.

CHAPTER FIFTEEN

"ENGAGE," ordered the captain and off-hand fired a burst right at the mummy on the other side of the room.

Five or six hot streaking rounds, each an individual trigger pull performed by a man who was no stranger to the trigger, found their mark and tore straight through the mummy's bandages, blowing dust and vapor and shredded bandage out the back.

Surprisingly fast, and unfazed, the mummy faded behind a grand golden sarcophagus, ornate and made of solid gold, and yeah, I said it twice. Ever seen one? It's pretty amazing. Especially if it's made out of all gold. Three times. The mummy must've just been woken by the white-robed priests who had scurried off through some unseen exit.

The gunshots still echoing through the burial chamber, the mummy began to laugh, and it felt for a moment that the temple floor trembled. Its dry laugh was papery and cruel as it returned fire a moment later, and the captain covered efficiently and quickly as rounds from Commons's rifle smacked columns and wall behind.

The chief popped around the corner, had no shot, and was back under cover, shaking his head at the captain across the space between them to indicate he had no sight picture to engage this new enemy.

I held fire and watched the flanks.

"You… Rangers…" cracked that cruel deep and ancient voice, and then the ethereal whisper, of the mummy. "Are a… tomorrow problem. Not today. Not yet. Not now. No need to die today… but die… you will… Ranger boys."

The walls shook once, hard and violent. As though the whole room had suddenly just dropped six inches.

The mummy laugh-croaked, its voice echoing in our minds and across unseen spaces within the burial temple.

And all that was super weird. But the weirdest part of all this was that the chief and Captain Knife Hand were now looking at each and making faces that seemed to indicate they were both processing something unexpected and communicating in some straphanger-operator speak I hadn't learned yet. They seemed to agree on something, the chief nodded, and the captain—his face in his predator form is unreadable as it's not human—merely accepted what was agreed upon without movement.

Stone-cold killer that he is.

But I felt some agreement had passed between them. I was sure of that. I just wasn't privy to it.

Operator stuff. Operating on levels mere mortals like me don't get.

Yet.

Yeah, I got dreams. It ain't a badge. But it is an achievement. If they can do it…

So can I, Talker said foolishly.

The captain shifted positions, quickly darting to another column faster than I thought possible.

Were-tiger gonna were-tiger.

Chief Rapp opened fire at the same time on the mummy's

position just to keep the thing from engaging with Commons's rifle.

Which… was a mystery.

Like… how does a mummy from the Ruin know how to operate an M4? A modern firearm that can't exist for long in the Ruin due to the lingering effects of the nano-plague.

Where he learn that, ask caveman Talker?

And yet, even as I thought this, feeling stupid and slow and not getting something that was right there in front of my face, I could feel the tumblers of the universe falling into place and pointing toward a solution I had yet to fully understand, or accept.

But… there was a sick cold feeling lingering in the background of my mind.

Fear.

It felt like fear, but I couldn't think what I was afraid of. All I could feel was it rushing all over and all around me. Like I was falling into some cold river I could never get out of.

Yeah, whatever. Fear isn't new to me.

I'm not new to gunfights or battle either. I'm mostly over that. But this was something else, some sickly gut-wrenching fear that was seeping through the room, and I had the suspicion it was coming from the mummy.

Like that was something it could do. Some Ruin-revealed ability in Kennedy's game of strange-shaped dice, pens, and paper.

Even through Chief Rapp's burst of return fire, the thing, hidden from us, had continued its constant breathy laugh of utter derision. The mummy didn't spook. You had the feeling it was no stranger either to a gunfight on levels I had never even considered.

Like… it *liked* them. Looked for them. Wanted to be… in them.

"Oh… Rangers," rasped the deadly mummy. "Everything is still violence with you… ain't it. Violence of… action. Isn't that what we used to say? Like… a religion… for you… ain't it, Ranger… boys. Ain't it always. Always… was."

The captain popped a frag and motioned that he was going to deploy it forward behind the massive sarcophagus and try to obliterate the thing.

Not optimal.

There would be overpressure.

Then, still holding the cooked grenade, the captain motioned with both hands that we'd flank and engage after the det.

Standard Ranger. Take away the enemy's momentum with shock, then make them pay with copious amounts of applied automatic gunfire violence delivered up close and impersonal.

Bonus points for knives and hand-to-hand. Teeth and garottes are just cray-cray.

But that's how Rangers roll.

Not to be confused with the Ranger Medic Ranger Roll.

The captain tossed the grenade, and a swarm of scarabs suddenly flung themselves off the columns, ink and paint suddenly come to vibrating humming life, and just…

… ate the explosion.

Weird.

One of the top ten weirdest things I've ever seen.

We did not flank.

We did not rush.

The mummy laughed, and it was clear, in the aftermath of the scarabs eating our grenade, that he had all the cards. And knew it.

"See… Ranger boys… chaos… is my jam," croaked the mummy from cover.

The room began to shake as a low earthquake shifted in the stone of the cliff… and didn't stop.

"Life is about… expectation… management. You came to find your… lost little Ranger. He's mine now, Ranger… boys. You're in doubt. You're in my jam, now. For me…"

One of the columns in the room suddenly collapsed, and through the hole in the ceiling came a flood of desiccated old corpses, broken rocks, and dirt. Human corpses.

Except they weren't dead.

They were… *un*dead.

They writhed lazily as all the dust and debris waterfalled down around them in their sudden pile, moaning on ghastly gasping sighs as they pulled themselves from the flood of rubble and began to shamble for us as fast as they could get free of the dirt cascade.

"… I'll be just fine now that we're… playing my game… Ranger… boys."

The captain shot a quick hand signal at us to pull back now to the entrance we'd just come through.

More columns were collapsing throughout the burial chamber. More corpses were entering the battlespace. More dried-out desiccated husks of the buried alive flooded down into the ceremonial burial chamber and began to rise like the floodwaters of death itself.

They were coming for us.

Still the mummy's voice was there as we pulled back, Chief Rapp covering from the door as the captain fired into the desiccated brown corpses surging for him, falling back deftly to the open bronze doors and dropping the undead as they shambled closer and closer.

"Life… is about expectation management, Ranger boys," the mummy's voice echoed. "You came here thinking… you were going to get your boy back. Now… he is with us in the Land of Black Sleep. Now… my master commands me… to destroy you. So…"

"Move to the exit now!" shouted the captain. "He's going to bring this whole place down on us!"

"Go, Talker, go!" shouted Chief Rapp, and he pushed me forward.

Honestly, I didn't need to be told twice.

That fear was fighting hard for a permanent place in my brain, and that pissed me off. But there was something about the order to fade that made the fear ten times more real all at once. Like every bad vibe, every bout of food poisoning from meat on the street, and even every overdue homework assignment had all come hurtling at me on a rain-slick Monday morning of not needing all this bad right now at this very moment.

So I ran… and was convinced we'd never make the exterior of the temple as dust and debris rained down on us and the buried-alive dead burst out of the walls and fell from the ceiling in great dusty waterfalls of death.

Then emerged from their rotting piles and reached out to drag us in with them.

We were running for the entrance to the temple, and the voice of the mummy with Commons's rifle chased us through all that destruction and horror just like in that first Indiana Jones movie when the laughter of his competitor echoes through the jungle as he races away from the headhunters.

"You took his general… the medusa… Ranger boys. And now Sût has summoned me for battle once again. And chaos, Rangers, remember… it's my jam. I will bury you… alive. Either here with me… or in the Valley of Death… Ranger boys. When the time comes… gonna bury… you… alive. Here… with me… Ranger boys. For-evah!"

And then… the mummy with Commons's M4 gave his Delta operator number.

But I didn't understand what was said at the time. And later it had to be explained to me.

CHAPTER SIXTEEN

VAST sections of the rock temple were in full collapse when I barely raced out of the dark and onto the temple steps, covered in ancient dust, choking, coughing, and trying to establish security and recognize threats as the first in the team into a new location we'd fallen back into.

Spoiler… we got pushed by this mummy general right into a blocker force.

I brought the M4 up and started engaging the shambling spindly-stick-body dead already struggling up from the sands and the river.

For me, and this is a side note, these dead really bothered me. Wasn't like some of the "classic" zombies or ghouls we'd faced before. These were like famine victims, their skin taut and brown. Their features misshapen by abuse and mistreatment in malnutrition before they were buried alive as a bonus feature to the worthy Saurian being entombed for the afterlife.

Their eyes were large but lifeless, and by what light there was available they looked to me more like aliens than human wretches. Saurian slaves, really.

They were small and gaunt. Their bodies little more than sticks wrapped in coarse rags that had probably once been the only clothing they'd ever owned as they toiled at this pyramid, that obelisk, or yet another grand monument to death eternal and the Saur.

It was clear their intentions were to harm us. So… I started blasting.

As they say.

Chief Rapp barely cleared the entrance, and then the whole temple collapsed beyond the darkness of the gaping open mouth of an entrance. I got hit from behind with a shock wave of hot dead air that smelled overripe with the sweet scent of the dead and the long-buried ages of papyrus-scrolled spells, eucalyptus balms, and burial spices.

I pivoted for half a second just to see if the other members of my team had made it, but there was literally no time to lose if I was gonna establish some kind of perimeter by gunfire for us to gather, organize, and move for the exfil.

Listen to me sounding Ranger and all.

Anyway… coffee would have been nice, but I was busy popping caps and smoking spindly dead slaves as fast as I could aim and pull the trigger.

Sometimes the fast-moving five-five-six got me a two-fer and blew apart a couple of the slave zombie skulls, but for the most part I had to put in the work of marksmanship, breath, timing, and urgency matching that of a ticking clock on a bomb about to detonate.

In that pivot back to check on the rest of the team, Chief Rapp and the captain, drilling two dead things that looked like skeletal corpses dipped in barbecue sauce and left to stretch in the sun, I saw the Green Beret reach into a cascade of dusty debris and falling rock of the façade of the burial temple, and watched as the operator yanked the stumbling were-tiger Ranger captain out from under certain death by crushing ancient temple.

It was literally all hands involved in the business of our group survival.

With a savage heave, Chief Rapp flung the captain ahead of him, narrowly avoiding another cascade of falling stone coming off one of the crocodilian carved titans guarding the entrance to the mummy general's tomb. Gaining his tiger's feet, the captain roared angrily and leapt savagely away, landing among a swarm of the dead who began to die violently having found themselves suddenly too close to Death Incarnate.

And Death was pissed.

I stalked forward, shooting down the dead as they reached out for the captain. The ones he wasn't tearing to pieces with huge and savage claw swipes, mindless of his primary and the efficiency and ease of modern weaponry. I shot thin bodies as fast as I could pull the trigger, moving to the double-tap and handing out two per on the walking corpses. That they were probably once slaves used to construct the ancient burial temple bothered me on some background app of my mind that was still human and not Ranger, but I kept pulling the trigger until they disintegrated or came apart like bundles of dry sticks.

As Sergeant Chris taught me... keep shooting till they change shape or catch fire. Whenever I remind him of that he just glares at me and says he's not the originator of the phrase.

I tell him, "Being as I'm the only one writing the history of the world now that all the other writers from our time are dead... guess what I say goes, Sar'nt."

To the victor goeth the coffee. Thus sayeth Talker.

We had a toehold on the other side of the death trap the

temple of the mummy-general had suddenly become, and then from out of nowhere swarms of biting horseflies come at us in clustering hordes, trying to get into our mouths and nostrils as they streak in angrily across the hot night like tiny little cruise missiles of hate and pain.

I know… it's just insects. But seriously, those bites didn't just hurt… it was like they were infecting us with rage and demonic anger.

And they jammed my chi.

I gotta give Bandage Bro that. It was a clever attack that suddenly had us fighting for our lives and messing up our ability to get organized, sectors to watch and on the route back to the bird and all.

The captain swiped hard at a corpse that had gotten too close, as he worked the flare off his chest rig where he had it near the bundle of ChemLights every Ranger possessed. The corpse shredded and flew into several pieces at the tiger's-claw slash, and the captain popped the flare, shooting it out over the river as the flies slammed their angry little horseshoe-shaped bodies into us trying to find any exposed skin in order to deliver that hard angry bite that seemed to distract you with an anger to only crush and smash the thing as best you could.

Never mind the dead still coming out of the river and the sands all around us.

There were a seemingly endless number. It seemed.

I know… that's terrible writing.

I was being bitten to death while the unquiet dead tried to rip me to pieces. And things weren't looking good. Even with the Green Beret and the were-tiger… numbers are numbers. And the ride out of here was a long way away with swarms of tangos between us and there.

Never mind. In it to win it.

Mag out.

Mag in.

Back on the gun. Principles of good marksmanship applied despite enemy efforts to jam my chi.

Someone put me in for an ARCOM. Even if it is posthumous. Name something after me.

Then I thought of Autumn and the… kid. And my promise to be there. So I got real meaner than the horseflies and took shooting down the enemy as personally as I could.

I caught most of these bites on the neck and face before I could get my shemagh up as my accuracy degraded and rounds began to merely "wound" the dead we were pushing through for the river now as the captain shouted orders and led us through all that swarming death, and I could feel there were other unseen forces out there in the dark besides the dead forming into walls and waves to push against our immediate and urgent gunfire to keep them back. I swapped mags and watched as the chief came up from behind shooting quickly and concisely at the clustering dead who'd suddenly made for me desperately as I released the mag, letting it fall to the sand and got another out.

The chief stopped for one hot second and mumbled something about blessings as he rested one dusty and torn assault glove on my shoulder and then moved on, shooting down more and taking the lead as the captain mag-dumped on a river hippo that had suddenly surfaced from the waters and was bleating angrily at us.

A. River. Hippo.

And yeah… its eyes were glowing red.

Hippos are super dangerous already. Even if they aren't demon-possessed mummy-controlled thralls. Which this one apparently was.

Still, beyond the dead I kept seeing tall… strange-headed figures out there for half a second. Then they were gone and I couldn't find them.

Then again, I was fighting for my life.

About that river hippo getting ready to charge and bite us with its massive prehistoric jaws… probably trample us too.

Seriously… river hippos don't play.

The captain walked forward, swapping mags without hesitation and then emptying the next kill stick into the bellowing hippo that tried to work itself up into a rage. So many coffin darts in and the bellowing hippo merely fell on its side thrashing like some savage dinosaur in the mud and reeds, breathing hot heavy gasps as it died under excessive Ranger gunfire applied like a boss with no time to spare as we pushed through the river muck and spotted the blades of the chopper winding up ahead across the dark river of death we still needed to cross.

But now, thanks to the Green Beret cleric's blessing, the insects that dared get near me turned to sudden fireflies and burned up in the hot sweltering night as we waded into the papyrus reeds and engaged the death at danger-close and spittle-flecked-insults range.

Like I said, ahead the Little Bird was already spinning up, and we could hear long bursts of gunfire from Sergeant Kang out on the sandbar because of course there were problems on the DZ too.

But that was an over-there problem.

We had to get through the over-here reeds and across the shallows to the sandbar, and did I mention the company of zombies swarming out of river drooling slime to get at us and drag us down into the darker and deeper depths of the Nile where the crocs can death-roll you and take you off to their dens for later snacking.

I'm not saying we were in over our heads…

But it felt like that.

And yeah, the Rangers who read this will say that's "just every day paying the rent on the scroll, Talker." Yeah, I get that. But there was some hopelessness that felt… magical and evil… that kept whispering in that mummy's hiss that we weren't gonna make it out of this one.

So anyway… I continued blasting.

Happy, Rangers? I Rangered. Even when it looked pretty bleak. At least I'm honest about things.

Warts and all. That's what I said.

I was dry on ammo and down to my sidearm by the time we made the wet sandbar and the Little Bird. Moving in a wedge, we slaughtered our way through the undead massing there and I probably burned my ammo and ended up Winchester on primary far faster than the Green Beret and the captain.

I know… lame. Amateur night.

When I called "Winchester," gasping because the suck of the stinking river mud and reeds and the overwhelming fear and fatigue was starting to want payment for services rendered, Chief Rapp just said…

"We almost there, Talker. Switch to your secondary and

keep 'em back, son."

My hands were shaking, my breathing was straight-up ragged. Demonic biting horseflies were turning to dying comets as they got too close, and that didn't help with handing out head shots to keep the dead down… but I did anyway.

When you go to Chief Rapp's school of awesome firearms training and trick shooting, he PTs you to death on the range—sprints in full gear, pushups, sit-ups, and plank holds—then makes you get up and start shooting targets for hits inside the box. What you learn from all that fatigue and stress is that when you actually have to shoot, move, and communicate under duress… it's a lot harder than just target practice at the range. Especially if you're firing from different positions.

But you get better at it and mainly you tell yourself to slow down, think, and make your shots count instead of just trying to be fast and urgent.

One zombie got close, and I had to shoot him several times as he grabbed onto my mag pouches and wouldn't die. Again.

So, that got a little urgent and excessive. But… it also got handled.

In the next moments with the exit in sight, I applied what Chief Rapp had taught me, stabilized the sidearm as best I could, and started squeezing off shots on the closing dead. And then this little technique suddenly appeared in my toolkit as we approached the crocodile-overrun bird on the sandbar…

I'd kick the dead, or dead-leg them with a swift and sudden kick, wait until they collapsed, they were little more than bundles of dried sticks, and then I'd drill them right in the skull point-blank down and prone in the shallow river water.

This slowed me, but I kept up the integrity of the wedge as we moved.

Sergeant Kang warned us of the swarming crocodiles coming out of the black-as-a-devil's-heart River of Night.

The moon was obscured when it should have been easily visible, and the air was hot and fetid with decay and death all around us. Sergeant Kang was down on one knee and swapping in a drum mag when we made the sandy stretch of the bar. He'd kept an open path he'd marked with ChemLights at the last second, never mind the shredded and thrashing crocs he'd shot to death to maintain the avenue of escape.

We loaded in, still firing at the prehistoric river lizards lunging and snapping for the skids—file that under, "Well that's a new one"—and I'd barely felt the *clink* of the retention lanyard on the airframe when suddenly we were desperately struggling for altitude in the night and hauling for the north up the black river of death and Sûstagul if we still had enough fuel.

For a moment the moonlight appeared as we climbed, and for a hot second I was able to see just how overrun the river, the fallen temple, and the sandbar was with the dead, crocs, more hippos, and… strange tall priests with what looked like animal heads, like the ancient deities of Egypt, walking among the unholy mass of enemies that had just tried to make us stay whether we liked it or not.

To me, climbing into the cool night as we got away from the hot stinking breath of the river, it was like a swarm of rotten maggots on meat gone bad down there, and not only was I surprised we'd gotten out of there alive…

… but amazed that we had done so at all.

CHAPTER SEVENTEEN

THE river teeming with the maggots of the mummy lord, whom I was shortly about to learn much more about, swirled and faded from view in the early night as the AH-6 turned from the river, picked up its course track, and headed northwest for Sûstagul.

Then the psionics had one more farewell vision for me. But it felt like a gut punch instead.

For a moment I felt like I was falling right out of the chopper, as though it had suddenly gone over on its side to make a turn and I was clipped in.

I might have even yelped.

But even as I did, I reached for my retention lanyard to ensure that in the chaos and confusion of shot-to-death and still snapping demon-crocs and all those moaning and sighing in torment swarming undead tomb builders sent at us, to die again, by the mummy, that I had somehow clipped into the airframe. Instead of doing something real stupid like not clipping in.

Honestly, I could definitely see me just clipping right back into me. My battle belt or plate carrier. Something stupid and guaranteed to make sure you never got to straphang beyond the intro level. Ever again.

My hands, as my eyes went into the vision I was suddenly having, found the lanyard by feel alone and ensured that I was, in fact, hard connected to the Little Bird's airframe even as I wanted to hurl and the world spun from the visions I was seeing courtesy of my psionics.

This is what I saw.

I saw Commons on a rough stretcher being carried by the white-robed and shrouded priests. There were no torches, and I wasn't sure if the priests were Saur, or humans in the service of Sût the Undying.

There were in fact such.

In the vision I was having, helpless to fight it off and only distantly sure I had not fallen from the AH-6, these shadowy and grim priests, chanting words I was sure were devilish blasphemies of some kind, hustled Commons out the secret rock entrance at the back of the collapsed tomb we'd almost been buried alive in, somewhere now in the crescent fracture that was the Valley of Kings and Priests, I was sure of it in my mind, and off into the night of shadows and glaring blue moonlight.

The landscape was lunar, and as noted tinged with blue. I could see other, more obscene figures like those animal-headed priests directing the ambush at the river and the sandbar. They were in the darkness all about Commons and the procession that bore him deeper into the Valley of Kings and Priests. The Valley of Death.

There were other tombs… other guardians…

But it was Commons. Unconscious. And clearly wounded in the vision.

He'd put up a fight. He hadn't gone down easily. But now they had him.

Then the world swirled back into reality suddenly and

I just hurled off the side of the chopper and covered both Sergeant Kang and myself in my own hot vomit.

Homestyle Vegetables in Sauce with Noodles and Chicken.

It was super awful.

The blades of the defiant and sturdy little chopper beat us senseless carrying us north with the night, and did little to cover the bouts of horrible reek that came off my vomit-covered fatigues and gear.

So… I got that goin' for me.

Still, despite this… I breathed a sigh of relief and laughed at where the mummy's fear had tried to consume me. It was gone now, and what replaced it was the opposite of what that fear had felt like.

Now, I had life. And hope.

The mummy's reek was far worse than my Homestyle Vegetables in Sauce with Noodles and Chicken hurl. It was the opposite of life. The opposite of hope.

But more importantly…

Commons was still in play.

And that… was everything to me.

CHAPTER EIGHTEEN

THE AAR back in the TOC was enlightening, and abbreviated. It was oh-three-hundred or sometime after by the time we got back and rallied in the TOC for the AAR and discuss next moves.

And there wasn't much of that because Commons was definitely in the belly of the beast and there just weren't the assets ready to go get him, even if we knew exactly where he was.

Which we didn't.

And that was really the problem.

And the fact that most of the detachment was out either blind drunk at this time of the night, with three days to go of leave, or doing their best to get to that state.

Old Man Sims, who was on radio watch in the TOC, wrinkled his face and snorted, "Yo, Talk… you smell like I feel most days."

I smiled and told him something not fit to reprint.

But he was right. The Homestyle Vegetables in Sauce with Noodles and Chicken still clung. And it wasn't good.

Anyway… don't worry about me, I had coffee. The smaj's blue percolator was ready when we got back.

We smelled of death, and Homestyle Vegetables in Sauce with Noodles and Chicken hurl, sorry Sar'nt Kang… and there were some minor injuries that needed attending to. The medics saw to the captain's injuries. He'd turned full human on the way back as the adrenaline faded as fatigue tried to take us.

And yeah... even flying over open desert at altitude, beaten by the wind and the night, after what we'd just been through, the adrenaline crash was extra hard. But coffee came to the rescue and what I'd seen in the vision kept playing over and over like some message that wouldn't un-alert from your notifications.

I stayed awake through the AAR and an assessment of this current "Commons Situation," trying to parse all the details of the vision and attempting to extract any meaningful intel that might be located within for the next mission we'd mount to rescue our Ranger.

Because that was one thing... that needed to happen. And it needed to happen right now.

That was like a broken record in my brain.

Command was all about running drone recon over the area to try and pick him up. Then we'd get some of the pipe hitters from the scouts and assaulters to go in on Little Birds, fast-rope in, and extract him.

We just needed to nail down his location for the rescue.

The only thing I'd told the captain over the comm on the way back was, "Sir, I believe Commons is still alive, and still in that area."

There was a long pause and all I heard was the soft *hummmm* of the comm in the silence as I waited for an acknowledge or an answer.

Then...

"Copy, Talker."

CHAPTER NINETEEN

SO, the Delta thing.

During the AAR both the chief and the captain seemed to be skirting around this issue as there were starting to be more and more people in the TOC besides those directly involved. Mainly the Air Force started showing up and trying to be helpful, letting us know they had drone coverage in the area and were running scans to locate Commons, if possible.

One of the Black Hawks was fueled, armed, and ready to roll.

Then, when the captain asked for feedback, which anyone involved is allowed to give, I piped up.

I'd just had my third cup of coffee from the smaj's perc and I was feeling saucy as the fatigue faded.

Call me the Comeback Kid, brought to you by coffee.

It was almost the witching hour, and the hour was either late, or early, depending on how you look at such things. The air felt dry and tired, and everyone's voice sounded like a three-day hangover.

Then there's three-cups-cheery old me sitting there all bright and bushy-tailed with tons of questions about all the weird we got involved in down there.

So… here we go… *Leeeeeerrrooooy Jenkins!*

As some of the younger Rangers say.

"Sir, when the… uh… mummy-guy… said… That's a

tomorrow problem… I noted an exchange between you and the chief. As though that phrase… was familiar to you. And the chief. Is that… important to the mission to find Commons?"

Then Knife Hand… in human form, thankfully… made that face. You know the one.

He took a deep breath, put both hands on his hips, and looked around.

He directed some personnel to exit the TOC. He asked that the jammers be activated, and we waited as Sims made this happen and the smaj made sure it was done.

I'd noted: even the smaj's ears had perked up when I'd said what I said.

That's a tomorrow problem.

Once all was secure, the captain told the truth. Which, in the Rangers, works both up and down the chain of command.

"The bad guy we faced in there is most likely a Delta operator. It has nothing to do with the rescue of our missing Ranger. But it is a serious problem concerning the reason we're down here: to terminate HVT Mummy. I don't know how he arrived here. I don't know the why or how he's involved with our HVT, but he clearly is working for them. But the phrase he used—*That's a tomorrow problem*—if you've worked with Delta… and them referring to us as *Ranger boys*, the newer younger crowd… it's pretty standard lingo. Add this to his acquisition and proper usage of Commons's rifle and gear, and both Chief Rapp and I believe we have encountered at least one of the survivors of the Delta team that went through the QST before we did and may have entered the Ruin up to eight thousand years ago. I believe in the dungeons of FOB

Hawthorn we found evidence of a group calling itself…"

"The Delta Kings…" I whispered.

Chief Rapp was stone-faced still and sat staring at the tent walls.

The captain merely nodded.

The smaj raised his gray bushy eyebrows, then sighed with audible disgust.

Sims pursed his lips and pretended he hadn't heard what he'd just heard.

Captain Knife Hand continued.

"Because you're more aquatinted with the… lore… Corporal Talker… of the Ruin… I need you to do an assessment of everything we've acquired so far."

He paused.

"Everything you've written down, and see what jibes with this newest intel."

"Can do, sir."

The captain nodded, lowered his head, and then proceeded again as we wrapped up the brief.

"Full disclosure… because this is us, we are Rangers…"

He looked around like he was pissed off to say what he needed to say.

"Both the chief and I have experience with The Unit. That's how we were able to identify his origin. To be clear… Delta is the best of the best. This bad guy is to be considered extremely, emphasis and I say again, *extremely* dangerous. He becomes a significant combat multiplier to our enemies. Some Rangers become Delta operators. Eventually. The OTC, Operator Training Course, is a gateway, and the Ranger battalions get the heads-up for the opportunity before the official email goes out. He is most likely us. And a whole lot of other dangerous trouble. That's just the nature of Delta. Each Delta operator has a Delta number, and there aren't many numbers."

Silence so heavy and thick you could wrap yourself in it and keep warm on a cold winter's night.

It was clear that our plans thus far… were out the door. This guy, this Delta operator now turned into a mummy and working for the enemy, willingly or unwillingly… was a game changer.

"Do you… know him?" I asked.

The captain stared at me with a look that was either total and complete honesty, or pure cold indifferent murder.

Warts. And all.

Sometimes I find Knife Hand to be the opposite of human. An operator on levels other than anything I should ever have known. Emotions and humanity shed somewhere in some forsaken hellhole just to make the next point on the land nav course of total unrestricted violence.

Very Dark Alleys, as the smaj had indicated.

I resisted the temptation to shudder. But I had asked what I had asked during an AAR, and I'd just been tasked to find out the answers. To know.

Knowledge is just another form of ammunition Rangers will use to kill their enemies.

So… all's fair. Everyone show their cards. Call.

The captain gave me that look. Total and complete honesty. Pure cold indifferent murder. Both at once.

"We are not sure, Corporal. We have suspicions. But his operator number is lower than both of ours."

CHAPTER TWENTY

I thought I was tired, but I found myself at dawn making my way toward Amira and her father's coffee pavilion in the port. The sun was rising, and for just a few magic moments the entire desert port city seemed to be made of gold and cool blue shadows.

Cats passed me, regarded me as though I were doomed and they felt some pity for me, then continued home from their night's haunts.

The city guards gave me a hard time about Rangers only being allowed in the cordoned streets given the damage and havoc we'd caused. I told them I was on official business and that my leave was over. I was no longer covered in blood and dust and Homestyle Vegetables in Sauce with Noodles and Chicken detritus from the battle at the temple.

I'd stripped, bathed in the trough, the water was cold and felt refreshing even though it was dark and before dawn, and asked myself, *How many times does this happen in your life?*

Then I changed into fresh clothes and handed my gear over to the guy we'd been paying coppers to in exchange for gear and laundry maintenance.

He bowed three times, murmured honestly about his great fortune in being able to attend to my Homestyle Vegetables in Sauce with Noodles and Chicken hurl, and backed away as I got into another set of fatigues.

I combed my hair.

I told myself I was going there because Amira's father's coffee was the best, and I'd been avoiding it because now I was back with Autumn and…

We have to be honest…

About these things…

But things had been going a certain, innocently but abundantly clear, direction between me and the honest and beautiful, and very earnest, Amira.

So I needed to… straighten things out. And don't ask me why I felt this way with Commons missing and the news that an equal to the Rangers, a premium tip-of-the-spear killer, was running the enemy game now.

Don't ask me.

But if you did… I'd say I felt something bad was going to happen, and I needed to be straight with everyone. Short accounts.

Portugon and the dead girl I'd tried to run away with… had changed me.

Autumn was part of my life… *was* my life now. Her and… the kid. So it was time to make sure this was settled and that the hard-working faithful daughter of the best coffee shop in town was… free to move about.

I was pretty sure, and I don't say this arrogantly, but I was pretty sure I was gonna break her heart. She was good like that. And I could tell… this was gonna hurt her.

Dawn in the city of Sûstagul is golden and beautiful. It's quiet. The day, hectic with business and trade and the shouting and cacophony of a dozen or more different languages all vying to be heard, would soon come and everything would change. But now, as I walked the streets toward the coffee tent of Amira and her family, I was alone. And it felt good.

It's a crossroads of the world.

The nights are busy with the pleasure and parties that even the meanest and poorest families seem to make their meals of every night. As if just surviving another day is enough for such a festive occasion.

Now, the work and heat of the day would begin. More legionnaires from Accadios would push through the port and head south. Veterans and boys getting their last look at what they were fighting for—civilization—before marching south to die before the Grand Pyramid of Sût himself.

Talker waxes eloquent.

But it's the truth. And it always has been. Soldiers die for the life they wish to live, if only so others may.

I stopped at the edge of the alley I had taken to reach the coffee tent.

Amira was there. Wiping down tables, busy at the business she kept alive with everything she could beg, borrow, and perhaps steal.

Her father was roasting behind the shop.

Her "whore sister," her words not mine… unseen. Probably asleep in some rich man's bed. She would be here later. The business would pick up.

And they would do everything they could to survive.

Even the whore sister.

And I thought about Commons and the fact that he was missing. In the hands of the enemy.

I walked forward and smiled and couldn't help but feel guilty.

What I said, ain't for this account.

Long story short.

She looked like I'd socked her in the stomach and knocked the wind out of her. She was, genuinely, hurt. But I gave it to her straight and said "I am sorry" in her language.

She sobbed once like all the love and life ever possible had been taken from her and there was no answer in the temples, or among the wise, that would ever make it better. Then customers were coming and her father was already stoking the hot fires of the sand pot where she would work all day.

And perhaps... forever. Now that I had told her I was... sworn... to Autumn.

I could see as she looked away to the work she would do at her father's side, that she too had big dreams. And that they were all gone now.

"Wait..." she said softly. Her voice husky. And then she went and made me a coffee. Her father tried to make it. She gave him a look, a hard one, and the man stepped back and she prepared the brew.

Grounds she ground herself.

Spices.

Hot water.

Three times it was brought to a boil.

And then she took a small and beautiful mahogany box with gold hinges up as she came to me with the delicate cup of brew.

She was fighting back tears. Bravely. Sobbing inside as her chest tried to heave and she fought to control it as she set the brew and the fine box down in front of me.

It was... a perfect cup, and I knew it would be the most

bitter coffee I had ever tasted. And I deserved it. Even if it was poison… I would drink it down, grounds and all.

"This…" she said, her voice little more than a whisper. "Is for you, m—"

She was going to say *"my."*

But she stopped.

"For you… Ranger."

She stood, straightened herself, and had all the class of a queen, even though she was not one.

But she was. In her own noble way. I see that now.

"The Kungaloorian sugar… you so *love*. I found some on a… on a junk for the east."

Imagine the worst you have ever felt.

She placed a cool hand on my forehead and brushed back my hair. Tears filled her eyes. And then she turned and went behind the tents.

I drank the coffee bitter.

I took the box.

Yes, I am for Autumn. But the sugar will remind me, for how much longer I have it… of Amira.

That is my sentence.

Then I left and never went there again.

CHAPTER TWENTY-ONE

REDEMPTION wasn't the reason I decided to volunteer for a suicide mission.

Amira stung. Yes. She'd live. So would I. I had Autumn.

And perhaps… this half-elf shadow kid whatever out there someday that might… need me.

The morning was turning to heat and rising sun in that beautiful city between the emerald sea and the sand of a desert that seemed to stretch off into forever. I feel that, somehow, I will remember for all the days I have left to me that the city was beautiful as the temple bells rang out their prayers and the people called to one another.

Work songs begun.

Trade underway.

Life… abundant.

But there was still enough morning cool in the shadows along the Street of Clay and Fire near the eastern wall where I'd gone next. I'd gone that direction to walk off Amira, and to get another coffee from a brew shop out there because of course… me.

And I told myself, there's no such thing, if Sergeant Chris is right, and I believe he is, as a *suicide mission* to a Ranger.

Rangers can do anything, Talker.

So I had this crazy idea in which it was highly likely I'd have to put that maxim to the test.

I drank the hot coffee standing there in the cool blue shadows of the wall as the merchants began to shape their clays and stoke their kilns, a little watery, no spices, and very dark and bitter with rich aromas of plum and butterscotch.

Coffee. All was right for a moment. And it too told me… *Rangers can do anything, Talker. You just gotta decide to do this.*

Oh, coffee… are you a liar, or an optimist? I don't know. I only know I'd be lost without you.

The sons of the roaster were in the back of the shop, and the heavy aromas of deeply roasted beans were intoxicating. Smiling and laughing as they roasted the sacks they'd hauled from the caravanserai that morning in the dark when the first trades began, the brothers working and talking of their adventures of the night before, and their hopes for the day ahead.

How do I know this?

I've been there in the dark. Listening to them laugh and brew and bargain. They are people just like me.

Again… a memory I'll take with me to whatever end awaits me along the trail ahead.

Right, Dad?

Right?

I watched those young men work and caught the quick glances of their wizened and ancient father working at the fire sand pit to brew the line of cups the silked and bare-chested customers waited for in order to start their day.

Junkies and addicts too. Meeting at their church. Laughing and sharing their stories, disappointments… and hopes for the day just as they did every morning too.

The brewmaster gave his sons stern looks, telling them to

get back to the work of roasting, or somewhere within the day there would be not enough, and they would be ruined.

The boys smiled, laughed, told some joke, and continued at their labors for that is what it's like to be young to someone who is getting older every day.

You have no worries. Only hopes. Right?

Then I caught the old man smiling with pride, or satisfaction… maybe… but actually I think it was something else. I think… it was gratefulness.

Gratefulness that he had sons. Children. They were his hope.

And that if anything should happen to them…

Then it hit me like a bolt out of the blue.

Commons was downrange and the Rangers couldn't get a rescue mission together at the moment for a lot of solid reasons. *Commons* was someone's hope.

The cold ring in my pocket was there and I felt my fingers hold it by its edges. An unconscious habit I'd picked up along the way.

I could go. I could go look for the lost Ranger. Me. Linguist. Gun team security. Some time on the scouts. The smaj's fixer. Occasionally.

I could go and find Commons in the Valley of Kings and Priests and Death. I could go because… I can become invisible. And no one else can.

We'd tested that, by the way. Other people using the ring. It didn't… work for them. They put it on, and… nothing. It didn't turn them invisible, like it did me. They just stood there awkwardly, looking extremely not invisible, and not a little disappointed, a shiny silver trinket on their finger. Just a cold piece of metal.

Vandahar had thoughts on this, as did Kennedy. Different vocabulary, but they both settled on the idea that when I'd first used the ring, it had *imprinted* on me. Like it was a baby duck that thought I was its mother, I guess. I'd seen videos like that back in the Before of ten thousand years ago. A bunch of ducklings, or was it baby chicks?, following around a human, or a dog, or even a beleaguered cat that seemed not entirely enamored of the situation it didn't know how it had managed to find itself in or why it should be punished so. Cute stuff.

But that wasn't this. That wasn't what was going on here, no matter what our wizards said or how they said it. No. It was, and I knew this in a way that I just… well, I just *knew*… I knew it was because of my psionics. That was the missing ingredient for everyone else. The necessary ingredient. The key. The catalyst. Or maybe the ring was the catalyst and the psionics was the… other part. The catalyzed?

Science isn't my jam.

The point is… the ring works for me.

I can become invisible. And no one else can.

And at the moment… that was important.

Kennedy would say to me, and *was* saying in my mind right at that moment as I held the hot steaming clay cup and seemed to be staring off at some unseen jumbotron of me on the move and alone deep behind enemy lines, that there were monsters, and spells, that could reveal me.

"Then what, Talker?"

I ignored him and sipped my brew, watching me flawlessly locate Commons and call in a rescue team.

Command didn't know that stuff about spells and

monsters, perhaps another lie I was telling me, thanks coffee. Perhaps with a bit of fast talking and reminding the captain the Rangers needed time to come off leave and get ready, and that Commons still needed to be located if any kind of rescue mission was gonna happen… perhaps I could go invisible and locate our missing Ranger ahead of time.

Then, by the time I'd identified his location, they could bring in a force on Black Hawks and Little Birds and rescue him…

"That's a suicide mission, Talker," I could hear Tanner saying in his own cagey way. Like yeah… it was. But that he'd be down for it anyway.

But I'd go alone. Because the ring only works for one wearer.

Me. Mama Duck.

Commons was alone and surrounded. I could go and find him. Then… the pros could come in and get him out.

It was a crazy plan. But it made sense to me and coffee, and that was enough to get excited enough to go and download it at the TOC and see if someone would let me try to get myself killed.

Commons was someone's son. Just like these boys roasting in the back. Someone gave him to the Army. The Rangers said they'd do their best to make sure he got out of there.

Time was burning.

I downed the coffee, didn't order a second, and walked fast for the TOC, working out my plan…

Knowing it was a suicide mission.

Chanting *Rangers can do anything* to convince myself that yeah… I could pull this off.

CHAPTER TWENTY-TWO

I laid the plan out to the captain and the smaj in the TOC and tried to ignore the looks of utter disbelief on their faces…

It was subtle, but it was there.

… as I ran through how I saw the situation, and how super-linguist recent Ranger could solve everyone's problems by being allowed to go deep behind enemy lines by himself with little more than a magic item.

My argument:

Rangers weren't ready to go right now to rescue Commons. Many were hung over, fatigued, and completely unaware of the situation. All of them would have been ready to roll in the eight minutes it would have taken them to get to their gear, get it on, and head for the LZ… but we have to be honest… these guys had been partying for close to two weeks.

Mission:

Commons needed to be rescued and that couldn't happen until he was located.

Execution:

Talker goes in with his magic invisible ring… or as Kennedy would term it, *Ring of Invisibility*… locates missing Ranger, and tracks location until assembled rescue force can be spun up for acquisition and extraction.

Commons in hand, the Rangers can then continue to

ready for coming combat operations, namely smashing the Saur at the Grand Pyramid before the Accadions crossed the line of departure and began the main assault, which the Rangers needed to be part of, undistracted and embedded within what were being called *hatchet forces* to make sure Mummy got croaked and the Saur were taken off the board for the End War in the north.

In other words… the rescue of Commons could jam everything up if it didn't happen fast.

And… could Commons be used as a bargaining chip by Sût?

This needed to happen now, and I was the only one ready, with an asset, that could begin to make events roll in our favor and protect the upcoming mission. I explained all this to the captain and the smaj, and now Chief Rapp and some of the Air Force officers who'd entered the TOC, all of them listening to me blather on and on as I tried to restrain myself from gesticulating wildly and seeming like some crazy conspiracy lunatic meme with a whiteboard of poison pen articles, strings, and mathematical equations.

One thing happened that totally worked in my favor though.

Drone recon by Pretty Blond Ponytail, aka Valkyrie, captured a force of white-robed priests carrying a litter, with a Saurian company-sized force acting as guards, toward a small human settlement located along the southeastern cliffs of the Valley of Kings and Priests.

The medusa had identified this as a place called Red Cliffs Village. A monument-carvers' settlement.

Many of the human populace still in Saur lands acted as

slaves and skilled artisans working on the many Saurian death monuments of pyramid, necropolis, tomb, and obelisk… features in abundance across the plateau, and even down through the crescent-shaped gash in the earth that was the Valley of Kings and Priests that surrounded the plateau.

The Valley of Death.

The mummy lord was tagged in the drone capture too, still strapping Commons's gear as the force made its way toward the village.

I added, "The Delta operator said, during the engagement in the tomb, that he had been summoned by Mummy to lead the battle against us. Perhaps Commons is some key to that?"

That's when they started looking at me suspiciously. I continued on with my brilliant plan and tried to resell it a second time in the unnerving silence that had fallen over the TOC. I pointed out that we could lose the operator and his force if they entered a tomb, many of which contained secret passages that climbed up toward the plateau and the Grand Pyramid.

But…

I am an E-4.

I am barely one of *them*. The hardened killers surrounding me who call themselves Rangers.

Halfway through my second time attempting to sell them, the captain raised one hand to halt my insane nonsense, rubbed his forehead indicating, to me, that he was tired of my immature lunacy regarding Army of One rescue missions, and simply asked, "Sergeant Major?"

The smaj made a face, and he usually doesn't do that as he is carved of granite of some unscalable mountain, and then, after another pause in which he seemed to study me and find me wanting of even having a Ranger tab now, much less a scroll, said…

"Solid plan, sir. A much as I hate to say that. Sir, we need to locate our boy, and the corporal here is the best asset to do that for two reasons. One, there's his magic ring trick. Two, if we lose him… he won't affect coming combat operations against the Saur as he is neither an Eleven Bravo or a small unit leader. We need to bear in mind that a rescue operation may incur losses, and I need every Ranger on the line when combat operations begin if we're gonna pull off the hit on the HVT."

The smaj looked at me, and I could tell that he, in his own way, felt slightly bad about what he was going to say next.

"Corporal Talker is no loss if the rescue goes bad. If he locates Commons, that makes it much easier to get our Ranger out and deprive the enemy of a move against us. I do have one reservation… sir."

"What would that be, Sergeant Major?"

"Rangers don't go alone, sir. He's got to take a security element. At least one other Ranger who's got his back out there when things go pear-shaped, and they're going to because that's the nature of the business. Problem is… that fancy ring o' his only works for one. Nearest thing we got that can pull that same trick in this particular situation, and this is my loose, emphasis on *loose*, sir, understanding of… the nature of things…"

Read: *Embrace the Fantasy.*

"… is Specialist Tanner. The dead kid. I mean… mostly

dead."

The captain made a face for a moment like he didn't know who the smaj was talking about.

"Kid with the messed-up face. Sir."

Knife Hand nodded.

"Given Specialist Tanner's current… dead… condition," the smaj continued, "he may also be invisible, at least to *some* of the denizens of that valley, given many of the tangos there are indicated to be undead."

If the captain's look of perpetual indigestion could have gone to college, gotten a master's degree in the study of itself, then published a best-selling self-help novel on how to Be More Indigestion, perpetually, that would describe the look on the captain's face as the smaj finished his say and sat down to pick up his Kindle, stare at it like he wanted to throw it across the TOC, then set it down and go all murder eyes and drink some coffee as he watched me.

The look on the smaj's granite stone face said, *I just bank-rolled all the credit I got for you, Talker. You don't make this happen, you better be dead.*

I nodded slightly to the smaj.

Message received, Sar'nt Major.

The captain hissed what may have been a curse.

Then the knife hand came out and everyone started getting their orders.

"Spin it up, Sergeant Major, and let's get ready to roll. I want the medusa back here in the TOC for a situation on the ground brief; get a bird headed south and pick her up from Captain Tyrus's command. She may have some insight for us. I want to see Vandahar. Barring negative input that kills the deal from these two, we will insert Talker and Tanner with the intention of locating Commons. Chief Rapp, I want a rescue team assembled and ready to move at a moment's notice as soon as Talker's on the ground. Coordinate with the Air Force for the birds."

The captain looked at me, seemed on the verge of saying something he'd regret, then stalked out of the TOC muttering, "Make it happen, Rangers."

CHAPTER TWENTY-THREE

JUST under twenty-four hours later, with dawn a thin red strip in the east, we boarded the Black Hawk that would take us to the insertion point south along the southern wall of the Valley of Death beyond the Grand Pyramid of Sût the Undying.

Sometime in the middle of the night, when the winds were good up on what was once called the Giza Plateau, they'd been feisty and gusting throughout the early night, the captain had greenlit a combat jump by Sergeant Thor and his spotter, Sergeant Reese, into the area to provide sniper overwatch on our insertion point. They'd shadow us along the opposite wall of the canyon and make sure we didn't have any unwanted attention as we made our way down the cliffs from an identified trail toward the monument-carvers' settlement.

I couldn't sleep and my gear was ready. And… I had coffee to spare. I listened to the TOC reports as the two snipers jumped off the deck of the hovering bird and came down on the plateau without reported injury.

The bird couldn't set down because the Saur were out in force, patrolling, and the plateau was littered with necropolises and obelisks. Command had identified a field the snipers could jump into and then hump toward the overwatch.

Just before midnight, they went in without incident and that was when I knew this was gonna really happen. Like it was real now.

I fingered the ring in my pocket and realized how much I'd just gotten myself into. Then I remembered that Commons had run to operate alone deep behind enemy lines in the river in order to do his job.

So, we could do this for him.

Tanner smiled and loaded onto the Black Hawk with all his gear and weapons. The spinning blades of the helicopter beat the cool dry morning air and pulled at his uniform as the stone-faced and visored door gunners ran system checks on their miniguns and made sure ammo would feed properly. Smoothing and adjusting the links here and there. Tanner smiled that half-undead rake's smile and I asked him if he needed help because he seemed so overburdened. In typical Tanner-ese he just smirked and muttered, "Ain't nothing but a thang, Talk." Then grunted and hauled himself into the bird and sat down, clipping into the deck.

He was carrying the SAW. Drum mags to spare. Forty pounds of C4 with the electronic detonators in a swollen assault pack, his plate carrier, helmet, battle belt, secondary, and a M110 Semi-Automatic Sniper System with a Sig Sauer TANGO6 1-6x scope. He had a short suppressor already on the SDM rifle and it was strapped to his assault ruck.

He was… comically overloaded.

Not as bad as the dwarves. But pretty close.

"Loaded for bear?" I asked as I studied all the mayhem and death he was strapping for our quiet little snoop into the canyon.

"Don't eat much these days so figured I could bring extra. We might need to keep it quiet before I go loud. Keep an eye on you with this," he said, reaching up and patting the M110 strapped to his ruck. "Forge printed it out last night and I zeroed about four this mornin'. Don't sleep much these days."

Then he smiled, and half his skeletal face didn't.

"You worried?" Tanner asked.

I shook my head that I wasn't because I was, and my voice didn't feel like it was gonna not rat me out.

"Might wanna be, Talker. Won't lie, buddy. This gonna be legit in it. Even I know that. But at least we got the wizard with us."

Kennedy trundled toward the bird as the SOAR directed him on board. He was carrying a large ruck. And the dragon-headed staff.

The captain's consult with Vandahar had obtained us Kennedy for the recon to find Commons.

In the wise old wizard's words, Vandahar put it this way.

"Ranger Captain…" he said to Knife Hand, which is what he still calls him. "It is time this young wizard goes forth on his own. Spells of detection and concealment I have taught him greatly, and he has much craft in the wizardly arts. I foresee that deep in that deathly valley he may be… of some use to your mission to obtain the lost Ranger you seek, for it is filled with Saurian sorceries of the darkest and most foul bent. And… the staff of his… well… it can lay waste the enemies there as though the end of the world is nigh, or perhaps one of your Rangers might call for a sky strike from the whirly birds that have come to join in our quest to smite Sût the Undying. I believe the term your young Rangers might use is… get wrecked on the enemy. Is that how I say this?"

It wasn't. But the message was understood.

"I feel he would be most useful to Corporal Talker concerning the demon's mouth this Ranger now seeks to tread… into. Yes… that's right," finished Vandahar, and then satisfied he'd said his piece, produced his long-stemmed pipe and set to blowing smoke rings.

In the TOC.

So Kennedy was going with us, and I was glad for that. He would provide his… services… and provide security for Tanner as Tanner stayed on close overwatch via squad designated marksman weapon, or laying the hate if it went kinetic while I was forward and invisible.

Kennedy knew his game. And the Ruin had seemed, many times, to *be* that strange game of funny dice, pens, and paper. So… I thought he was a good choice. The three of us could be invisible, each in our own ways.

And we had Thor and Reese across the canyon too. Sniper and spotter.

Yet another form of invisibility.

The blades of the SOAR Black Hawk began to reach full pitch. We were cleared by the ground crew, the warrant officer flying the Black Hawk lifted off, and we headed south with a sharp turn.

Down below, in the dark, I could see the Rangers following the smaj in PT gear as they ran the walls. Once around the city and then right into Hardt's dwarven-built Darby Queen.

Leave was over. Hell was back in session. The smaj would have the captain's Rangers ready to roll in short order.

Tanner smiled and raised both thumbs indicating we'd dodged that one.

The desert and the dark consumed the suffering Rangers

as the Black Hawk climbed, and I could almost smell the alcohol pouring out of their systems as they began to be PT'd to death. And then brought back to life.

But that was just my imagination. And… I wondered if they'd be the lucky ones as we flew toward the dawn trailing a Little Bird on overwatch and loaded with miniguns and missiles.

If the insert went bad, the Little Bird would lay the hate and we'd wave off.

Twenty minutes later, the morning dawn sky was filled with locusts all along the south like some developing storm front. Kennedy cast a short spell and got on the comm with the Black Hawk crew. According to the Ranger wizard, the locusts were spell-summoned from the south. They'd try to overtake us and jam the turbines and crash us. Kennedy suggested the chopper wave off as the morning sky suddenly turned to seething, undulating, midnight host, and it was clear armies of locusts were coming for us and that they'd try to take us down.

"We ain't turnin' back," drawled the warrant over the comm. We've seen this in scouts we've been runnin'. Ain't nothin' we can't get around. Besides… we got a Ranger on the ground and in serious need o' friends. Nightstalkers'll get you in. That's what we do. We get you out too. We also do that. Hang on, Rangers. Papa Bear to Gunfighter… bait and switch on my command. Execute. Execute. Execute."

The Little Bird flying overwatch popped flares and broke off to the west, blurring tracer ammo into the looming swarm just ahead.

The Black Hawk at the same time went east, dove for

the badlands near the River of Night, and went to the deck over the river, speeding down its sparklingly blue length as the sun began to come up in full to the east. We flew south undetected, and the swarm chased the AH-6. Eventually we started our climb for the cliffs and the canyon.

Two hours later, the crew hovered over a high ledge near the trail that led down to the valley floor far below, and we fast-roped in.

Gloves smoking.

Then the bird pivoted, the warrant officer saluted once, and we darted and halted in the shadows of the rocks until the Black Hawk was gone, waiting up there along the canyon wall and listening to the wind and the silence as the sounds of the helicopter grew distant and faded and then, eventually, were no more.

CHAPTER TWENTY-FOUR

WE made contact with the snipers in the silence after conducting our SLLS. I was the patrol leader. And immediately, of course… things began to go pear-shaped.

This was not my perfect mission I'd envisioned under the influence of street coffee, I protested to myself as Sergeant Thor gave me the increasingly bad news after literally little more than two minutes on the ground.

Command, to their credit, listened to the sitreps and let us work the problem without either ordering the Black Hawk back in to pull us out, or the AH-6 to come in and cleanse the area by fire.

"Mongoose, this is Python…" said Sergeant Thor over the comm, his voice brief and businesslike.

Snipers were Pythons on this. The scout team was Mongoose.

"Predator in the area," he continued. "Lay low, he seems to be interested. Predator is at five hundred feet directly overhead."

What the hell.

From my position in the shadows between two large rocks, I looked skyward into the midmorning sun and spotted the dracosphinx up there in the sky.

It was circling just above us and getting lower and lower as it did so. Within a minute it settled on the high red rocks well above us and perched there, scanning the rocks and crevices below… for something.

For us.

We waited and held our breath like that would make a difference.

Thor would make the decision here. We were to remain quiet and follow his route observations until we reached the canyon floor below.

Then… I would take charge of the stalk.

I felt the ring in my pocket. It was good I hadn't forgotten it.

I had my M4. My sidearm. An assault pack that should have had less coffee in it than it did. And extra mags. For all of us. Like a good patrol leader.

I also had *Coldfire* strapped to my assault ruck. The dwarves had made me a sheath.

The Valley of Kings and Priests here narrowed from a small valley to little more than a wide fracture in the land.

"Stand by…" said Thor a minute later, and I exchanged looks with Tanner as we held position and continued to hold our breath. Kennedy was staring skyward and gripping his twisting and gnarled mahogany dragon-headed staff we'd taken off the dead sorcerer at the beginning of all this back on Ranger Alamo Island.

I'd seen him roast fire giants and orc hordes with it. It was clearly some kind of staff of power and fire, and I was sure Vandahar had helped him master it and unlock its secrets.

But… as patrol leader… I had to ask myself if Ranger Wizard Specialist Kennedy could take out a ferocious sphinx that had a penchant for ambush and combat if the lore

Kennedy had told me was correct.

The giant sphinx-thing pecked at rocks, clicked to itself, and seemed to be murmuring some Muppet-like language to itself. That fascinated me. Language, me likey. Hey... who knows dracosphinx and has two thumbs?

This guy. Me pointing both thumbs at me.

The flying monster seemed to find a snake, and it quickly snatched the viper up and gulped it down in one crunchy bite that echoed off the walls as it studied the rocks and silence of the mysterious Saurian canyon near us.

"It knows..." mouthed Tanner wordlessly and then silently adjusted the SAW, stabilizing it on a rock and giving him an angle to engage the beast with.

Rangers gonna Ranger.

I shook my head and made the hand signal to wait.

"Engaging..." said Thor tersely, and half a second later the M107A1 anti-materiel rifle he called *Mjölnir*, suppressed with a QDL suppressor, fired.

I had no idea where the snipers were firing from. All I knew was they were hidden on the other side of the canyon.

Yes. I am a pro patrol leader. Not.

The Barrett, firing unsuppressed, is normally a loud *boom* and a barking *ROAR*. Unsuppressed that is, and no, suppressors are not silencers like in the movies, but at this distance, and with the mirage cover over the silencer... it was an almost mere indefinable click as the legendary Ranger sniper engaged the impossible flying sphinx on the other side of the canyon. Our side.

I'm not good at distances but... it was a tough shot.

That was taking a chance for most snipers. The range was

extreme. The QDL suppressor would degrade performance over that range. To be sure.

Thor made the shot.

And there was wind.

A slight morning breeze.

But the math was fatal and the giant bird, which is really what an dracosphinx is, took the round, must have taken it in the head, Tanner thought he saw bone matter and brain spray… and was Yahtzeed just like that.

We didn't hear them say that. But… you know they did.

The beast's head rocked from the round moving at twenty-four hundred feet per second… perhaps Sergeant Thor had even used a Raufoss round in effect… then the great multicolored and feathered lion body of the thing started to slide down the canyon wall, tumbling, its great raptor's wings flailing and breaking, bouncing and striking ledges and outcrops as it passed the ledge near us and went off down farther into the rocks below.

We waited.

"Hold…" said Thor a moment later. Then… "More."

A Saurian patrol, six lizard men, were on the trail far below us. They'd been sunning themselves on the rocks, blending in with the colors like chameleons, as the sun rose in order to warm up their cold blood.

Now they reacted to the great sphinx that had just been domed and tumbled into the rocks not too far off.

Clearly they had no idea what had happened.

Then they began to die as *Mjölnir* silently began to shoot them down from range. It wasn't until the last two were left that they figured out they weren't just dying by magic, but that some unseen force was patiently murdering them. Then they tried to hide.

The sniper team adjusted Thor's fire to get these last two, like a couple of professionals working a math problem, and the Saurians died peeking out from the rocks they were covering behind.

Then… "Mongoose… clear to proceed. Python out."

An hour later we reached their position and passed silently by the dead lizard men flung about on the gray and dusty rocks, their huge dark eyes lifeless. Their black blood sprayed and drooling into drying puddles.

It was as quiet as a cemetery, and the snipers had done their work without a trace, or alert, or even a hint that they'd been there.

Because they hadn't.

We passed on and continued down the old shepherds' stairs that had been long ago carved into the rock of the cliff wall.

Clear to Proceed.

CHAPTER TWENTY-FIVE

WE made our way down into the valley as the day turned toward noon and the sun began to reach directly overhead.

The days were shorter, we were in fall now, but for some reason the heat clung to the world like a wet blanket that would not dry even in the noonday blast of the sun.

"At least it ain't humid," muttered Tanner and spit dip off the edge. He shrugged his back with an effort long gone unconscious in the Rangers, patted the SAW with his assault gloves, and continued on ahead.

The trail that wound down the cliff wasn't vertical, but it was near enough, and on top of that it looked like it had been carved by nearsighted cavemen ten thousand years before even we'd leapt through the QST time to arrive in the Ruin. It was as dangerous as it was precarious. But... "You gotta be half mountain goat to Ranger," as Joe would say. Otherwise... "you gonna be an Olympic diver. Dangerous bein' a Ranger... who'da thought."

We were headed down into the Valley of Tombs, the Valley of Death far below, and the progress was painstaking as the wonky little trail crossed back and forth down the face of the cliffs.

Yeah, it had a lot of names, the Valley of Kings and Priests, Priests and Kings, but as we got closer and closer to the floor it was anything but some fracture in the earth. It was a place of death and unholy rites, and I didn't need to be a Cleric of the Hidden King like Chief Rapp to figure that out.

And… you could feel it, the closer we got to all that long-buried death that wasn't… *dead.*

Sleeping was more like it.

The whole valley, or canyon, floor was like an Egyptian cemetery down there. Strange monuments of ancient Saurian worthies carved into the rough cliff walls marking the entrances to fading grand tombs. Towering obelisks marking some important long-forgotten moments, or according to Kennedy, maybe used to maintain permanent spells of warding or binding of some dark and demonic forces in service to the Saurian thaumaturges, and thus it was best to avoid those areas once we came upon them.

The safety brief was ongoing as we caught glimpses of what we'd be getting into. All the while minding our steps, our boots growing hot with the work and the load and doing our best not to fall down into what we must enter.

There were strange temples down there, empty and devoid of life, gray sandstone that seemed barren of love or passion, steps, stairs, platforms, columns, and invariably a wide pavilion adorned with markings of the black sun that could be seen from our elevation. All with no sign of life, neither human nor Saurian.

Places of sacrifice. But who was sacrificed was the question I didn't like the answers to.

Hazzim had said the Saur conducted most of their unholy rites at night and with moonlight to watch the flickering torches and hear the gagged cries for help.

The Saur were buyers of slaves, and raiders of nearby

races. Anything not them was for their use no matter how dark the subject.

It was day, and as we moved slowly down the side of the cliff, winding back and forth, our bad steps sent skittering rocks and small too-loud slides down onto the rocks below. At night we would need to move much more cautiously if we hoped to avoid the patrols of the Saurian legion and the temple guardians.

Red Cliffs Village was little more than a multi-leveled cliff-walled dweller village, and as I observed the settlement along our slow trek down the side of the cliffs of the great fracture, I scouted my route in. The route I'd take once I'd slipped on the ring and headed in to look for the procession of white-robed mysterious priests who'd accompanied the Delta mummy strapping Commons's weapon.

And who carried our wounded Ranger.

From high up here I could see no trace of them. But I could see humans though, like us, in ragged clothing, working at carving stones or moving between the buildings to conduct their business. They were small in stature. Bandy-legged, brown-skinned, and dark-haired.

But they were human, and part of me wondered if they could be... *allies*.

Chief Rapp had warned me to be on the lookout for those who could help us and be turned to the cause of liberating the oppressed from tyrants.

De Oppresso Liber.

The motto of the Green Berets.

But there'd been more to that last-minute no-time-to-spare conversation with the special warfare chief who'd accompanied the Ranger detachment into the Ruin.

In fact, I'd had two conversations that played again and again in my mind the closer we got and the more and more the sound of the hammers and chisels, working desultorily against monuments and markers they'd been forced to carve, grew louder and clearer as we made our approach to the monument-carvers' village along the southern rim of the Valley of Kings and Priests.

One conversation was with Chief Rapp. And that was more of him downloading his concerns on me.

The other was the medusa brief after she'd been flown back to the TOC from her position at the front helping Captain Tyrus get the Accadions ready to march on the Grand Pyramid and give battle against the forces of Sût the Undying.

Chief Rapp would be running the extraction force. He and I interfaced, and we agreed, him really telling me, on comms and signals and what he expected of us once we located Commons down there and how exactly we'd extract.

"I need you to maintain visual contact on Commons once we're on the ground, Talker. If it's a situation where we need to breach a location to get ahold of him, then I need solid intel on all exits and entrances into the location he's being held in. Windows and everything. As we move to the staging position, I need you to interface with me on the ground, *hip me* to the location and the bad guys, then take my blockers and position them at the approaches where the enemy might bring in a QRF if they try to shut us down. After that, you and your team will move to the birds independent of my force and secure the LZ for extraction. The birds do not depart unless I visually confirm you and yours are on board and all accounted for. Agree, Talker? We ain't leavin' anyone behind."

I agreed.

"Then that's all good, my man. Now, I got one other thing to lay on you and this ain't part of the mission because if it comes down to it, Corporal… we gonna smoke his butt. But the Delta operator…"

He paused and looked off like he was gathering his thoughts for a moment. The giant black Green Beret wiped away sweat. We'd been working hard to get the first Rangers ready to roll working together as assaulters, support, blockaders, demo, and everyone else down on the roll with just a few hours from dusk till midnight to get a loose structure for the extraction team to work with once they came in.

Chief Rapp suddenly asked for a drink of my coffee and then drank the whole thing down.

The whole thing.

That hurt.

He exhaled a gusty, "Awwwww yeahhhh. Tha's good stuff. Now listen. The mummy—not the HVT, the Delta operator—like I said, we gotta smoke him… so we gonna make that happen. Straight up. But one thing to consider, Talker… and maybe this is just between me and you 'cause these Ranger boys, they killers and we gots to be honest about that, they smell big game now because they pure predator… but…"

I interrupted him. "Ranger boys."

The chief stopped and looked at me dead frank. No Chief Rapp smile.

"Yeah, Talker. Told ya I was part of the Unit. Special missions unit. Intelligence support activity. Stuff that doesn't really exist on paper. Truth is there're lotsa parts to Delta, and not everyone knows each other. And here's somethin' else I want you to know about Delta maybe ain't been conveyed to you by these Rangers, or even my OG unit… which is SF… which is what I am. I had some time runnin' in Delta doin' a particular thing at a certain time. But here's somethin' you don't know about 'em… they good. They not just good… they like… the Knights Templar, Talker. Rangers is killers. You need somethin' or someone dead… we all agree, Rangers is who you call when someone gonna die.

"Green Berets… there's a lotta gray there. Some shady stuff. Some shady deals. Some shady dudes I still call brothers. That's the nature of the work. And it's necessary to get the bad guys. Or at least that's what I had ta remind myself of sometimes along the way.

"But Delta… that's different. They the real true warrior devoted to the cause. There's no lies there and ain't nothin' gray. Listen, Talker… there's gotta be a spark that remains of who and what he really was… is. Because if he'd really wanted us dead, we woulda been right there. Maybe he was just toying with us to make it look good to Sût and the priests that probably spy on him for ol' Sût. Maybe I got it wrong. Maybe I don't. But I run with Delta. Once. And I can tell you what I just told you. If you get a chance to turn him, and I know I'm askin' you to maybe bet your life on this… and tha's your call, Talker, if you don't. But he still good. He might just be… a slave right now. And maybe… jes maybe… he need a shot at redemption. Someone to break them chains they got him all spelled up in. If my prayers can do it… I'm gonna give it a shot. But even still… I'll have my rifle center mass on his butt, and I will double-tap him if I can't get him to flip. Hell... who'm I kiddin'... I best use the whole mag on him, Talker. But... it's just somethin' to weigh as we go in, and I don't like it, and it certainly don't help matters. But he Delta, and them cats has saved more lives and put it on the line in some hairy places no one ever knows about. He deserves at least an offer to come back. Tha's all."

Okay. So there's that.

And then there was the medusa and her entrance into the TOC...

And what she had to say about the situation on the ground.

CHAPTER TWENTY-SIX

THE medusa entered the TOC ten minutes after the chopper that brought her in was down on the LZ. She was dressed in her shining Spartan armor, fabled gleaming sword hanging from a belt of woven gold coins rumored to be charms and wards of great power. Even here she was carrying her giant round circular shield, embossed with a screaming... medusa. She took off her helmet and suddenly the asps in her raven-dark hair began to undulate and quietly seethe at everyone in the TOC.

We'd gotten used to it, but still it was fascinating to watch. Because she was a genetically aberrant medusa in that her looks didn't turn you to stone. But she *could* emit a high, piercing note and unleash a powerful and devastating sonic wave that could cause a mass petrification out to several hundred yards. She'd done that against her own troops. And because of that... we were safe.

As long as she didn't use her scream against us.

She got down to business, like time was of the essence, and it was, and gave us the brief on what we could expect in the valley. She was in a hurry to get back to her troops and preparations with the Accadion war leader. We were in a hurry to pull off the rescue of Commons.

Apparently there were factions down there in the Valley of Death. Even among the Saur.

She'd learned to speak English pretty quick. And it wasn't rough. She was adept, though her voice was heavily accented Mediterranean. The words she didn't know and what she had trouble with, I cleared up for the command team.

She barely acknowledged me. Not because she was haughty; people mistook this in her. But because she was all business. Total warrior. And the Rangers could identify with her on this.

The people she led had their lives in her hands. She didn't waste time, as it would waste them. She understood the responsibility of leadership.

And it was hard to believe she was anything else but this alone. Never mind the rumors that she and the captain of the Accadions were pretty torrid.

What she downloaded in the TOC basically went like this.

"The Saur are not as united as they might like the world to think, Rangers. I was sent by my terrible sister, the once-queen of the medusae, whom you slew at the citadel—and for this great service I cannot thank you enough—as a hostage and a bargaining chip for her with the dark lord that is Sût himself. I was sent, and I was charmed into service against all who opposed his cruel will."

She spit on the floor of the TOC to show her contempt for the Lich Pharaoh.

Which was funny… because she's beautiful like a very cute actress who would have been the star of some TV show about a young girl making it big in the city or at some profession, doctor or lawyer, but she's super angry and… more than a little fierce. That, to us, the Rangers, comes off as cute.

But then again, explosives are our playthings and we tell jokes that make people nervous.

We don't laugh at her though.

The asps in her hair, and what she can do, go a long way to reminding you just how dangerous she is.

But she's beautiful cute, *hawt* as some of the younger Rangers say… and to see her spit… in anger… I'll be honest, I had to suppress a small giggle.

Tanner can't keep a straight face around her.

"She purty, Talker. And I know I got no chance with her, lookin' like this, but… I get a shot? I'm gonna shoot it. Even if she does have that jacked war machine from Accadios wrapped around her alabaster finger. I'd fight Captain Tyrus for her. Prolly win 'cause I'm agile. And wily."

That was one way to read it.

It looked like Captain Tyrus had *her* wrapped around *his* battle-scarred hands if you asked me.

She clearly dug that kinda dude and she was totally into him.

He was pretty much warfare itself in a way Rangers aspired to be. We have to be honest about that. And the Rangers were, about the legionnaire. And some, myself included, wondered at seeing how much Ranger knowledge and tactics the Accadion war captain took to, very fast sometimes, such that it was almost like he already knew it all, had forgotten it, and then just remembered.

He was a Ranger without being one. No one disputed that. It was just weird that he was so like the best Rangers in the detachment. Even the grim hard-as-nails demeanor and quiet competent professionalism.

Even Kang and Hardt, the guys with the most contempt for anyone not meeting standard… seemed to quietly be in awe of the guy.

It was… weird. That's the only way I can put it here. So of course she dug him. She likes warriors. And he was the epitome of one, even among the epitomes of warriors that are the Rangers.

There in the TOC she told us what was what in the Valley of Death we were soon headed into. I was all ears as this was my probably terrible plan.

"The Saur are a venal group of thugs who are always scheming and conniving to have power over one another. Ignore their trappings of wealth, power, and immortality. It is all stolen or fake. Undeath… is not eternal. It's corruption prolonged. That and nothing more. If they could slay Sût and take what he has for themselves, then they would do so in the time it takes to draw the blade. There are the Priests of the Dark Sun who believe that the being they worship is the true power and not Sût himself. And there are the sorcerers and the Saur who have fallen under the sway of the Nether Sorcerer who has offered them great powers if they would give that strange being the treasures of the Land of Black Sleep. Make no mistake, they would dethrone the powerful pharaoh could they but do it, and quickly hand power to the Nether Sorcerer so they could realize their dreams of bringing the world under their claws and heel for their own dark pleasures. Both sides, and this is the true nature of the Saur… believe that whatever power they make their dark pacts with, the being of the Dark Sun, or the Nether Sorcerer, they believe they can betray each entity and rule, establishing a new line of Saurian pharaohs that are either them, or under their direct control. Removing the heavy yoke of Sût from off their shoulders."

She paused and looked around.

"But Sût is not stupid. And he is still very powerful. So powerful that their own powers come from him, and they could never beat him even if they united together all their sorceries and demonic pacts in order to defeat him. He is destruction itself. They know this. But because they are Saur, because they have dark desires and immortal dreams… they seek to betray him even in the hours of their most loyal service."

She pointed at the projected map where we had marked up the insertion point and the possible location of Commons.

"This area of the valley is controlled by the Priests of Amoc. Amoc was an ancient pharaoh, early in the line of pharaohs, who discovered the being of the Dark Sun through dark ceremonies with other… forces beyond time and space. They worship the Destroyer, as they call him, and they have been given the power of immortality… or… the mummification rites. Undeath. They have long curated the line of Amoc and see themselves as the restorers of the true pharaonic line. The only reason Sût has not destroyed them is their control of some of the most powerful clans of Katari assassins who guard the temples of some of Sut's most powerful heroes."

The warrior medusa looked around at us, her voice and eastern rhythms enchanting and intoxicating. I had to admit… she told a good story.

"The heroes… like Su-haptep, the one you fought in the temple by the river… are all sleeping. Cards to be played in Sût's game against you that we make ready to begin. Su-haptep was once a great king in the north. A brother to a band of mighty warriors who came from the skies and did battle against the fabled frost giants of the Dire North. In time, they leagued with the Dragon Elves and established that empire and saw its rise… then journeyed into the east to reach the Cities of Gold that once were found in the wastelands before the great star struck the Ruin. It was there, at the front of a great host, on the verge of victory, that Su-haptep—his slave name—was captured and became a warrior in service to Sût, seduced by the power and darkness the Lich Pharaoh wields in stunning and decadent abundance. Whoever he once was… his real name was lost to time. As the Spear of Sût, as Su-haptep was later known, he beat back the mighty forces of the Cities of Gold and smashed their alliances through craft and expert guile. He was a brilliant general, and he led a vicious campaign in the deep south of the unknown lands against the Chetani cat people and sacked their forbidden ivory palaces, bringing many slaves and much gold to the vaults of Sût in tribute. In the south he is known as… the Devil Who Cannot Be Seen."

She turned once more to the map, and her voice lowered.

"He was once a man… like you. And I think… he must have been one of you, come much earlier than you to the world as it is now. Before the Fall. The Ruin. As general of the forces of Sût, when I was such, I had access to the secret papyri in the Temple of Ar-Pythas that spoke of such things… and even some of the fragments of the *Book of Skelos* itself. I know of these things. But… once, he was a man. And men are mortal. In time, the Spear of Sût fell in battle… and his dead body was returned to the Land of Black Sleep and made immortal by the high priests of Amoc for Sût.

"Throughout the years he has been summoned to fight time and time again for the Lich Pharaoh. Time and time again there has been much slaughter, darkness, and chaos in his coming to the battle front. And every time the forces of Sût the Undying have been victorious. Even in the face of odds that cannot be measured. But as the years have passed, the cost of summoning Su-haptep has grown great, for even Sût must carve off more and more of his dark energies to keep his best general undead and leading his forces in the wars the Lich Pharaoh has set himself to. It has been many, many centuries since we have seen the summoning of the Spear of Sût. Not in my lifetime. That the pharaoh has called him forth from his tomb once again, one last time, means that even Sût himself is worried, and has summoned his best."

She paused and looked around, conveying utter seriousness.

"This is not the good news you might want it to be, Rangers. The Spear of Sût is a formidable general who has never been defeated in the immortal state in which the Lich Pharaoh has held him. Before that, he was a hero of great renown who did mighty deeds that have been lost to time just as his true name has been. Myths and legends abound of his doings. But because we must face him, together, in battle, I urge that you consider him a priority enemy we must remove from the board… at any cost. Otherwise we must consider his many triumphs and lament that we may be… his last."

She lowered her head and bowed, indicating she was finished with her say as was her manner.

In the silence, the captain cleared his throat.

Then he spoke.

"He is… or once was… one of us. And his name is Tom Sloan. Master Sergeant. And yes… he's very dangerous."

CHAPTER TWENTY-SEVEN

WE had eyes on Red Cliffs Village. Thor had some view of it too, mostly the external walls. Tanner had a view inside the common areas where the carving was done and the living under the whip of the Saur was endured.

As of late afternoon there were no Saur in the area from our observations and that of the sniper team. But to me and Tanner there was a feeling that something had gone down just before we arrived. Kennedy was more quiet than usual, and that was saying something for him because unless you got him talking about his game of dice and imagination… he was generally pretty reserved. It's a wizard thing I guess. We need to get him a pipe, so he looks thoughtful.

We had established an LP/OP, listening and observation post, higher up on a little-used trail that led down into the cliff village, and Tanner and Kennedy could see down into that and would be able to cover me as long as I stayed out in the open. We'd also identified some areas where coverage was not good, like I was talking to my cell phone provider, if my cell phone provider provided outgoing fire in either excessive doses from the SAW, or something surgical with the SDM rifle.

Tanner was a good shot.

Kennedy still needed a lot of work and had been getting a pass due to his magical studies with Vandahar.

Still… the smaj wasn't happy about that.

"Everyone's a shooter. Even the damn cook," was the smaj's regimental policy regarding all Rangers.

Then Vandahar would intervene with instructing Kennedy in creating floating discs that could transport gear over any terrain, or a powerful Ray of Disintegration spell he'd recently learned and had yet to master.

Though all agreed that the Disintegration spell, the one time we'd seen it used against a giant desert troll who'd hit one of the towers in the defense of Sûstagul during a raid in the days after the second battle… was legit Carl G. Or as some of the Rangers who'd formed a cult based on Brumm's iconic "Carl G don't care" termed it… "Carl would approve."

Kennedy disintegrated the bottom half of the raging desert troll swinging a ball and chain the size of a car and charging the tower.

I say again… the bottom half.

For the next ten minutes the legless roaring hideous thing flopped around and died in the sand, swinging its massive chained weapon at its own orcs and destroying the entire raiding force.

Those that survived, fled.

Legit Carl G.

I was waiting for someone to start saying, "Ranger Wizard don't care!" But… so far no one had.

I felt that was a missed opportunity and only a matter of time before Kennedy earned it with the even more destructive spells he was learning from Vandahar.

"Well," I said over the comm as I approached the walled village and an open gateless arch where a blind old man with wild gray hair sat begging, "here goes nothin'." Then I slipped on the ring and turned invisible.

"You gone now, Talk," whispered Tanner, confirming that I was now visually undetectable.

I'd shucked much of my gear up on the ledge LP/OP. Gone over everything I was carrying into the village, tightened and tapped and secured what I could, and tried to stay as quiet as possible while jumping and climbing a little up there.

I was getting pretty good at that. Moving silently. And I felt I was doing much better than in the tomb with the captain and Chief Rapp just a little over a day ago.

I was thinking about my steps and starting to slide a little quieter as I moved.

I took only my sidearm and *Coldfire* in. I wanted to have my hands free so that I could use them to keep myself quiet. The ground was uneven everywhere and I wanted to be able to catch myself. The last thing I needed to do was trigger an alert because the locals got freaked out by an invisible man they'd heard take a bad step and start stumbling down one of the lanes inside the cliff village before smacking into a wall, gear and all.

Slowly, I made my way past the blind man and for a moment was concerned that I had been a little too loud as he turned his head and tracked me as I walked past. But when I looked back he was staring sightlessly off into space, and I went with *perhaps it was just timing that had caused him to move just as I passed.*

In any case, he didn't seem concerned.

So I went in further and tried to figure out what I could

figure out regarding the white-robed priests and the mummy operator who was once called Tom Sloan.

About that…

After the brief, the smaj volunteered Master Sergeant Tom Sloan's operator tag, as guys in the special missions unit often run with call signs.

Cool guy stuff.

Nightmare.

That was his tag.

Apparently there was a story behind that involving the fact that he had nightmares and talked in his sleep and it almost got him tossed from one of the schools he went through. Probably OTC.

Something to razz him about that just stuck because that's how guys are in the Army. You ain't gonna get a cool guy tag on purpose. And… you ain't gonna think one up for yourself.

Fortunately for Master Sergeant Tom Sloan… *Nightmare* became prophetically true. The story goes, according to the smaj, Master Sergeant Sloan and his team tormented a national force under some tyrant somewhere in some horrible place in the world Delta wasn't supposed to be in, during a very unsupported mission back in the day… meaning it wasn't supposed to happen… and the torment got so bad that the local petty tyrant ended up telling a reporter that the suspected insurgent force was giving him nightmares, " haunting my dreams" as he "tried to bring peace and prosperity to my country" from behind the walls of his twenty-six-thousand-square-foot mansion complete with a "Lambo garage."

The nightmares got so bad the guy ended up killing himself with a gold-plated forty-five.

Or so the official story goes.

Nightmare.

As Tanner said in that half-dead whisper to me after the smaj had finished telling his story over the blue percolator, which, let's be honest, had my attention shall we say, Tanner whispered in his dead serious dry voice with his half zombie grin…

"*Nightmare.* Fun, huh, Talker?"

That was a clue for me, later, about what was gonna happen between Tanner and this guy.

But that was later, when everything went pear-shaped and there were no tricks left.

CHAPTER TWENTY-EIGHT

CREEPING the village collecting intel. With my Ring of Invisibility!

So… it wasn't as cool as you might think it sounds… or as dangerous, though it did get hairy there for a hot second… just as I made it out, too.

In a small alley, Tanner put a round through a Katari assassin that had been stalking me by smell.

"Talker," said Tanner in my comm, which was dialed down way low. "Hold. Guy's been following. One o' them cat-people ninjas."

Thankfully, Tanner's dead guy vision, or whatever it is, sees a shadowy image of me and that allowed him to track me through the ville. It wasn't great but at least he had a vague idea where I was.

I didn't even know, at that moment in the collection, they were even in the village. This one had been left behind by a small force to see if they were being followed, which we'd find out later is a standard Katari operating trick.

No one else was in the alley and the cat was creeping up with his sharpened little khopesh blade. A crescent dagger really.

Then Tanner drilled him once in the chest. The shot was suppressed and the cat fell on his back. Tanner put two more in him and the cat was dead.

"Get rid of the body, Talker," said Tanner in my ear.

"Where? How?" I asked, still incredulous that invisible me had been stalked. And those rounds had gone pretty close to my head because that's how imminent the backstab I was about to receive had been.

"Back of the alley there's a low wall. Throw him over."

So I did. The cat left a blood trail. I kicked stone dust over that as quietly as an invisible man can, and thankfully there was a lot of that, dust that is, because it was a monument-carver village after all.

Long story short, the *ville* was boring. Besides almost getting assassinated.

Mostly it was just listening and trying to put all the pieces together of what exactly had happened here.

And where… was Commons.

Intel collection, which is what I was doing, isn't what everyone thinks it is… or what *I* thought it was. James Bond stuff. It's a lot of, for scouts, sitting in a hide, keeping the bugs off you, and watching a bunch of dudes out in the jungle doing super boring daily stuff in hopes that you will learn their routines, guard changes, sleep cycles, training, et cetera, so that when it comes time to whack 'em, you can do it with optimum speed and violence and minimum loss.

Surprise, losers!

And if that sounds worth it because laying the hate on some bad guy from surprise with either a sniper rifle or traversing *and* plunging fire from a light machine gun is your jam…

Note… ever since *Nightmare*, the mummy operator Delta guy… I know, that's a mouthful, but this Big Bad we were facing had a lot of hats…

But ever since Nightmare had used "Chaos is my jam!" when trying to back us off, when according to Chief Rapp he probs could have smoked us in there in his burial temple… I've now begun to use "my jam" a lot.

I bet you can guess what my jam is.

Correct. It's coffee.

And so the phrase has been popping up in my conversation and this account more and more. I've gone back and assassinated it a few times. But my apologies for suddenly getting all "my jam" about everything. Lame. In my defense… I know, I know, I'm even worse about that phrase and a few assassinations are in order there as well… but *in my defense* part of being a linguist is being a sponge, soaking up everything about a language, its nuances and even the foods the people who speak it eat. So I have a tendency to soak up things and make them my own. Especially if they're cool. Like… *My jam is…* and then insert whatever you dig.

All right, got that out of the way and wasted some valuable ink, and your time. I can hear you guys complaining…

So… sitting in a hide, keeping the bugs off you, and watching a bunch of dudes out in the jungle doing super boring stuff.

Intel collection.

Not James Bond stuff.

In the walled cliff village all I did was wander around and listen to the villagers who spoke mostly Arabic, easy and getting easier for me by the day as that's pretty much the root language down here in the Land of Black Sleep, mixed with Gray Speech and a few other Mediterranean languages, throw in some Chinese, which again, no probs for me, and I followed what was going on.

I'm getting a lot of practice with this patois of languages and I'd even say I'm downright fluent in a few that weren't even part of "them all" back in the days when I first dreamed of learning them all. Talker, get yourself a prize outta the prize drawer.

We all know what the prize is.

But yeah, it was all pretty boring.

It took the rest of the day and the early evening to piece together what exactly had happened before we'd shown up.

The priests and their procession had arrived in the village the night before. The white-robed ones, and the mummy, Nightmare. And they were still carrying Commons.

The villagers talked about this among one another as a prelude to what happened next because many of them had gone and hidden in the "Cool Caves" they'd carved out in secret at the back of the *ville*.

They felt they were safe from the Saur there.

So when the white-robed priests grabbed one of their own, once the procession was inside the *ville*, and started drawing circles in chalk and conducting rites, the villagers knew bad things were afoot and began to hide themselves.

The white-robed priests sacrificed a young village woman, a girl really, her name was Moasi, and cast spells.

"What kind of spells?" Kennedy asked me.

But Tanner only muttered, "Bastards must pay."

I described what I'd heard in a small square hidden against one of the main walls the village had used as a kind of festival and religious pavilion. The white-robed priests had performed their dark rites and sacrificed the girl there.

She was fifteen.

Like I said, I described what I'd seen to Kennedy, and he surmised that it was most likely some kind of protection spells and his guess was that somehow, whatever they'd cast, it had obscured the priests' movements to the drones we had overhead and that was why the Air Force didn't catch where the priests and Nightmare went next.

"Operator Puke probably guessed we'd be running drones now that he knew Rangers were involved after your little tussle in his bedchamber," said Tanner bitterly.

I concurred.

Then the priests and the mummy boogied and the villagers thought they were definitely headed for the Serpent Stairs farther to the west up the Valley of Kings and Priests.

The Valley of Death.

But that's not where it ended. I continued listening to the villagers, wandering slowly through their streets and listening as they downloaded their horrific ordeal to one another as the day ended.

This had all happened in the dark of the previous night and some of it in the morning. They'd gone back to work despite the horrors they'd lived through because the Saur didn't accept excuses for work not being done and the villagers lived in total utter fear of the lizard men overlords.

And of Sût himself, whom they made signs to ward off curses every time the Lich Pharaoh came up in their accounts.

Then, before we got there to the village, while we were still inbound down the River of Night… the Katari showed up.

Deep Blood Clan.

Apparently.

Servants of the Priests of Amoc. Uneasy allies of the Lich Pharaoh and possessors of grand dreams of a new pharaonic line according to the medusa.

A Deep Blood Clan kill pact consisting of six Katari assassins had been dispatched to assassinate Nightmare before he could reach the top of the Serpent Stairs, or the Stairs of the Great Serpent as one of the village's elders called it. A carved set of massive twisting and turning stairs that led up to the back entrance to the Grand Pyramid from the floor of the valley.

The Katari had questioned the villagers, and in the questioning had revealed much of the nature of their mission. For the Katari may be deadly killers, but they are also quite chatty and have a tendency to constantly chant on and on about what they're about as though it's some kind of prayer. So said Vandahar. Disapprovingly.

These Katari were tasked with taking out the mummy champion of the Lich Pharaoh so that Sût would fail and perhaps be destroyed by the Accadion legions assembling against him in the north.

Then the time of the Priests of Amoc would arrive…

Like I said: factions.

The Katari kill pact had decided to take a shortcut through a nearby tomb and come out halfway up the stairs via the back entrance at a place the maps marked as the Spring of Sullus. It was a well halfway up the winding stairs that led to the Giza Plateau and through the Temple of Un, a fortress necropolis under the control of Saurian praetorians known as the Viper Guard.

A nasty bunch if previously collected intel was accurate. The Accadions called them "witch warriors."

So, if Nightmare reached the Temple of Un then he would be beyond their reach and able to lead the Saurian defense to victory, according to the chanting Katari kill pact.

The Katari agreed among themselves, murmuring and chanting over and over right there in the village, that this must not be allowed to happen as there would be no stopping the "Spear of Sût" once it did.

And then there was Commons.

He was never referred to by name in the accounts I heard. Of course not. No Commons. No Gill. No Aqua Ranger.

But he was referred to, in a way that was worse than all of those names, and I knew it was him that was spoken of.

In the accounts I overheard he was mentioned only as "the sacrifice."

"Not on my watch," muttered Tanner when I downloaded this portion of the collection back at the LP/OP.

It was heading toward midnight by the time I got back to the outpost, passing out of the walled village, sneaking once more by the old blind man in the night. Still sitting there with his copper begging bowl. Still staring sightlessly into the dark night.

And then, just as I crept past him, he suddenly spoke.

"Bless you, friend."

His voice was thin and ragged.

I froze and said nothing.

"You will do right now, will you not, listener?" the blind man asked the air around me with a smile. He was speaking in Arabic.

I said nothing.

"You have been sent to help us. Even a blind man can hear you moving about the village, listening to the great wrongs that have been done us this day. I have listened long enough… that yes… I expect good from this one, the King tells me so. That is what I have said to myself. That is what the Hidden King speaks to me. Blessings, silent one. Prayers for what comes next will be made. All will be well… even though you may think that you have lost something valuable, my listening friend. Have faith, all is not lost. And… one day…"

He smiled and cleared his throat.

"Even for a blind old man like myself… one day, listener… all things sad will come… untrue."

I pulled two gold coins from my pocket and listened as they fell into his copper bowl.

A fortune for him.

A fortune for the village.

"Blessings, giver."

And then I was gone.

CHAPTER TWENTY-NINE

I thought about what to do next before I made contact with the snipers, knowing command would be in on it and they might shut down what I had in mind. But the clock was ticking, and the stakes had just gotten a lot higher. Nightmare reaches the temple, he's out of reach, and apparently he's a real game changer.

If we lose in the battle against Sût…

Then the Saur go north to help in the battle against the Cities of Men. The last bastions of civilization.

I thought about the Accadions. The Portugonians… and all the other small cities barely hanging on against a vast overwhelming tide of evil.

A world that would become just like this village of stone-carving slaves. Hiding in caves. Thinking they were safe. Hoping they were.

And then being sacrificed on a whim.

We'd be splitting up to make this happen if we were gonna do it…

I saw Tanner as I ruminated over these things, strapping the SAW as he stood up in the dark of our silent little LP/OP on the high ledge. I drank some cold coffee and munched on a stale cookie from the MRE.

He walked down the trail, stopped, and began talking in a low whisper to someone I couldn't see.

This has happened before.

Ghosts.

He sees them. We don't. Generally.

Usually the dead who have been wronged.

After a few minutes of talking to that someone I could not see… he reached out and put his arms around whoever it had been.

Someone who wasn't there anymore.

He held her, because I'd find out who it was later, he held her for a long time. And then, after it was done, after she'd gone off to wander in grief, he came back.

"She was going to be married after the next rainy season, Talker."

I knew who he was talking about. The girl the priests had sacrificed.

"Village boy who sometimes sneaks off to work as a porter for the expeditions of thieves that come into the valley from a city across the sea to the east. A place called the City of Thieves. He was going to marry her when he came back. He really loved her. She loved him. He's gone now. Like us. Off on an expedition in a tomb south of the valley. Tomb of some minor official. Easy money, he told her."

Like us. That stuck with me later. Told me about Tanner things I didn't know.

Tanner gave a dry, heartless, dead chuckle at this.

"Makes sense, I guess. Thieves from the City of Thieves."

He was talking in his dead voice now.

"She said that once they were married, they were going to escape to there, this City of Thieves, and have a life, a much better life than this. Children. That was important to her. Children, Talk. That was what the girl wanted. A child. She was so sad, Talk. Couldn't believe she was dead now. She couldn't stop crying."

And so you held her, I thought and didn't say to my friend. You held the ghost of a dead girl who'd been murdered and had everything she ever wanted taken from her, my friend, because that's who you really are.

Not who you've become.

But who you really are, and have been all along, and why, for your whole life, you've been fighting everyone in authority.

Like some champion.

Some half-dead, messed-up-face, champion for the dead.

You'll fight for any lost cause, won't you, Tanner. Because that's what makes you… you, my friend. You will fight to the death for those who can't fight for themselves anymore. No matter what the odds are. It's what makes you… you.

"She was so sad, Talk. Couldn't stop crying."

And then you swore you'd get her… revenge.

Because that's who you are now. That's what you do.

And I stood up and got Sergeant Thor on the comm, knowing that command could pull us out in a heartbeat if they didn't like what I was proposing.

Knowing that Commons was… a sacrifice for Nightmare. A sacrifice to Sût the Undying.

And that wasn't gonna happen. Not if we could stop it. And the only way to do it was to do it now and do it quick and there probably wasn't time for a rescue mission if it wasn't now.

"Mongoose to Python… Nightmare is on the move. Stand by to reposition and intercept."

CHAPTER THIRTY

I laid out exactly what we'd learned and what we needed to do to acquire visual on Commons if this was gonna happen, which was the mandate for the stalk I'd been given by the captain.

Acquire visual ID of Commons and maintain visual ID until the rescue force with Chief Rapp could come in and extract our Ranger.

To do that… we needed to follow the Katari to the tomb.

Tanner said we needed to kill them once they had the tomb open. I didn't say that on the channel that command was listening to as I told the snipers what was up. But I was down for it.

We'd need to get them out of the way before we intercepted Nightmare and his team. The Katari kill pact was going to try to kill Nightmare, which, okay, thank you, except we couldn't allow that to happen because Commons was right there and might be killed too.

So the plan was to shut them down in the tomb they were on the move for right now in order to reach the Spring of Sullus via the back door and assassinate Nightmare. It was an old tomb dedicated to a priest-architect. Which was kind of a big deal to the Saur. The mummy builder and designer of the Grand Pyramid… Papht-Un… or, as he was known by the villagers, the Mad Puzzle Master of Outer Darknesses.

This was a tomb that had remained basically untouched over many long centuries, and through which only the Katari, in their role as tomb guardians, were allowed to access.

That's how the Katari got about so fast. That and the fact they were *cat-ssassins*!

Talker words FTW.

And in the event we were unsuccessful… something could still be done, which I felt was something, because Commons was hanging out there in the wind.

"Python… suggest you reposition to an overwatch with an eye on the spring halfway up the Serpent Stairs. The package…"

This was Commons's tag in terms of the mission. The package.

"… will emerge from there. This is an ideal point to intercept. But to acquire and maintain contact Mongoose will need to follow their trail and may be out of contact. Mongoose over…"

Mongoose is us, as has been mentioned.

I waited and listened to the silence of the comm as everyone listening asked themselves… Who the hell does the linguist think he is?

But these were Rangers and I was one of them. I'd been trained to lead small units by them. That was Ranger School. I was the guy on the ground with the best picture.

For Rangers… rank and job didn't mean as much as Ranging. And this was what I was doing as I'd learned it from them.

Still… I was kinda surprised. *I* wouldn't listen to me. But hey… life comes at ya fast.

Command was also listening and had said nothing so far. So that was… positive?

The reposition for the two snipers would be a long belly crawl and delicate creep to avoid the many Saur patrols up there along the plateau near the fortress temples that ringed the Grand Pyramid as a defensive network.

"Mongoose, this is Warlord Actual…"

Captain Knife Hand has entered the chat.

I waited to be shot down.

"Mongoose… how long to reach the tomb to transition to the back door?"

I'd already map reconned this.

"Warlord Actual… I say two hours to get to the front door. Five to six hours to reach the back door and put eyes on the package from the ground."

If both snipers moved low and slow they'd be in position on the overwatch a few hours before that to glass the spring where the procession of priests carrying Commons and led by Nightmare would soon appear.

I had no idea what was in that tomb. What we'd face in there. What we'd have to go through just to see the other side.

But we'd make it happen. Whatever it was that was in there.

The comm crackled and Sergeant Thor spoke. "Warlord… the plan looks solid, and this might be our best chance. Launch the extraction team at oh-four hundred and they'll be over the site at daybreak. They can fast-rope in and take control of the package. We can extract from there. Nightstalkers can handle the action. We can draw the site and update extraction force once we're on the ground in a few hours. Python over."

Silence. I could feel the captain thinking this one over hard from hundreds of miles away.

A Black Hawk, at least, would come in, drop Chief Rapp's team via ropes. Door gunners on the minis laying the hate in all directions. Sergeant Thor and his spotter doming the priority targets…

Nightmare, of course.

If anyone was gonna do Nightmare, Sergeant Thor and *Mjölnir* was the bet I'd lay down in the casino of violence this was all about to become within six hours.

My team, Mongoose… all we had to do was trail and block. If Nightmare got crafty we'd follow and alert. That's all. That's what I told myself then.

Ranger snipers, a Green Beret–led team full of Ranger pipe hitters, and backed by a 160th Nightstalker Black Hawk… that seemed like the perfect combination to get Commons back.

I cautiously treated myself to a quick drink of coffee because it felt to optimistic me… that my stupid plan was about to totally execute with minimum screwups from me.

Take that, Sar'nt Major. You won't have to have Kennedy dig a ditch and bury me after shooting me with your own sidearm, will you?

But still, the comm was silent and Knife Hand said nothing. Then…

"Solid copy, Python. All elements cleared to proceed. Warlord out."

CHAPTER THIRTY-ONE

"WHOA!" said Tanner. "Lotsa dead down here…"

We were on the move and on the move fast. The clock was burning, and we had to catch up to the Katari, which we did pretty quickly as we hustled down off the cliffs. Kennedy and I went to NODs to see in the dark as there wasn't much moonlight down here in this section of the canyon. Tanner had DeadVision or whatever.

We got going quickly down onto the monument-littered valley floor. There were obelisks, statues, and the entrances to old tombs that had been robbed long ago everywhere.

And there were bones. Lots of bones. And broken weapons and gear.

"Lotta expeditions from that City of Thieves got murked right here, guys," said Tanner.

Murked. It's catching on.

"They're everywhere, Talk. From all ages. It's some wild and crazy stuff. Even Saurian funeral processions, like parades of ghosts. Buryin' some old pharaoh I guess."

This was stuff we couldn't see. Dead stuff. And right now… the dead weren't our concern and so me on point and leading the way, Tanner in the center with the SAW, and Kennedy bringing up the rear with security, we moved rapidly toward the tomb we suspected lay near a sharp spur on the far wall of the valley.

High above on the plateau the snipers were knee-deep into repositioning.

The medusa had been contacted, forward at her location at the developing front line, and we got some reference points from her that meshed with our village intel and the rough map the detachment had been developing of the valley already. So we had a pretty good idea where the cats were headed, and like I said we picked them up shortly.

Beyond this spur they were headed for along the far wall, the valley curved northwest, and halfway along that curve we suspected Nightmare and his team were making their way toward the Serpent Stairs where they began their long haul up toward the plateau.

The tomb at the spur would allow us to get going upward faster and arrive at the well ahead of them. The well was halfway up the stairs and wide enough for a caravan, or funeral procession, to rest.

On the comm the snipers were silent, and it was clear they were creeping on their location.

Drone recon did a flyover and identified us but not Nightmare's team. So their spell cover was working. I thought of the dead girl and watched Tanner's grim half face in the dark working dip and revenge he was gonna lay on those priests once he caught up with them. He was like… broadcasting it. And the empath feature of my psionics was picking it up loud and clear.

Speaking of clear…

We were clear of Saurian patrols as confirmed by drone recon, so we hustled after the cat-ssasin kill squad, or whatever it was.

Within the hour we caught up with them and we followed their split-up formation from a distance as they made a zigzag course toward the tomb. We spotted the carved obelisks, two of them, that marked the entrance to the tomb of the Mad Puzzle Master, and we watched as the three separate groups of Katari, they'd been traveling in pairs, came together before the entrance, readying to open it via their arcane techniques.

Hunkered behind the fallen statue of some long-lost-ago Saurian titan that had cracked into three pieces, Tanner spoke up, suggesting how we do this. He spit dip on the Saurian's croc sneer and sketched his plan in the sand.

"Listen up, boys. These Katari… they see ghosts. I been watchin' em… and they're reacting and steering clear of all the ghosts we keep runnin' into out here tonight. Must be some kinda superstition they run as part of their jobs as guardians of these places."

I waited. Interesting, but I wasn't yet seeing how it helped us.

Tanner continued.

"We go kinetic in the night, even suppressed… chances are the Delta dude out there may hear us way-afar off and know he got a Ranger problem on his six. That might cause him to switch his route up. I'd do that. So if we can get it on with these cat ninjas *quiet*-like… then maybe we keep Delta Dude trackin' toward the ambush we got waitin' ahead for him."

I nodded. We'd already discussed this. But I could see Tanner had an idea.

"How do we do that, Tanner?"

He turned toward Kennedy. "You were telling me about

that new spell you learned…"

"Yeah… the slow spell."

"Yup, that's the one. Okay, here it is. I haven't really talked about this, but I kinda got it figured it out so I can… well, best way to say this is I can camouflage myself like a ghost. Okay? For a short period of time. If I think about one, real hard, and really concentrate, then to other ghosts I can appear like one of them, to them, for a little while. Happened when I saw one of 'em that made a big impression… this, like, knight guy in sweet dark armor who'd been hung. The other ghosts came up and started talkin' to me like I was him. So… that's why I was locking in on the Katari seeing ghosts. They been skirting around them as we get close. So if I *camo* as one of them, there's a chance I can quote-unquote *wander* near enough, without triggerin' 'em, then I get it on hand-to-hand. If Kennedy uses his new spell…"

He looked at the Ranger Wizard. "Like *how* slow, Kennedy?"

Kennedy thought about this for a long moment.

Out there, across a field of sand and broken stones, near the entrance to the temple, the Katari were now busy at the great stone door. We could hear them meowling like house cats in the night and that was weird. But in unison. Like an eerie cat-choir.

"Most times I've cast it," said Kennedy, "the target seems, to me, like they're moving around in thick syrup. To me. I think *they* don't realize it though. I cast it once on you, Talker, and you didn't even notice."

"I didn't? What'd I do?"

"You were drinking coffee. You didn't care."

Sounds like me.

"Plus I got some other spells I can throw once they're slowed."

Tanner handed me the SAW. "You run this. Even if it's canned its gonna make a sound he may pick up, and he'll know for sure what it is 'cause I'm more than sure he knows his way around a suppressed SAW. Delta got all the toys back in the day. But if things get weird or get away from me… then I guess we gotta open up with it."

"What are you going to fight them with?" I asked.

Tanner shrugged and popped his flick knife. He smiled that half gruesome smile.

"This I guess. Works so far. Got two guys in a bar once with it that I'm sure CID was still askin' questions about when we jumped forward. So… why ruin a good thing?"

It was the standard Benchmade.

I pulled *Coldfire* off my assault pack and handed it to him. Hilt first.

"Sweet," hissed Tanner. "This'll do nice."

CHAPTER THIRTY-TWO

TANNER'S fight went down fast… but in slow-mo.

Pretty cool stuff, and it gave me, once again, a newfound respect for Kennedy's growing wizardly skills.

Powers, I'd started to call them, and I wondered, later, after I reflected on all that went on in that tomb… how long he would remain… him.

Just like Tanner, he was becoming something new. We all were. In our own ways. *Ruin Revealed* ways. And I wondered how much longer I could hang on to what was familiar, and needed, in my own life.

Listen… I've never been like this. I'm a minimalist. But my time with the Rangers had transformed me, and there was a part of me that knew I needed to hold on to every moment, every one of them, because of what I feared was coming.

What?

Change?

The end of the mission?

The end of all things?

I didn't know yet. Only knew that it was. And so, I reminded myself, all things must.

I set the SAW down on its bipod where I could get to it fast if I suddenly needed to suppress a bunch of them or engage some new threat we hadn't factored into the planning for our attack. Instead I opted for the M110 SDM rifle Tanner had brought along. I scanned the night and chose which out there among our enemies was going to die first. I sighted and watched the cat. Waiting for Kennedy to kick it all off. Then I looked away from the scope, giving my eye a rest.

One shot, suppressed, was likely to go undetected and might be the game changer we needed once things started to go hot. So I'd use the squad designated marksman rifle.

And yeah… this was one weird fight. I'll just tell you that now.

Rangers with weapons and spells versus cat-ssassins.

The AAR was gonna be lit.

The Ranger NCOs back with the detachment were going to roll their eyes. But… we're gonna win. I'd made up my mind about that. If it all went sideways I was gonna go with the SAW, stabilize, and blast our way through it. Even if I hit Tanner he could take a round. He was dead. Probably don't want to him in the head though.

Heads up, Talker… don't shoot your buddy in the head.

Roger. Can do.

So Tanner starts breathing deeply and we don't see the change… but he says he's got it now. It's this kid that got shot with like a dozen arrows he saw one time back in Sûstagul.

Tanner thought he was a thief or something that got caught, and that was how they executed him. The people in the city. The merchants. But the thing that always bothered Tanner about the ghost was that Tanner would see him a lot, and the kid was always trying to return the money he'd stolen. Carrying it about in a sack, asking if anyone had seen some name he kept going on and on and on about. That he needed to make it right.

No one saw him. No one but Tanner.

And so he wandered around constantly until Tanner finally decided to ask around himself and see if there was some way he could help make things right for the kid.

"He's just a kid, Talk. But I can tell he felt real real bad about what he'd brought on himself and his family. And it was like his ghost thought he could make it all right and avoid all the grief he'd brought on his fam for what he'd done. I asked this old beggar dude, he looked older than dirt, I asked if he'd ever seen anyone executed that way in Sûstagul. Y'know, shot by a dozen arrows at least. He said he hadn't and that wasn't how they executed people anyway. They usually drowned or hung them. But then… he said about thirty years ago, when he was just a guard, before he'd lost his hand in a fight with orc raiders from out of the desert, that was actually a good story but now's not the time… he said that there had been a kid who'd stolen from the wrong wizard. And that wizard had the kid tied up and had his best assassin shoot him several times atop the southern wall near the Gates of Eternity. Shooting not to kill, but to wound. One arrow every hour. Twelve hours later the assassin fired the fatal shot and the debt was considered paid though the money was never recovered.

"The kid's family was ruined. The wizard drove them from the city and they were never seen again. Always felt bad for that kid's ghost, Talk, and I've been lookin' for a way to make it right. But I ain't as smart as you. I bet you'd know how."

I had no clue.

The mystery was like decades old. Everyone was probably dead. Yikes.

So now, apparently, Tanner was ghost-camouflaged as that arrow-shot kid, and slowly, Tanner rose from behind our cover and began to wander, haphazardly, toward the Katari at the entrance to the tomb.

I switched over to the M110, flipped the night vision optic on, and watched as the Katari finished up their prayers, or preparations, at the tomb door.

It was slowly sliding open of its own accord. So that was creepy. But that was also not necessarily a tomorrow problem as much as a later-after-this-ambush problem.

That's how we movin' in the 'goose. One baby step at a time. Add up enough and we got ourselves a completed op and no dead Rangers.

Except Tanner. He's mostly dead.

Look at me acting like an NCO. I gotta get these corporal stripes off me and get back to the mafia.

One of the Katari noted Tanner's ghostly approach, made a sign that seemed to wave him away as though he were dispelling or cursing ghost-Tanner, then turned back to the work the Katari were finishing up at the open tomb door. They had bags rolled out in the sand with what looked like tools, and now they were wrapping these up. Other tools were coming out in their stead. Bars. Poles. Picks. Scrolls.

They certainly were preparing for something that lay ahead in the tomb, and they seemed more concerned with those preparations than with Tanner's ghostly child arrow pincushion slowly wandering toward them.

When Tanner was within twenty feet, Kennedy began to mumble his spell quietly. The words to me sounded slurred, and yes, even slowed down…

Go figure. It's a slow spell, Talker.

Then Ranger Wizard Kennedy leapt up and *threw* the spell right at the Katari, while balancing himself in the sand with the dragon-headed staff.

We'd considered using that powerful staff and just roasting them all with a fireball, but its fiery nature might cause excessive illumination in the dark valley and Nightmare might pick up the "illum" from a distance if he was still near enough to our location, put two and two together, and come up with Rangers on his trail.

Then how we gonna *Surprise, Ranger Smash*?

So this is what I saw after Kennedy fired the Slow Spell…

The spell shimmered like star-shine out in the night and away from us as it got lobbed, arced high, and landed perfectly among the Katari cat-ssassins.

It landed and then exploded, in normal-speed motion like a dozen translucent stars suddenly bursting forth in every direction all at once. Then the stars started moving slower and slower as they streaked away from the detonation point among the killer cats.

Some of the cats, and of course they would do this, they're cat-ninjas remember, had lightning-fast reflexes, and they leaped away from the starburst impact in the instant it detonated with a soft… I don't know how to say this… not everything is grand and epic and all, y'know, all "YOU, SHALL NOT, PASS!"

But the spell detonated and made a loud fart sound, yep, when it exploded among the cats and suddenly everyone caught in it slowed down like they suddenly went into slow motion.

Like in *The Matrix*.

Even the leaping cats were suddenly slowed.

Tanner was outside the… range of the spell. I hadn't even thought about that, but Kennedy timed it right. "Game on!" shouted Tanner, and he drew *Coldfire* with a soft hiss from the scabbard he'd been carrying in one hand. He tossed the scabbard and moved in to assault. The blade was already glowing a pale cold blue like it did in the presence of dangerous enemies when Tanner attacked the first Katari with zero finesse.

Zero.

He just ran forward, heaving the longsword with both hands overhead, and brought it down savagely in true Ranger fashion right on the nearest cat, right through the thing's triangular head.

Very abrupt.

No art.

Totally effective.

The cat-ssassin watched in slow-motion horror as Tanner practically cleaved it in half down to the collar bone.

Before it could hit the sand, Tanner whirled, yanking the glowing blade free and hurling it sideways right into the next cat, edge first like a boss, catching that one right in the ribcage as it slowly reacted to the fact that the fart sound had detonated seconds ago.

Seriously… it made a fart sound and that was pretty funny even as I pulled the trigger on the farthest one away from Tanner and sent a round into that one. My aim wasn't great, and I think I hit it in the belly when I was aiming for the sternum. I adjusted and the cat-thing merely slow-motion reached for where I'd just shot it as I took my time, let go of my breath, and sent the next adjusted round through its mouth.

I'd aimed for a dome shot. Top of the skull since I was high.

Instead I blew off its chin.

Get good, Talker!

It was still reacting, meowling in wide slow horror at having been initially shot in the belly when I ruined the bottom half of its jaw.

That was cool, and I may have shouted "Magic is awesome!" as I picked up another target in my scope. But I'll never admit to that in the AAR.

Kennedy in the meantime threw a volley of magic meteors, they glowed a venomous green, but not too bright, that streaked right into one cat and tore straight through it.

The cat watched with that same slow horror as it was shotgunned to death by magic stars all at once.

There were two left, and Tanner had just run up to the second-to-last, unceremoniously thrusting *Coldfire* right into its belly, when we noticed that one of the cats had dodged all the effects of Kennedy's farty slow spell and had just run for the entrance to the tomb like its life depended on it.

"He made his save," hissed Kennedy.

Which the cat did, and I went rapid-fire squeezing off a shot and then chasing it with more rounds to get it down on the ground.

Noting this here for the AAR…

Without a spell like the one Kennedy fired off, Katari are almost impossible to kill by targeted fire. They… are… *fast*.

I chased that one with five rounds as it tumbled, dashed,

cartwheeled and at one point finally just leapt for the darkness beyond the tomb door and made it safely away from us and into the tomb beyond our ability to engage it directly.

I swore.

Five of the cats were dead though, and Tanner was pumping *Coldfire* like it was a game ball in the endzone.

Then he spiked it in the sand and shouted, "Yeah! 'Merica!"

He wasn't yet aware that one of them had escaped. But… it *was* a pretty cool fight. And Tanner looked cool standing amid dead cats with a glowing sword spiked in the sand.

I'll give him that.

CHAPTER THIRTY-THREE

WE found an old map on one of the dead cats.

It looked like a very fine antique map, well done, of the tomb that we were about to enter. But though there were markings, and this is not a pun… they were little more than cat-scratch and I couldn't even take a guess at what was annotated along the yellowing papyrus.

But it did show the route through the tomb and the back door we needed to reach in order to gain visual on Nightmare.

We had a long way to move, and there were clearly some danger areas within the ancient tomb. But at least we had this.

We went back to our primaries, Tanner took point, and we went in knowing there was an assassin aware of our presence somewhere inside the tomb, and probably many, many traps and possibly even some guardians.

"Don't worry, Talk," laughed Tanner. "We got 'nades. Very few problems in this life a well-tossed grenade can't solve. Know what I mean?"

Then we went in.

Three chambers later, in what looked like some kind of trophy room, we ended up in a fight for our lives against a stone golem that looked like a Saurian pharaoh.

The grenades didn't work.

CHAPTER THIRTY-FOUR

IT'S time for that download on who the Saur really are.

Here we go.

Hazzim was right. He told me everything, he just told it to me in an antique and ancient Bronze Age Ruin kind of way. Told me everything, right there as plain as day in his own singsong broken voice as we sat there late into the night among his dusty books and crumbling papyri, him taking me back through as much of the crazed history of the Ruin as I could take.

I thought I knew what was going on.

But I didn't.

Not until we began to enter the first chamber of the ornate and beautiful tomb on the stalk for the remaining cat-ssassin and the rendezvous to intercept and rescue Commons. The walls were painted in gold within the old tomb, and the story on those gold walls, in the hieroglyphs of the Saur, was nearly insane. But as I watched it all unfold, watching the corners and watching the shadows, Kennedy casting Detect Traps…

It all began to make sense.

The first chambers were a maze.

Kennedy detected the first trap, bringing us to an abrupt halt with a "Hold, guys."

We held.

It was dark even in night vision.

Total horror show.

"Kennedy… what is it?"

Kennedy: "There's a torch on the wall. We need that. Night vision isn't gonna work in here if we're gonna avoid all the death in the walls."

Death in the walls. Great.

Tanner frowned at us. "I can see just fine."

We flipped up our NODs and Kennedy lit the torch on the wall—he studied the sconce as though it too might be trapped—and then cautiously, almost delicately, plucked the lit torch from its sconce.

He waved it around and moved in front of Tanner.

"There…" he whispered, pointing toward a certain section of floor. The floor was marked in Saurian hieroglyphs too.

They were everywhere.

"Any square with that black sun on it… treat it as trapped. And no… I don't know if that means it's going to explode like an IED or toss us into another dimension or shoot poison darts out of the walls at us, probably from the mouths of these crocodile cartoons on the wall… but just avoid them if you wanna go on living."

I nodded soberly.

Tanner laughed, and I could tell what he was laughing at. He was already not *going on living*. He was dead. Poison dart away.

Still… best not to tempt fate.

We proceeded deeper into the dead quiet tomb, and the farther the first maze of corridors went into the cliffs, the more the story of the Saur was finally explained to me. Like

Hazzim had already explained it to me. The difference being, this time I actually understood.

So, here's the big reveal.

They're us.

Ten thousand years ago, the Saur got changed, courtesy of the nano-plague, into lizard men. They were once part of the great tribe of humanity. And if you followed the story along the walls that the mad architect had left behind, and now that I think about it perhaps it was more of a confession than anything else, they, the Saur, not only knew it was going to happen, the coming plague, they welcomed it as the herald of a new age for them.

An age of death, tyranny, and destruction.

Who were the Saur ten thousand years ago?

Who were the orcs?

I've made some guesses. I'm sure you have too. Conversations among the Rangers have often gone this way as we've wondered how people who were once like us… became elves, or orcs, or monsters in the aftermath.

The Ruin turned McCluskey into a vampire. Me into a mutant with mental powers called psionics. The captain into a were-tiger. Sergeant Monroe into a minotaur.

Not everyone. But some.

And when you understood that most of the Ruin had become something else, and that humans were the minority species… that was something to think about.

The Shadow Elves were basically Korean.

Many of the other elves seemed to be reminiscent of other races we'd once known. The Deep Elves that Sergeant Joe and I had been hunted by in the desert beyond the Atlantean

Mountains, the ones that worshipped a Spider Queen god, they seemed Indian from India.

Hazzim says, as do the pages of the *Book of Skelos*... that the Ruin reveals the true nature of a person, a race, or... a way... over time. Make of that what you will. The fragments of the *Book of Skelos* we've recovered so far indicate that the revealing isn't necessarily fair.

So there's that to consider.

You get that some people changed, became something other than human, because this savant spectrum coder, angry about some great wrong done to her even before I was born, decided to turn the world into a fantasy game she'd played one summer via the nano-plague and the ability to rewrite not just DNA, but molecular structure.

It's an insane tale. A work of nonsense by some hack writer.

And it makes no sense.

Then you look around at the writing on the walls of a lizard man tomb you're crawling through, filled with traps and treasure and deadly magic, and you see why she made the Saur.

They're what we already called, some did anyway, ten thousand years ago, *the lizard people*.

The people of power.

The tyrants who seem... inhuman in their high towers.

She knocked those towers down, thinking she was equalizing the playing field. Teaching them a lesson.

But they built pyramids and embraced their chosen dark destiny.

It was like this...

Like she'd fallen for all the "conspiracy theories" that turned out be just… conspiracies… all along.

Never mind the theories. That too was a trick they were playing on all of us right there in plain sight. As in… *It's crazy to think we'd actually be doing the crazy things we're doing. Right?*

I know… madness. And listening to Hazzim I found myself convinced the old sage had indeed lost his mind.

But it's been right there all along.

Buried here along the ornate gold-painted walls of an ancient tomb deep in the desert, and right in front of our eyes out there in the Ruin.

Did she hate criminals and suicidal jihadis bent on destroying the world by sword and fire? Yes. She did. And she coded for orcs using databases and genetic algorithms.

Did she think lawyers and financiers and the greedy were parasitical scum? Yeah. She did. Vampires and other monsters came into being.

Did she believe in princes and noble races like elves and dwarves? Yep. That too.

She coded things that I would have thought impossible, and she came up with some insane logic none of us will ever understand, that in her mind… justified her revenge at having youth, and love, and even personal destiny stolen from her because some big brains were planning for the nuclear annihilation of the world back in the sixties and they decided they'd need warriors, tacticians… and brains.

And she had brains to spare.

Revenge kept her alive. Except she thought it was love. She was confused.

The fragments say that much.

The whole book... someday I think we'll find it. But already... I think I got the story. It just took this mission to reach a place where it was all written down... as a confession.

Yeah. I think, now that I look back... yeah... it was a confession.

But in the moment she hit... I don't know... *send*. Or *enter*. Or however she hijacked biolabs and released her weapons... she changed the world, destroyed technology, and made magic real.

Maybe she was trying to make a better world than the one we were dealt. I've played that game. Haven't we all.

I think some other stuff happened beyond her input. The dragons. The Nether Sorcerer. Hazzim indicated, in his frail old singsong voice...

"Those are from outside, Talk-ir. From the darkness beyond the light. They are not of this time, or place."

So... there's that.

But who are the Saur?

They were exactly the tyrants they are today.

The powerful. The elites. The inhuman.

Those who shirked love, grace, humanity, and freedom... for total control and an obsession to rule over others no matter the cost.

Robbery and war were their tools. Genocide was always their final solution.

It still is if you read the hieroglyphs correctly. Even without the nuances.

And if you followed the story on the wall long enough, which starts with Saurian glyphs that look like little human figures in cities, and follow it through the darkness of the Ruin and watch as on the wall they turn into the monsters they've become… then you understand it all.

You understand the Saur.

Who they were… and who they are now. Same. Same as it ever was. Just… right there in the open.

And here's the crazy part. As if all that wasn't crazy enough…

They knew it was coming before anyone else. And instead of warning others… trying to stop it even, according to the story on the walls of the tomb… they *wanted* it to happen and saw it as the final stage in gaining total control, mastery of the world that would become the Ruin, and the destruction of every human.

They were no longer anything like the human cattle they ruled over and were better than. What they'd once been.

They were gods now, mortals. Kneel and suffer our wrath and damnation.

The writing on the wall said so.

And they had the longevity technology at the beginning.

The tomb was old… but the glyphs and figures said the Saur were old even then… the tech CEOs and politicians and celebrities, the rich and powerful, the secret and hidden running the show and playing everyone off against one against another… they were older.

And they were… still.

As in… they'd *never died*. The powerful of the Saur could be as old as the Ruin itself.

That is, if the writing on the wall was anything to believe, even if it was a confession.

There are probably Saur… that I once knew from some news article, social media post, movie, book, TV show. Maybe even voted for.

We are from ten thousand years ago. But look what's become of us.

Even the figure of Sût the Undying himself, a lizarene Saurian adorned in gold with alien narrow eyes, a crown and a throne and slaves and gold… follow the figure across the walls of time written on the uncorrupted tomb… and you'll find him in human figure at the beginning as the plague began to spread. A powerful magnate shown ruling over a city in guise and by craft and hidden means.

Stunning stuff.

Too much to process on the tension-filled crawl through the trap-littered tomb. But there on the tomb walls passing the traps either Tanner seemed to have some natural skill in finding…

… thin wires to cause blocks to fall from ceilings.

… pits painted to look like the floor.

… poisoned darts that sprang suddenly in soft hisses and laned in his rotting flesh to no effect.

Or Kennedy detecting them by his barely heard magical incantations…

The story was all there on the wall, the story of who the Saur really were. And are. Now.

They were… they are… the monsters they've always been.

And even now, they lay out there under the sinking sands in many undiscovered tombs and hidden pyramids out there beyond the known lands, waiting to rise once again and try to "cleanse" the world of human cattle.

Genocide. Same as it ever was.

So in the end… it will be them. Just them and not you. And only ever them. For all time.

That was written on the walls. Right there in front of your face right now. You just gotta believe what they're saying.

Or as Kurtz one time told us as we improved defense against another mass-wave attack by the orc hordes… "When someone tells you they're coming to kill you… believe 'em."

Yes, Sar'nt. Roger that.

When we entered the final trophy room where the mad architect had admitted to all the crimes of it all in hieroglyphs and stunning and intricate models in miniature that showed the world that once was, the world we knew, deep down there in the Saurian tomb, and the fabled structures he would build later as the Saur began to go forth and conquer after the long dark of the first thousand years of the Ruin…

Pyramids. Temples. A tower that looked like a challenge to the gods themselves…

Warring.

Slaving.

Sacrificing to a dark sun that hated humanity. Hated everything.

We saw it all on the stalk, intent on our mission, noting it all… well.

That was when the golem attacked in the chamber of wonders.

CHAPTER THIRTY-FIVE

WE faced three guardians in that nightmare tomb on our way to the back of it to get eyes on Commons. Add other formidable foes and the traps, then the climb up the hidden well… and we barely made it to the spring just in time to watch all our plans go up in complete smoke as everything went sideways.

But as we pushed through the traps and monsters, using gunfire and explosives, Kennedy's spells, and every skill we had that the Rangers had mashed into our brains and bodies… and yes, grenades… we only knew that the swifter we moved, the more Commons's chances improved.

And that was our mission.

Nightmare.

The smoking of Sût.

But all of that came after getting our Ranger back. I can say that with complete truth about all involved.

The stone golem came to life in the trophy room of miniature models and grand Saurian dreams. The story of the Saur, the *whole* history, and what must have even been prophecies of the Saur to come regarding the invading of other dimensions and realms, even other worlds, was all there all around on the walls of the great trophy room of the mad architect.

We thought the golem was just another statue carved and

constructed in tribute to the mighty glory of the Saur… until it came to life and tried to kill us. That it was merely some artistic feature watching over the treasure and tribute of the fantastic room we'd entered as we made our way through the mad tomb.

There were so many gold artifacts there, and it was easy to get distracted studying them.

I guess that was part of the trap.

So many gems set here and there in these fantastic pieces…

The ceiling was even a map of the galaxy, but made with gems for many of the stars… and the blue there that made up the galaxy was one of the most beautiful colors I've ever seen.

There was strange gold lettering and lines up there I couldn't make out.

The golem came to life and tried to kill us, grinding and moving, stalking slowly toward us with intentions that were clearly homicidal. We were smart enough to realize rounds weren't gonna do much to it, so Tanner got ready with the explosives, falling back with his assault pack and working on the method of detonation as I stood there and couldn't think of what to do. Kennedy hurled magic missiles and a few other spells at it… nothing to effect.

I had my doubts about the explosives. We were deep underground… We were probably going to kill ourselves…

I scrambled and the thing began to smash everything in colossal strikes as it tried to crush me.

Tanner lobbed grenades and they practically gave us concussions from overpressure inside the space. We'd finally fallen back to the passage we'd come through when Kennedy shouted "Hang on!" and fired off his disintegration ray.

The golem halted, then shook it off like magic was nothing to it.

"Sometimes..." mumbled Kennedy, "certain monsters can have anti-magic shells."

That would have been good to know earlier.

"Glad I brought this," Tanner grunted, and he hefted the explosive-laden pack and the detonator that would destroy it, all of it, in one go.

"Uh... that might be a bad idea..." I said as the stone titan closed to smash us all.

"Applied explosives have solved many a problem and have been responsible for good times I will remember always," Tanner laughed, then spit some dip on the gold walls of the tomb. "Trust me... I'm kind of a pro at bad ideas."

He set the timer he'd installed in the ruck to two minutes.

"Here's what we do," he said.

The thing was almost on us. We either needed to head back the way we came, or...

"Is it run around it real fast, Tanner?" I asked desperately, because time wasn't running out... it *had run* out.

"Yeah... do that," said Tanner, then he armed the detonator and set the explosives-laden assault pack down in front of us. I wasn't an EOD expert, but that thing was probably going bring the whole chamber down on us, if not the entire tomb, when it went off.

Seriously.

"Kennedy, you still got that shield spell?" said Tanner calmly, like we were running demo at the range and learning how to be better at it when it came for realz and game time.

Kennedy nodded and opened his mouth, but nothing

came out. The adrenaline had ahold of him and he was having trouble breathing.

"We run for the far exit once I arm the timer," continued Tanner, still calm despite the circumstances. "We get to the passage on the other side of this chamber, cover, and Kennedy throws up his shield spell. Maybe that buys us something against the overpressure and blast. Maybe it doesn't. Best I can do. Otherwise we lose the chance to acquire Commons."

"We run. Forward. Let's do this." That was me. Saying brave stuff and feeling absolutely certain that death was so near I could reach out and slap it.

Kennedy held up his hand. He was hyperventilating.

"Wait… got something… better."

"Okay, but no time," said Tanner. "Run and use it when we get there!"

We ran from the passage right directly at the giant stone statue of a crocodile, leering toothy smile coming for us, scrambling to get away from its legs and massive stone arms as it swung immense crushing mauls for fists right at us.

Statuary and gold artifacts were destroyed. Walls and lines of Saurian hieroglyphs exploded in grit and debris.

But we made it. Made it past it and out of its immediate kill radius.

Then, once we hit "open ground," we ran like gazelles because that's all you can do when you're a young Ranger. You run just to keep up. And all of Kurtz's endless death runs around FOB Hawthorn paid off as we surged for the doors at the far end of the great chamber, counting off the seconds we had left to live before the explosives ruck detonated and brought the whole place down on us.

I was first to the doors because I'm fast, and all my fears did not come true as the doors were neither locked nor trapped.

They were, in fact… not even real.

The doors were an illusion.

I passed right through them.

Into a dead end.

Small. Round. Smooth walls. No exits.

Or so I thought until I looked up and saw that the smooth walls had jutting stones designed to climb up into the darkness way up there.

And that was the only way out of this.

We'd find out later, mere moments later, the hard way, that some of these stones were false and designed to make the potential tomb robber fall from a great height instead of reaching the upper treasure vaults before the final burial chamber.

"Climb!" I yelled, and started pulling myself up along the jutting stones, hauling for all I was worth as the seconds left to live expired.

Kennedy began to climb after me.

Tanner, counting out loud, came last.

I was worried that Kennedy was breathing so hard he wouldn't be able to speak the needed words to activate his spell. He was gasping as he climbed.

I think I was too.

We were up, not that high, when Tanner reached ten and started on nine and Kennedy let go with one hand and directed that hand toward the illusory entrance in the wall we'd come through to reach the well, that's what it felt like anyway, we were climbing up.

Then he cast… as he told us it was called later…

Wall of Stone.

Gasping… but he got it off like a pro.

All of a sudden the illusion began to solidify into gray granite down there where we'd just come through, the fake doors becoming real wall and sealing us in as Tanner counted down the last five seconds before det.

To me… the wall wasn't going to be totally solid in time to deflect the blast.

CHAPTER THIRTY-SIX

THE entire well rocked hard in the sudden blast and we hung there in the darkness as Tanner's C4-laden ruck detonated and destroyed most likely the golem and probably that entire level of the tomb.

If not the whole tomb itself.

Suddenly, I was more aware than I ever thought I'd be that we could be totally trapped in here.

Kennedy's Wall of Stone had been enough, had come together hard enough at the last second, to redirect the blast and overpressure from pulping our bodies and then collapsing the well we dangled in now from uncertain and perhaps false handholds.

Then, as other portions of the ancient tomb could be heard collapsing and falling apart, vast sections of the area we'd just come through no doubt crushing everything we'd passed, an earthquake followed as we hung there and swung in the dark. Bits of stone including one sizable chunk, unseen in the dark, probably a climbing stone or two, streaked toward us and slammed into the now-solid floor the Ranger Wizard had summoned into existence to protect us at the last second.

"Neat spell, Kennedy," I whispered. My voice was dry, and it barely worked. There was dust in the air everywhere and it rained down all over us.

"Yeah," said the Ranger wizard. "I'm still learning it. I

thought… what the hell… gotta go for it otherwise we're dead. Surprised it worked. Pretty cool though, huh?"

The tomb had fallen silent and we just hung there in the dark.

"Yeah," I said. "Pretty cool."

We'd almost just been killed. But… he had a spell he was… still learning.

I pulled a red ChemLight, snapped it to life with one hand, and dropped it. We weren't too far up from the magic floor.

"Everyone cool?" I asked.

They were.

"Let's drop down and consolidate."

We made our way down, and it was strange to stand on a magic floor that seemed much like freshly poured concrete. As patrol leader I got busy with figuring out how much gear was left.

Both Kennedy and I had kept our assault packs and weapons.

Tanner had lost the SAW back in there while working the explosive solution on how to deal with a living statue come to life and trying to do its best to smash you with its giant fists. The squad automatic weapon was now on the other side of the magic Wall of Stone, and probably flattened like a pancake.

That wasn't good. We'd need that game-changer weapon to suppress if we had to block Nightmare's force if they decided to pull back and away from the chief's extraction team and Sergeant Thor's supported fire by *Mjölnir*.

We were the blockers. Nothing says *Don't come at me bruh* like suppressive fire from a SAW going high-cyclic.

There was gonna be lightning riding and maybe even forbidden popsicle.

Or you could be crushed to death, here, Talker. Buried alive.

I pushed that thought away, but I had a hard time of it, and it was starting to get to me.

Tanner still had the M110 SDM. He'd slung that before getting busy with the det ruck. So, we had weapons. We had ammo. We had only a few grenades left, four between us. All frags. There'd be no shock in our awe if we had to breach any chambers higher up, but… we'd just have to shoot everyone. Whatever form of undead they were.

And that brought up the question…

How much of this tomb was still intact.

The destruction caused by the det ruck had been colossal, and if it weren't for Kennedy's spell we'd be dead, and stopping Nightmare would be someone else's Today problem.

"We're still in play," I muttered in the darkness as I pushed away all those shadowy thoughts I was having about what it would be like to have been crushed down here by our own explosives. Or… buried alive.

I seriously doubt we're…

Don't think about that. Don't think like that. You don't mind, it don't matter. But it made me start to sweat, and take things a little more serious than I usually do.

That's when I muttered we're still in play.

Then…

"Clock's burning, let's roll. We got a date with a mummy."

And… getting Commons out of this was still possible. I pushed away the dark thoughts of being crushed alive, wiped at the cold sweat that had broken out, and got ready to climb our way out of the well we'd ended up in.

"Don't take it so serious, Talk. Ain't ya never almost been crushed to death?" said Tanner dryly. His old sly self.

Kennedy laughed.

I love these guys.

CHAPTER THIRTY-SEVEN

WE emerged from the tomb… barely. We almost lost our lives twice more. And probably a few times we weren't aware of.

It was day, morning just, by our Timex watches.

Oh-six-forty-five.

The furious howling sandstorm enveloping everything was in full blast and it was clear there'd be no extraction team unless they'd gotten on the ground before this haboob hit.

The secret door we'd found at the back of the tomb, courtesy of a Kennedy Detection Spell after Tanner had saved us in the last chamber, had pushed away with all of us putting our backs into it.

Then we were standing on a small rock platform, cut into the serpentine stairs we'd aimed for, flying grit and sand blasting in all directions, visibility not more than a few feet.

"I'll try the radio," I said, covering in the entrance to the secret door, which seemed nothing more than ordinary rock face on this side. "Tanner… try to figure out where on the stair we're at, and where Nightmare's force is."

The radio was dead. Too much interference from the sandstorm. I pulled my phone from my admin pouch and checked text messages.

Yep, text messages. The Air Force had drones up and we had established a rough network south of Sûstagul that reached almost to the Accadion front lines forming around the Grand Pyramid…

But the pyramid, for some reason, played hell with our signal.

I got lucky. There was a text message from the TOC more than two hours ago.

And then a series of messages in the hour before alerting us that a sandstorm had suddenly developed and pushed in—yep, we've noticed—and that the extraction was on hold until the skies cleared enough.

It was just after dawn, but the golden light of the sun and swirling red sand along the high stairs that cut into the plateau made everything seem like some hellish alien world we'd arrived at on the other side of a long space flight through a vast universe of death and loneliness.

But that may have been a lingering effect from the horrors and temptations we'd just faced inside the cursed tomb.

The last message from the TOC read, "Extraction not possible at this time. Hold for storm passage. No expected time."

As Kennedy peered into the dust and tried to see what he could see down the stairs that seemed to be drowning in a tempest of flying sand, Tanner came back through the swirl, took a knee, and briefed me on what was what.

"Spring's five hundred meters more up the stairs." He nodded in that direction. "They halted there… maybe waiting out the storm but I don't think so, Talk. I got a feeling he *summoned* this storm for cover for him to reach his OBJ. No sign of the snipers. No sign of the bird or the extraction team either."

Then I told *him* what was up with the radio and texts. We were all on the same sheet of music now and I felt an urgency to move, attack, strike, and destabilize the enemy plan.

But three blockers were not an assault force.

What Tanner had given me was good intel. I had no idea how my friend had collected all that accurate data that fast. In the middle of a sudden sandstorm. And like a good patrol leader I had to know. Had to verify what I'd been told. Then I could make a plan and execute.

"How do you know where they're at, Tanner?"

He rubbed the side of his face that still had skin. The bone on the other side remained in its perpetual rictus.

"The priests are alive. I can… feel 'em up there. Just ahead, Talk."

He was using that dead… *other*… voice now.

"I…"

Tanner stopped and seemed to be working through something.

"Remember when I said they'd pay? Back there… with the dead girl."

I did.

"I'm stalkin' 'em now. Got this… *ache*… to settle them up. I can't think of the word… but it's like a thing for me now."

Vendetta. That's the word, Tanner. I didn't say it. Just listened to what my friend had to say.

"I think it's part of who… *what*… I'm becoming. Y'know… as I fade. I don't know, but that's what it feels like. So, I can feel 'em all alive and ready to be harvested right up there five hundred meters away all close to the wall of the cliff and the spring. Can't feel Commons 'cause I don't have a beef with him. He ain't who I… *gotta get*. Know what I mean? But I can feel *them*, those white-robed priests that did that to the girl to protect themselves from the drones up there plain as day. And somethin' else, Talk…"

My friend *was* becoming different. That's the best way I can put it.

"I can feel him too. Nightmare. He's like me. But he's powerful, Talk. *Real* powerful."

The sand hissed and skirled all around us and there was no way even the Nightstalkers were getting through. We were on our own for now.

And then Tanner said something so unlike him. Words like Vandahar would use.

I mark it down for the permanent record.

They sent a cold chill through me worse than the cold sweat of almost being buried alive in the tomb we'd just barely escaped from.

"He is a being… of greater power than we suspect."
Yes. My friend is becoming… *different.*

CHAPTER THIRTY-EIGHT

AFTER climbing up the well, and barely not falling to our deaths thanks to the false handholds the mad architect had installed long ago, we made it up into the upper treasure vaults of the tomb.

We lit the torches we found along the wall and continued forward down a small passage, avoiding the black suns cut and carved and inked into the ancient stones used to form the place.

They were like deadly black spiders full of doom to us.

We found that the Katari we'd been missing had tripped a trap and had been crushed by a stone that fell from the ceiling as poisoned spears suddenly pierced him from every side.

What was left was gruesome.

But one less cat-ssassin to worry about.

Soon we entered a vast treasure room, and… it was by far the greatest one we'd yet encountered. Even better than that of the dragon the Rangers had slain in the remains of the Dragon Elven capital that was once Paris in the long ago of the Before.

Or what the Ruin now called the Savage Lands.

Piles of shining gold coins, centuries untouched, were suddenly illuminated by our torches where they lay in vast great heaps. It seemed to me that all the gold in the world that had ever been, was there. I reached out to pick up one antique coin, and Kennedy stopped my hand and whispered…

"Don't."

Then he cast his trap detection spell, murmuring his arcane magic words and waving one hand over the vast vault like some Jedi from the movies.

He made a small "humph."

"What," I asked.

"It's not trapped."

"Score," whispered Tanner, and I could tell how many slashed and wounded dancing girls he was gonna show the time of their lives with as he considered how much gold he could stuff in his cargo pockets.

Gold is heavier than you think.

But yeah, a few handfuls and he'd be the king of Sûstagul as far as those fading beauties were concerned. At least for a night or two.

There were chests of gems. By torchlight they illuminated and sparkled, changing the color of the light in the dim chamber, causing it to shift like we were in some funhouse arcade. One gem, I guessed, would have been the equivalent of all the gold Tanner could have humped out of there had he not blown his assault pack to bits saving our lives.

And there were suits of ancient ceremonial armor. Golden and polished. Carved with eagles and glyphs. There were spears that seemed to shine of their own light. A shield made of silver with a massive hieroglyph I'd learned to identify as the moon. A shining khopesh on a pedestal that must've been a magic item as some low note seemed to sing within the room whenever you looked at it too long.

Like the blade was trying to communicate with you. If

only you'd just listen.

And other fantastic treasures. Potions in crystal vials set in golden racks. Scrolls lying across a great golden, teak, and emerald painted table.

And in the center of it all, an empty small gold-inlaid throne set with more moon symbols.

Across the seat, two fantastically carved rods lay crossed, and I had no doubt they were either valuable beyond belief, or magic items of might and power.

What lay in this undiscovered vault… was lifetimes of riches. And it was one of the most fantastic sights I've ever seen.

That's when the shadows began to come and creep about like living things.

We heard them whispering, like some soundtrack in a horror movie everywhere at once and close up in our ears. The menacing sound of the shadows made it clear we were about to get attacked by barely unseen enemies.

"Shadows," whispered Kennedy quickly. "In my game they drain you of energy using the negative plane until you're little more than a dried-out low-level husk. Then a long slow death. Then… you're a shadow. But…"

"We know, Ranger," muttered Tanner slowly, already going *other*. "That's in your game, Kennedy. Might not match."

And then… in that unholy language of the dead that Tanner knew, and didn't know, he began to speak to the shadows of the dead thieves who'd spent their lives trying to reach this chamber and loot its vast wealth for themselves, and had lost their lives in doing so, becoming mere shadows protecting what had cost them… everything.

Tanner spoke to them, and they waved off their sudden greedy attack to keep us from taking their wealth.

"They're worried we want to take what they've come for," Tanner said slowly, facing them, his arms out like he was projecting some wall by sheer force of will that kept them back from us within the guttering torchlight.

Out there, across the vast glimmering and gleaming treasure field that was the vault, we could see the shadowy images of the men they once were. Hiding from the light. Hiding behind the riches that had cost them their life. Seeking to get close if the torch should fail… and make *us* like *them*.

"Weren't for these torches, they'd already have gotten us," muttered Tanner. Then spoke to them more in that dead language.

"They say if we leave, they'll let us go."

"Then we leave," I told Tanner. "We're here for Commons. Not the gold."

"Solid copy, Talk."

He told them that, and the hissing and whispering began to die down and the shadows grew still in the half light, watching us to see if we'd honor our word.

Barely… and just… I could see their greedy eyes alight with envy and fear, watching us. Even in death, they wanted the treasure that had robbed them of their lives. If just to stay here forever and hover over it.

There was something… terrible in that, and in some way… I understood it. Understood how terrible it was to be addicted to something that had total power over you.

But I was better than that.

I took a drink of coffee from my backup spare emergency canteen I keep at the bottom of my ruck where other important lifesaving gear is supposed to go, like food and socks.

We backed away.

"Ask them which way out?" I told Tanner.

He shook his head sadly.

"They don't know, Talk. They don't want to leave here."

So we moved on and passed through other lesser vaults and libraries filled with crumbling scrolls and deathly silences. Then we found the stairs, removed the traps because we are Rangers and that's our thing, and made the final level of the crypt, which was a lone room in which a stone sarcophagus waited in a vast and empty silence that was so thick it felt like a living feral thing that would consume you in time.

Which was ironic, because the only thing in that room besides the stone sarcophagus… was the crypt guardian.

And his temptations.

CHAPTER THIRTY-NINE

IT asked us…

Who we were and what we'd come for in the chamber of its master.

The thing in the tomb. The crypt guardian.

It was little more than a skeleton floating about the sarcophagus in a tattered black monk's robe, the skull grinning and glaring at us in the dark. Its two eye sockets filled with a hypnotic red light in all that bare light and darkness.

"In the game," whispered Kennedy, "that's called a crypt thing, and it's pretty powerful. Immune to certain spells like *hold* and *charm*. It can teleport you by touch in any direction it wants. If there are other undiscovered levels in this tomb, it could possibly send each of us, if it gets ahold of us, into those other levels, or even underground chasms to be lost forever. But…"

"We know. Things may not match your game. What's it want?" I asked.

"To ask a question," muttered Tanner in his dead voice. "And whatever it asks… guys, don't listen."

I had no idea what that meant, and then… I heard its voice in my head and knew that it too was a dead thing just like my friend… was becoming.

It was grave-dust cold. It laughed without laughing at how weak you were, and then gently, it asked what you wanted most…

But there was no pity in it. No love. No life. No mercy.

"Don't listen, guys," said Tanner again and stumbled forward. He was fighting some battle we weren't privy to.

"Searchin' for the hidden exit… It's here… Don't listen, guys. Hang on…"

Kennedy told me later that he tried to cast his *silence* spell but the floating skeleton guarding the crypt messed with his head so much that Kennedy got all ate up trying to remember the spell.

What did it whisper as Tanner searched for the exit as fast as he could?

And it did seem that Tanner, using DeadVision or whatever, could see his way to the secret exit. Or to at least know a general location for it.

Perhaps the ghosts of the dead who'd been slain by this thing were showing him the way unseen to us.

My friend is becoming… *different*.

But while that happened… the thing offered us… everything we ever wanted.

All we had to do was open the sarcophagus. It was that easy. And then everything…

Everything.

Even… godhood.

"Found it," said Tanner dully and waved for us. We stumbled away from the skeleton and toward the section of the wall Tanner was pushing inward on.

Not a black sun, but a stairway to the sun represented in Saurian glyph.

Everything.

Power.
Fame.
Women.
Magic.
Might.
Knowledge.

The skeletal guardian offered everything if we'd just but stay and approach the lid to the sarcophagus… and see what was inside.

Even just writing the words down doesn't do justice to how tempting those whispering lies of acquisition and immortality were. It hurt to say *no* to them as the crypt guardian seemed to reach into our minds and show us…

Luxuries and pleasures beyond imagining…

If we would just push the lid of the plain and featureless ancient Saurian architect's resting place, the fiend who'd built the dreams of avarice that were the Saur, and set him free.

The door was open, and Tanner, promising and telling us to keep our ears… or was it our minds?… shut, pushed us through and onto the rough stone-cut stairs that led up and out of that damned place through a dark and narrow passage.

… a place of damnation.

He saved us from it all.

But…

My friend is becoming… *different.*

CHAPTER FORTY

I would find out later that the extraction bird had been hopping its way south and the pilot had lifted off despite weather being bad on the LZ.

Again…

"We got Rangers that need friends… this is what we do."

Then they saddled up and went for it, making small stops when the storm was bad, and trying to fly around, or through what they could.

They got close, but not close enough.

They went circuitous, approaching the boiling storm front from the east and getting as close as they could until they set down and switched everything off.

The storm was too heavy by that point and visibility was zero.

There was doubt among some of the air crew whether the bird would even fly again due to the fact the sand they'd been flying through was so heavy.

But they were close. Twenty minutes.

They sat there in the bird, the extraction team deploying around for security as the storm seemed to get worse and worse by the second. To them, according to the door gunner, there was no way they were going to make it to get Commons out of there.

Then, his words, "Chief Rapp exits the bird, walks a ways

off, gets down on one knee, and he starts talking to himself. Head bowed and all. Some of the Rangers gave him hard looks… you can tell, they been through stuff, seen a lotta death, they got things to work out… but I know what Sunday school is. I unhooked from the gun and a few others did too, and we went out there and just knelt down with him. First, I felt stupid. Then I remembered I'd do just about anything to get a man in trouble off the *X*. So… there I was on my knees in a sandstorm with a Green Beret praying to God for a break for some Rangers that was in it. Storm was scrubbing the skin off o' us, and… well, I didn't think it was gonna work… but, you know, Corporal Talker… I wanted it to. So… maybe that's all ya need. Don't know. I've seen some stuff."

Ten minutes later the skies cleared, enough, not by any safety standards anyone would greenlight back in the world, and the cowboy pilot spun up the blades and the extraction bird was once again en route to our hit location at the top of the stairs.

We didn't know that right then as radios were still down and I wasn't checking for messages on the device in my admin pouch.

And because we were already engaged hot with the Saurian praetorians at the Spring of Sullus and the white-robed priests as Nightmare made his run for the top of the stairs now that he was close enough to the Temple of Un.

Now it was a straight-up brawl, and twenty minutes was a whole other world that would never make it for some of us.

CHAPTER FORTY-ONE

"HE'S on the move, Talker," said Tanner. "He's already ahead of the priests. He knows he's got enemies."

I had no plan.

So…

"All right… that works for us," I said, like I knew what I was talking about. "We just need Commons. We hit the procession from the rear, we can snatch Commons and let Nightmare push into either the snipers or the extraction team."

I checked my rifle and made sure it was mostly sand-free. The other two did so with theirs. I handed my grenades to Tanner.

"Kennedy… you handle the Saur." The white-robed priests had at least two squads of praetorians. "I suggest your staff of fireballs or whatever it is… but if you can smoke a Hill Giant then that shouldn't be a problem."

I turned to Tanner.

"You got the priests. I'm going for Commons. Once I grab him, I'm either gonna pull back to here with him to keep him outta the fight, or if we get some signal from the extraction team, then I'll push on the bird and you cover me. We avoid Nightmare and let any fight develop between him and the other elements. I don't think we can take him."

Tanner stared at me stone-dead-faced.

"All right," I said. "Let's do this."

Five minutes later we engaged the first Saur at the Spring of Sullus.

CHAPTER FORTY-TWO

THE battle at the Spring of Sullus was a hot mess.

The Saur had broken into two groups, one leading forward and trying to keep up with Nightmare, who we could see was now farther up the curving stairs and heading for the top.

Yeah… he was trying to make a run for it. His Delta senses, honed by years of wily action, must've been tingling that he was in a bad position and probably surrounded.

He was cutting his losses and leaving Commons for bait.

The snipers were already engaging the group of Saur trying to keep up with Nightmare, the storm having cleared enough for them to just begin opening up with accurate fire as we crept close to the spring to begin our assault, creeping up the stairs as we did so.

We had no flashbangs, and we couldn't use grenades because of Commons… so we were going to move and fire knowing the Saur had bows and spears to return fire with.

And the priests had spells. That's what they could do to us. But if we could hit them with violence of action—y'know, speed, aggression, surprise—then maybe we could shut that down.

In hindsight… I should've had Kennedy target them.

Just as we launched our attack, me in the center, Tanner on the right, and Kennedy flanking left into the flat open space that was beside the spring, we heard *Mjölnir* open fire unsuppressed from the cliffs high above and on our right up there on the plateau.

The Saur beyond the spring and taking point to follow Nightmare up the stairs, bore the brunt of the sniper fire as lizard men began to die, twisting and turning shot through, blood and brain matter spraying across the well-worn dusty old rock of the carved stairs.

We caught a break. We launched the attack with max surprise and then we opened fire.

I put rounds into the two priests nearest Commons, who was lying on the ground near his litter and not on it. To me he still seemed unconscious. He looked dirty, and there were clearly some wounds.

Unfortunately for him I was gonna Ranger-roll him to get him out of the conflict as fast as I could, and as I moved forward swiftly, following my boots and placing accurate fire in consistent shots on both stunned priests, I'd cleared the area enough that I broke into a flat-out run at the last second, charging Commons's prone form, and tried to get the Ranger-roll right this time first-time-go.

Gonna be honest…

Not my specialty.

The Ranger-roll is a technique perfected by Ranger medics to get a downed man out of harm's way— read, under fire— and to someplace where he can be treated. It involves doing a combat roll as you reach the man's boots, ending up lying on his stomach with your back. Then quickly reaching around to grab his far leg with your arm, wrapping it under the thigh, and then continuing the roll as you as you begin to stand up and hook his other arm over your shoulder, and then, holding them both limbs in one arm 'cause you're working a rifle, standing fully up.

Easy, right?

If I've made this sound like a series of steps… it's actually done in one fluid motion.

Not gonna lie… I'm not great at it. I used to drop Brumm all the time when Sergeant Kurtz made us do it with all our gear on.

Arrows whispered through the air in every direction as I charged and made my attempt to get Commons to safety. As I reached the Ranger, I noticed Tanner had already been hit by some of the Saur firing at us a few times. Arrows stuck out of him. He didn't seem to mind and continued his massacre of the white-robed priests.

Tanner was busy shooting them to death like it was a bodily function.

Kennedy went live with his dragon-headed staff and used it like a napalm thrower, covering in hungry fire a group of Saur that had been bringing up the enemy rear. The Saur hissed and ran. One threw himself off the cliff.

I Ranger-rolled Commons, grunting, "Got you," and got it mostly right in that I ended up on my boots with Commons wrapped around me.

He was out of it, and he looked pale.

But I could tell he was alive.

I stood, pivoted with my rifle, and fired one-handed at a nearby Saur who'd charged me with a spear. I kept pulling the trigger as the lizard man closed until he changed shape, but he didn't. He just kept coming.

Then he caught fire as Kennedy paused from laying waste with his flamethrower staff and shot a volley of magic meteors with his off hand into the guy coming for me and Commons.

These meteors blew holes in that guy.

Now I needed to run for cover…

That was when Sergeant Thor shot Nightmare.

Sometimes you can overcomplicate things. You don't always need a team. Blockers. Extraction.

Sometimes you just need Sergeant Thor, an M107A anti-materiel rifle named *Mjölnir*, and a fifty-caliber BMG Raufoss round with an armor-piercing tungsten core.

Thor drilled Nightmare, blowing dust and bandages out through his chest along the stairs.

Nightmare didn't die. He laughed over the dying winds of the storm. But he was trailing bandages and it was clear he'd taken heavy damage. His hit points were low, as Kennedy would say. He stumbled, then turned, his gritty voice echoing out over the valley as he cast a powerful spell to knock the snipers engaging him off the cliff.

Earthquake. That's what Kennedy told me later was probably the spell. Nightmare would have access to such high-level spells, probably acquired over lifetimes of travel and war throughout the Ruin.

He was indeed a being of great power.

It didn't push Thor, who continued to try to engage Nightmare despite sections of the cliff coming down around him, but it did destroy my option to retreat as a section of the collapsing cliff gave way and destroyed the stairs below the spring.

And then… the stairs began to collapse *upward*,

disintegrating around us like someone had just dropped the Mother Of All Bombs down in the valley.

"Run forward!" I shouted and hustled ahead with Commons on my back, pulling for all I was worth to reach the stairs ahead. In seconds the stairs behind me were collapsing in great cascades of ancient stone and falling into the Valley of Death far below.

CHAPTER FORTY-THREE

WE buddy-carried Commons up the stairs and out of harm's way as the extraction bird came in hot, door gunners laying the hate on a large force of Viper Guard responding from the Temple of Un at a dead run like savages from some insane Bronze Age epic of tribes ululating and war-whistling into battle against the few who stand against them.

But there was already a new battle underway up there on the plateau at the top of the stairs Nightmare had reached before us. Bent but not broken.

We moved fast, the stairs still collapsing behind us in great sections, cracks and rents appearing ahead of us as we carried Commons as fast as we could.

We could hear the battle ahead and it was already insane.

There was gunfire.

Lightning flashes and thunderclaps.

Fireballs rolling like ominous bowling balls. Then massive explosions.

Spells of magic meteors and other offensive rays, beams, and spell-fired plagues were rattled off by Nightmare as he worked his way forward to link up with the Saur who were coming out to rescue him. All the while running Commons's primary and shooting at anyone who got in his way.

He too was in it to win it.

Weren't we all.

He threw *hold* spells at the door gunners in the extraction bird and froze them into immobility.

Then he engaged and shot Chief Rapp and two other Rangers.

Rapp was only grazed. One Ranger was hit bad enough to start first aid on himself. The other shattered a plate.

Then the running and gunning mummy lord hit the bird with a lightning strike he called down from a clear sky. And if that wasn't enough, he sent a swarm of locusts at us as Tanner had started to engage him. Kennedy took a turn and carried Commons as I got my breath and readied for the final push at the top.

Locusts from out of the sky slammed into us and tried to take our eyes out. They tried to crawl down our throats.

Eye pro and shemaghs up, we pushed forward, and the swarm dissipated as fast as it had come up.

The extraction force was now holding the area around the bird, but they were overrun dealing with spells from the mummy lord that Nightmare had become, and the Delta operator turned and suddenly launched a *Cloudkill* spell at Thor, who kept getting rounds on target but deflecting off some kind of magical shield Nightmare had thrown up as he limped forward and tried to reach the surging Saur that could soak up some incoming for him.

He'd been shot in the leg now too and probably a dozen other places, his wrappings were flying loose and there were visible holes right through him, but he was still pushing forward when we reached the top.

Kennedy was immediately on the radio when he saw the *Cloudkill* fire off and told Thor and Sergeant Reese to run for their lives ASAP.

That poison cloud would kill them as it unnaturally raced across the sky toward their position on the rocks like it was a living and very hungry thing.

Kennedy later told me it was another pretty high-level spell. Nightmare was full of surprises.

Then the Delta operator turned mummy lord pivoted, and working the rifle, started shooting at the pilots of the Black Hawk to get them to abandon the bird, or just kill them, despite the fact the blades were still spinning at idle power. The pilots covered, and the door gunners were still frozen motionless by the *hold* spell.

Chief Rapp was hit, but he was still in the fight and now not firing as he dragged a wounded Ranger, this one hit by a lightning bolt fired from the shroud-wrapped hands of Nightmare, for cover behind a nearby rune-covered obelisk half that was little more than a stump.

The guy would live.

I could see Chief was breathing heavy, but he was still in it. He waved for us indicating we should push for the extraction bird. They'd buy us time.

It looked bad. Tanner raced past a couple of the Rangers who'd been hit by a *sleep* spell as Nightmare reached the stairs, then Tanner started engaging the Delta operator with his SDM rifle.

Casually, Nightmare turned and fired a fireball at Tanner from less than twenty-five meters.

It hurtled right at him, expanding, and Tanner took the ball of bright flaming fire right in the chest and burst into flames, falling to the ground suddenly and unceremoniously.

I think I screamed.

No, or something.

This had been *my* plan. And now…

Nightmare was on the move for the miniguns on the bird, but he turned toward me and engaged me psionically… just to make sure I wasn't gonna be a problem.

Yeah… he had those powers too. And then some.

He was… *powerful indeed.*

A psionic battle feels like it takes lifetimes. To the people involved in one.

In reality… it's like two seconds.

I thought I had him and just bore down with everything I had, trying to hit him with my powerful mental blast. You know… my one good trick. Never mind the headaches. And who cares… we were getting Commons out of this…

Nightmare just laughed inside my mind, absorbed or deflected the mental blast, then shattered my mind with something that sounded like breaking glass.

I went down, hearing gunfire and fireballs streaking across the battle space. Seeing nothing and sure my mental faculties had just been bell-rung down to infant level.

I wasn't out for long, and when I came to, Tanner, burnt to a crisp, was on his feet and tiredly dragging up a SAW one of the sleep-downed Rangers had been carrying.

He was still on fire in places. He looked like a monster from some horror-show zombie flick.

Nightmare was almost to the chopper…

Tanner, all smoking flaming burning zombie, started to lay the hate.

Nightmare's shield was no match for the volume of

incoming. He was flung about from the barrage of impacts from the SAW. His rifle fell from his hands, and the mummy lord was spun to the ground near the chopper.

He tried to get to his knees.

Tanner, his skin and face a black nightmare, just continued to fire, dumping the whole pouch into the downed mummy that was once a Delta operator.

Once one of us.

By the time Tanner finished, he was standing directly over Nightmare, emptying the last of the gun almost point blank into the torn and fluttering bandages of the mummy operator, those rags being driven and whipped about already by the blades of the Black Hawk.

I got to my knees.

Kennedy had Commons. I took over. Kennedy was beat. He couldn't take another step.

The Saur were starting to get close with effective arrow fire to boot. Arrows whistled through the air and slammed into the hard dirt all around us. I started toward the chopper, my legs burning, my shoulders crying, my mind ready to watch Tanner drop over on fire, the adrenaline after being destroyed, or was it revenge, only carrying him… so far.

Slowly, I pushed for the Black Hawk for all I was worth. Kennedy got the downed Rangers up and moving to the bird.

Chief Rapp had the Ranger hit by lightning by the drag handle and was pulling him too. The guy came to life, spitting and swearing as he got to his boots and made it the rest of the way on his own, though limping and looking uncertain of exactly where he was.

The cloud that could have killed Thor and Sergeant Reese

was nowhere to be seen, and now both snipers were running for all they were worth across the ground between the cliffs and the extraction bird.

The door gunner, free of the *hold* spell now that Nightmare was probably dead… if he wasn't dead I can't understand how… began to lay the hate with the minigun on the approaching Saur force hurling spears and arrows.

A few more magic missiles got shot off at us and slammed into the side of the chopper.

Chief Rapp took Commons from me and then he and the medic got him aboard and started working on him.

And I turned toward Tanner.

He was on his knees in front of the flapping remains of Nightmare.

I reached out, but he was still smoking. His face and skin, what remained, was burnt to a crisp. He didn't have much longer. Who could?

"Not as bad… as it looks."

He was dead.

"Man…" I said. And could think of nothing else to say even though I wanted to say everything.

Tanner stood. Unsteadily. I helped him. Then… slowly we started toward the bird, smoking and all. I batted out the flames still on him, gently.

"Not…" he began with a grunt, the Rangers helping him aboard, "… as bad… as it looks."

We clipped in, and the extraction bird hauled herself away from the body-littered top of the plateau.

I was sitting next to Tanner, and he smelled like death.

But he was pretty alive… for an undead guy.

CHAPTER FORTY-FOUR

WE flew north in an overloaded Black Hawk, due north because we didn't have the fuel to go around the Grand Pyramid. We had no idea, or at least *I* had no idea as the bird beat the air and the Rangers sat there looking grim and hard, that the battle for the Grand Pyramid had just started at dawn. I gotta admit, and they do too… we were all a little stunned we'd made it through that one.

Thor smiled at me and then laughed.

Unusual for him.

He looked like a savage covered in dirt and sand and soot. So did most of the other Rangers.

Chief was working on Commons, and we all waited for the assessment as he and the medic started doing their best to make sure he was gonna make it.

The wind and the day beat the deck and drove the battle out of us, making it seem as though we'd left all that… back there. Some other life not this one.

"That was hairy…" said the pilot over the comm we were all connected to. "You guys want some music?"

No one said anything.

Chief Rapp looked over his shoulder and gave me a thumbs-up, pointing down at Commons on the deck.

He would make it.

"Tear It Down" by Def Leppard started to play over the

comm.

Nightstalkers got toys.

It was cool.

That's what we were gonna do to Sût.

Tear it down. All of it.

The war had finally begun that morning. Old Sût, convinced the odds were stacked against him, had ordered his troops forward to hit the digging-in Accadions in a surprise attack and hopefully break them up for slaughter by the orc hordes even now streaming across the desert like an unholy plague of darkness.

Maybe Nightmare had convinced the Lich Pharaoh via some kind of spell-comm that this was what needed to happen.

Nightmare was dead now.

One of the Rangers had left a burning thermite grenade on those windblown bandages that had once been a Delta operator back there on a body-littered LZ.

Just to be sure.

Don't mess with Rangers. Even if you are Delta.

Below us, as we crossed over the pyramid and the plateau, the legions were already engaged with the Saur swarming out of the fortress temples. Orc hordes were hitting the flanks. Spells and arrow fire got flung in sudden waves like those locusts Nightmare had used against us.

Def Leppard went to eleven, reached down, and played their hearts out.

Yeah. This *was* pretty cool. All things considered.

I looked at Commons and reached out to touch his boot. I held my hand there.

He'd used every trick in the book and then some to make it.

Then I saw the JDAM go right into the front of the Grand Pyramid, exploding away in every direction, blowing rock and debris everywhere as we flew north.

It was on.

Captain Knife Hand didn't play around. He'd just throat-punched Sût. The Forge had ginned one up and the Air Force had made it happen.

Good on them.

It's good to have friends for Rangers.

That was the response to a Saur surprise attack. Hit back, and hit back hard.

Give the Rangers time to get involved and take the necropolis forts down there, the great bridges, the tower-defended stairs and all the other fortified points leading right up and into the pyramid where Sût the Undying himself was hiding.

That would come next.

Def Leppard screamed about tearing it all down and getting ready.

And Commons…

I held his boot.

And…

Commons lives.

Next would come the Battle for the Great Pyramid, and the Rangers would *sua sponte* that. As they say.

Of their own accord.

But for now, all that mattered was… Commons lives.

EPILOGUE

IN time, and I add this note much, much later… we would leave that city and the ruins of the Saur empire we had destroyed.

But Commons, and a few other Rangers, would stay behind as a force. Aqua Ranger would rise to prominence in the city, and in time… have a family. And it would be said that there were no better swimmers than his children. And grandchildren. And yes… even great-grandchildren.

He lived.

He prospered.

He was loved.

He was a Ranger.

Commons… lives.

The End

The Rangers will return in Forgotten Ruin Book 9:
Sua Sponte

Visit **www.WarGate.store** for exclusive Forgotten Ruin merchandise.

To learn about more titles like this one, or to be notified upon the release of the next book in this series, sign up for the WarGate Newsletter at **www.WarGateBooks.com**.

ALSO BY JASON ANSPACH & NICK COLE

Legionnaire
Order of the Centurion
Savage Wars (2020 Dragon Award Winner)
SGT. THOR the Bold

ALSO BY JASON ANSPACH

Wayward Galaxy
Void Drifter
'til Death

ALSO BY NICK COLE

American Wasteland:
The Complete Wasteland Trilogy
SodaPop Soldier
Strange Company

9 798889 220534